For four centuries Magnus has lived according to the dictates of the moon, his heart isolated by the domination of his wolf nature. Now fate has brought the beautiful, independent Sian to his house at Darnwell and their irresistible attraction has exploded into a white-hot passion. Yet she is not wolf, and the time has come for her to embrace the change. But once she completes the ritual and claims her place next to Magnus, the rivals will appear on the horizon…

Visit us at www.kensingtonbooks.com

Books by Daisy Banks

Timeless Series
Timeless, Book One
To Eternity, Book Two

A Matter of Some Scandal
Fiona's Wish

Published by Kensington Publishing Corporation

To Eternity

Timeless Series

Daisy Banks

LYRICAL PRESS
Kensington Publishing Corp.
www.kensingtonbooks.com

To my husband.

Prologue

A little outside the village of Darnwell, in England, stands an ancient estate. The woods are dark, the wrought iron gates black, the vista hidden. A foggy haze rises both dawn and evening along its quiet cinder paths. The majestic house, beyond a wealth of trees, carries within a cruel secret, or so, after a pint or two in the pub, the Darnwell villagers will tell any traveler. Most visitors smile or nod at the tales, one or two might seem interested, a few even take a walk to try to see the house, brave enough until they arrive at the gates. Often then, business commitments force them to leave.

One woman has ventured to this place. Sian lingers where she has discovered love, but with the rare, precious sweetness, she's found a fearful threat lurks. If she can't learn to control the danger, her love will be nothing more than dreams. If she can't control the dreams, her love will be nothing more than danger.

Lust and love battle for ascendency. Autumn mist rises like smoke from the dark water of the lake. A horror reaches out to be assuaged. Love, tenderness, and hope linger in the daybreak, in the evening shadows, too, for not all evils are without redemption.

Chapter 1

Thank God. No claws.

Magnus examined his hand, a man's hand, before he clasped Sian's offered palm and met the massive dark pupils in her gaze as she set the padlock down. Naked, grimed by the process of transformation, he used her help to haul himself up from the floor.

She slipped the silver necklace with the key to his chains inside her shirt.

He grimaced as he wiped the scraps of crusty dust left after his transformation from his arms. October's full moon had proved nothing like the last. This time there was no delightful shared dream.

Instead, Sian had met more of the wolf he carried within him.

Heaven help him, tonight she bore an injury to attest an encounter he couldn't recall.

God.

He gritted his teeth. His gaze fixed on her. "What happened?" He nodded to her bandaged arm dreading her answer. "How did you get hurt?"

"Here, Magnus." Sian draped a warm robe around his shoulders. "I'm fine." She glanced to her arm. "This, it's not more than a scratch."

He staggered away from the cage, where the beast spent his days, leaning on her for support. "I scratched you?" he managed to ask, begging for confirmation of his fears.

"It was my fault. I got too close to the bars. We'll get you to the bathroom, then I'll go make us something to eat."

He dragged one slow step after another. Sian slipped her arm around his waist, and with her help, he made it along the corridor to the bathroom. She opened the faucet on the bath while he drank two glasses of water. All the time, he kept his gaze on her.

"You bathe, I'll go cook. Please, Magnus, don't worry." She smiled. "We've survived this month's full moon."

He ached to kiss her, but not like this, not with the grime of transformation ingrained on his skin. She deserved better. Sian—his goddess, the woman he'd die to protect—deserved the best he could give her. "We'll talk after I bathe."

She nodded so her thick brandy-colored curls moved to lure his fingers. "Yes. Don't be troubled."

Reaching out, he touched the bandage on her forearm. She winced.

"Impossible," he whispered. "I adore you, but I've hurt you."

"It's not what you fear. I remain mortal."

"That's how I want you to be. How you should be."

"Hmm." She turned off the taps. "We have to make a decision, Magnus. I'd like us to decide soon. I can't bear this. Everything would be solved if…"

"I know. After I bathe, you can tell me what happened while we eat."

Sian placed a kiss on the end of her finger and pressed it to his lips before she left. His heart ached for her hopes, for her confidence that she could make all well. He dropped the grubby robe, climbed into the tub, and closed his eyes. This full moon had pushed the usual boundaries. The additional power of Samhain seemed to have supercharged his appetite, but there was more than he'd anticipated. Though often he returned from transformation confused, his body still attuned to the senses of the wolf, this evening every muscle clenched tight, filled with lactic acid, as though he'd been rigid since Friday night when the full moon shifted his consciousness. Somehow, in his transformed state as the wolf, he'd spent hours fighting to keep himself still. The reason for such strange behavior in the beast eluded him.

He tilted his head back into the water, so the warmth might ease his corded neck muscles. The sensation of heat welcome, he sank lower in the tub until the water covered his hair. He hoped this would soothe his skin and his pain, but until he spoke with her about what had happened, nothing would pacify his fears. Annoyance that he couldn't recall the acts of the beast swept through him. There had been times like this before. Even when he'd killed, a savage act any creature should remember, he could recollect nothing beyond the satisfaction of blood. But, if he'd harmed Sian, the wolf would have howled its sorrow until the walls echoed his repentance.

If only there were a way to force himself to remember. Truly, he was cursed.

Tired, his muscles clinging onto the edge of tension, he flipped on the shower attachment. He stood as the water drained from the tub. Angling the showerhead, he turned on the water and sucked in a breath at the cool blast. Skin tingling from his rinse, he clambered out of the bath. At least he now stood clean. Once he'd dried off, he put on a fresh robe, cleaned his teeth, and combed through his hair, following a morning routine despite the evening. Finally, he shoved his feet into rattan house shoes. Full of fear at what Sian may say, he made his way down the green, wrought iron, spiral stairs to the kitchen.

Sian sat at the broad table sipping from a big blue mug. Coffee from the aroma, bacon and eggs, too, were ready. Under covered dishes, the food was hot from the stove. The residue of wolf senses fought with his man-brain to analyze all the information. Tonight, a ripe, powerful scent haunted his kitchen unlike any he'd known in an age. The odor of blood, an iron rich tang, packed with a sultry promise, smoldered around him.

Female blood.

"I must have wounded you deeper than you think," he said, reaching for her arm but not touching in case he might cause further pain. "You must be bleeding still."

"No." She shook her head and glanced at the bandage. "It's not the arm. It's another kind of bleeding. I think it made things worse this month. I should have left the room once you were caged."

"Oh," he said, registering her meaning at once. "That's something I'd not thought on." He accepted the mug of coffee she put in his hand. Her hormones prodded the wolf senses with a fragrant lure. Instead of lying dormant as they should have after his transformation, they set an echo of desire through his bloodstream. "Yes, it may well have provoked the creature."

"Hmm," she murmured. "You could say that."

He slid his arm around her, bent his head to her shoulder, and pressed a kiss to the warmth of her neck. "I'm sorry. So sorry."

She stroked over his damp hair, brushing it back from his forehead. "It's all right. I'll know next time—it's my fault—it took me a day and a half to understand what was going on. I was so worried about you, I'm afraid I got closer than I should have. I looked for you in the dreams as well, but no, not this time. I think you were buried deep within the wolf senses this month, much more than the last time. Me..." She glanced down. "Me being like this made things worse. Please, sit. You must be hungry as well as exhausted. You didn't eat all the steak I gave you."

"I didn't?" He sat.

"No, so you must be hungry." She lifted the lids on the covered dishes. Glad to wean back another sense from the wolf for the here and now, he luxuriated in the smell of food.

Sian dished up several slices of bacon and added a generous helping of scrambled eggs, two cooked tomatoes, plus several mushrooms.

He accepted the plate. His stomach growled as though the wolf spoke from within, yet still he had to force himself to pick up the fork. "Forgive me?" he whispered.

"Of course." Her gaze held his, a shimmer of moisture in her eyes. She swallowed hard, her smooth throat moving fast. "It wasn't your fault. We both knew this month would be hard, with it being October. I didn't understand your need, or the way I affected you. I'll make sure it doesn't happen again, but I think this must be another reason why you should consider making me your true mate."

"Not yet!" A fresh wave of guilt barreled through him at her teary glance in response to his tone. His hopes to control the vile process of transformation lay in a ruin. Last month, the rage Franklyn had provoked in him by attacking Sian, empowered him to take control of the wolf and change at will. He'd hoped from that time on, he could control the shift even at the full moon, but no, the moon still dominated his world, his life, leaving him fearful for Sian. She could eventually control him, but she needed time to learn how to use her innate skills. "You are my true mate, my woman. But, please, don't force more, not yet."

"Eat." She wiped beneath her eye with her knuckle. "There's lots of time, you've said so."

He swallowed a mouthful, then another, unable to meet her gaze right now, lost in the strangeness of the restoration of human needs. Most of all, he floundered in his anguish, for he'd explained so little to her. She remained at the mercy of the moon tides in his blood. He'd thought ensuring her safety from Franklyn's cruel obsession his foremost duty, but he needed to do much more to help her find her path in the convoluted ways of the wolf. "You're not eating?"

"No." She shook her head. "I'm too tired."

He shoved the plate away. "Then come here, we'll go up to bed. We'll sleep. Tonight we can dream together. In the dreams we're free."

"I'd like that, Magnus. Right now, I'd like to be free, just us, with nothing else to think of at all."

He moved around the table as she pushed back her chair and stood. She gave a sigh as he took her into his embrace. Nothing could have spoken so loud as her soft breath to tell of the fears she'd tried to hide. "My brave,

Sian," he whispered, brushing his lips against her forehead. "I promise you next month will be easier."

"I know"—she glanced down to her arm—"this isn't too bad, Magnus. Perhaps, if we'd met in June things would have been different."

"Yes," he said, as they made their way up the spiral staircase. Every step he took, he hated himself for a coward. If he'd met Sian in June, things would have been easier for a brief time, perhaps, but she would still have had to meet the beast in its hunting state at some full moon. This month, the wolf within him had longed to hunt.

He stretched as she kicked off her sports shoes beside the curtained bed. She stripped off her shirt and cropped jeans before she lay down on the crumpled sheet. For the first time in a century, he regretted the arrangement he'd made for his housekeeper to not return until the first morning after a full moon.

Sian should have fresh, soft linen for her tender skin. He licked his lips and savored a taste of her warmth on the air.

The ache of need still squeaked through his muscles. A craving nagged in his body that had never followed him through to a waning moon's dawn. Not the need for blood, or the wish for the savage hunt in the starlit night, but another primeval hunger. Lust. He covered her with the sheet, the quilt, too, until she appeared comfortable. "Sian," he whispered.

"What?"

"I'll sleep apart from you tonight," he said. Palms up, he took a pace back from the bed.

"Oh, why?" She sat up, her eyes wide.

"Because I understand the power of this. I have no wish to harm you more. We'll wait a day or two before we share the bed again. Tonight would be a mistake."

Her glassy gaze searched his. She blinked, breaking his eye contact. "I know," she whispered.

"Remember, you are more important to me than anything in the world." He turned toward the door, ignoring the little catch in her breath, though it tore at his heart. Her ripe fragrance lured him too much, made him want her with a savage need, a hunger no woman might understand. A she-wolf would, but Sian wasn't yet a she-wolf. She'd not enjoy coupling with him as though she were. He closed the bedroom door behind him and strode down the corridor.

A sudden flash of memory hit. The reason for the solid painful muscles, protesting every movement he made despite his soak in a hot bath, thumped between his eyes. For three and a half days in wolf form, he'd wanted to mate, had lusted for her. Somehow, he'd held the savage need under control—just. The pinpoint vision of the moment sent a fiery flash to his groin so his cock twitched.

Confined for the time of the full moon in the small room with the cage, he had found her fragrant, sensual lure tortuous. When she had crouched on her knees to peer at him, all he'd wanted had lain beyond those solid bars. In the hope of gaining surcease, he'd reached through to grab her, scoring her forearm with a thick black claw. He'd sucked in a powerful blast of her scent as she had cried out.

Another inch would have made her his.

He'd have held her close enough to tear off the garments she'd worn and taken her. His damned wolf body would have reveled in the cure for his painful need. The beast had no conscience to trouble it.

He gripped the rail at the top of the stairs, could see nothing in the evening's gloom but the vision of her sleek, pale beauty, the silken flesh of her parted thighs, the springing auburn curls, the juicy heat lodged within that promised bliss. A fresh hot spasm throbbed in his groin. His body demanded he find fulfillment. How he had wanted her. He still did. She was ripe to mate, ready to breed. He could taste her in the air. His seed would fill her. Their cubs would be bold, clever, bright, and sleek.

"No!" Kicking off the rattan shoes, he dashed down the stairs, along the corridor to the drawing room where he opened the secret doorway below the window. He ducked through and dragged in a breath as he ran along the terrace overlooking the lake. An icy thin slime of frost met his feet. He skidded, regained his balance, then pelted down the path. He raced onto the spikes of grass that yielded with the heat of his tread. Down the slope, into the night, he bounded in an effort to escape the pain. The frigid air cooled his ardor, exorcising the lust from his body with every breath he inhaled.

A fragile, starlit lattice of ice stilled any movement on the lake's surface. He hurried across the causeway to the pagoda.

Each step on the boards of the jetty crackled and crunched, snapping the delicate icy crust from the walkway. Inside, in the gloom, he huddled in his robe on the day bed where he and Sian had first made love in the flesh, what seemed like so long ago. Though the search for peace drove him here, her scent still lingered to tease his senses. Memories of peeling her from her cashmere business trousers stoked the embers of his desire. He tried and failed to close off the recollection of her pleasure cries. Tonight they powered through his body as they had that day, charging his desire, tormenting his senses so he ached with a terrible longing.

Fearing he'd not be able to control his brutal need for her, he sought solace. Though he'd learned years ago self-satisfaction was a poor substitute for a woman, it proved one-step better than none at all. Tonight, he fought to achieve release. Only with her image in his mind, and with the lust of the beast rampant, did he reach orgasm.

It shouldn't be this way.

He clutched a cushion as the moonlight diminished. A thin gray line defined the horizon. When the wedge of light, banishing the waning moon, spread wider, pale gold and pink hues smeared the sky to pronounce dawn's arrival, no matter his darkest desires. He blinked gritty eyes, but found, at last, some semblance of peace.

Chapter 2

After her careful one-armed shower, Sian undid the dressing to check her wound. A nasty, red heat burned along her forearm. The bright slice mark, about three inches long, throbbed. The pain hadn't decreased in the night. She squirted another layer of antiseptic onto the tender skin. If her arm showed no improvement by lunchtime, she'd have to make an appointment with the doctor. This scratch hurt more than her palms had done when Franklyn had shoved her down into the road at the beginning of the month. She didn't recall her hands ever blazing this hot, not even after Magnus took the gravel lumps out with tweezers.

She rewrapped the current injury, making sure the bandage didn't press too tight on the fresh piece of gauze overlaying the wound. The last thing she wanted to do was make a fuss and pile another layer of guilt on Magnus. He bore quite enough as it was. She pulled on her robe before she walked back through to the bedroom.

The neat side of the bed where Magnus should have slept screamed his loss.

Where is he?

She'd checked the guest suite before she took a shower. The room offered no sign of him. He wouldn't have used any of the other unaired bedrooms. Perhaps in the kitchen? The household staff wouldn't appear until about eight-thirty this morning, so until then they had to look after themselves. Hopeful she'd find him downstairs, she descended the stairs to the kitchen.

No Magnus. Not even an empty cup to show he'd been there at all.

She made coffee and decided to take it upstairs to drink in their bedroom before she got dressed. The silver coffee pot held enough for three or four cupfuls. In the hope Magnus might join her, she put an extra cup on the tray.

Her period, the cause of the problem between Magnus-wolf and her, had thankfully almost finished. The last three nights spent observing him in the cage had obliterated any sentimental ideas she might have had about the creature Magnus always referred to as "the beast."

In wolf-form, he lived in the animal's reality. She quaked at the memory of him sniffing, inhaling the air, his howls and snarls, along with the powerful pawing at the ground despite his chained limbs. Most frightening of all—the incredible compelling eye contact. The image of golden wolf eyes would haunt her. If not for the restraints and the cage, she'd have run for her life.

He would have caught her in the same way he had done on the beach in their first dream together. A sprint along the sand should have been easy since she still had the speed she developed in high school, but in that dream it wasn't enough. The essence of the capture confused her for a time but she finally recognized the truth. Her body knew its needs better than her, but it was Magnus the man who held her in their dream, not Magnus in wolf-form.

She didn't want to consider what might have happened if the wolf had caught her.

"No, not possible," she whispered. Magnus as a wolf would have ripped her apart with his savage teeth, not fulfilled her passions. "For goodness sake. The change is over for this month. Let it go."

She peered into the mirror. The dark shadows beneath her eyes told their own tale. While watching over him, she'd not slept after her first failed attempt to find him in the dream state. His howls had dragged her from her fitful doze the first evening. Her fear he might be ill in wolf-form swept everything else aside. She couldn't stop watching him. Lost in her unease for him, she'd hesitated to take the sleeping pills she'd used at last month's full moon when she had first witnessed his transformation.

He'd been so different this month, she'd worried something dreadful had gone wrong in the process. Though he'd explained about some elements of his change to wolf, there was much she still didn't understand. Her concerns had forced her to remain conscious.

He hadn't lain in the cage as he did last time. This full moon the thick-furred wolf stood and eyed her as if she were on the menu. After the first few hours, when he got no response to his howls, he had struggled against the bonds, much more than last month. Even the second night, when she had finally guessed what prompted his wild-eyed interest in her, she didn't want to leave him alone while she curled up on the chaise and slept. The sadness in his gold-flecked eyes had kept her focused on him, drowsy as she was, until, at last, the moon changed and the process of his return to normal had started.

"Magnus," she said as he entered the room wearing the thin house robe. "Where did you go last night?" His strong features held the look of living granite. The pain etched onto his broad cheekbones hurt her. His beautiful mouth, the full firm lips she hungered for, appeared thin today. If only she could ease his sorrow. This cruel tension diminished him to a parody of himself. "You look awful."

"I know." His lips moved to create a taut smile. "I'll shower and dress. We'll talk after." He strode past her into the wet room.

Her heart flipped as she swallowed down a new dose of anxiety. She went into her tiny, private boudoir to put on her makeup. This space he'd given her had once been his powdering room. She tried to imagine him with a white powdered wig, with the kind of satin and lace garments she'd researched for the *Timeless* film. He must have been stunning. No wonder Julia had fallen for him. She couldn't understand why Julia hadn't married him when he asked. She sighed, lost in the sadness of the tale of their relationship.

We won't end like that, not if I can persuade him to make us permanent.

Love should be about romance, tenderness, hopes for a future together, but for her it meant many other things. She swiped on her blusher, but the bronze pink only seemed to highlight her pallor. A quick slick of lipstick did nothing to help her. She didn't bother with more than one light coat of mascara.

In the dressing room they shared, she sorted through her armoire for clothes. Though her current mood screamed Gothic Queen, she donned some lime green leggings with a long silk shirt decorated in a Celtic lattice design. She peeked out the tiny window. The day looked cold with an ice-blue sky. From the sway of the tall trees, it was windy, too. She rummaged through one of the drawers and found a clingy knee-length sweater.

Heartbeat rising with concerns for their discussion, she went through to the bedroom. She dumped her sweater on the chair before she opened the door to the wet room. She caught a glimpse of his slick, dark, wet hair dripping on his broad shoulders. The water cascaded down his back to his firm-muscled ass. Still, his pain beat at her like a night fury. Not anger, but an aching hurt she could do nothing to relieve. She called into the shower. "Shall I pour you some coffee?"

The full power of the spray, along with a waft of steam, drowned out his response. She closed the door. Rather than wait, she poured two cups anyway. Curling her hand around her cup, she settled herself in the huge, oak chair in front of the hearth to wait for him to join her. The carving at the end of the curtained four-poster bed, of two wolves with bodies entwined, spoke to her the same way it had the first time Magnus brought her into this room he'd kept as a private sanctuary for so long. This hand-chiseled image, a reference to his parents who had commissioned the monumental bed, gave her hope. They'd loved, as humans and wolves, their pairing bound in a permanent connection. They'd produced offspring. A son, this magnificent, wonderful man, wolf, person. A wave of emotion brought a lump to her throat while she weighed the possibilities against the current reality. Blinking fast, she swiped at her eyes.

This mood would bring her no good. Crying wouldn't solve a thing. She'd end up with a sore throat, red eyes, a swollen nose, and none of it would help. If Magnus found her in tears, it would stoke his guilt further. He might even try to send her back to her flat in London. The line she trod with him demanded the balance skills of a gymnast on the beam. Yes, he cared about her, she was certain…up to a point.

Maybe he loved her enough to send her away. Fresh tears welled for she could imagine his explanation. *I can't hurt you like this anymore. You must leave.*

Heaven help her, he'd mean every word of it. He'd send her away, then bury himself in majestic misery here while he waited for her to age and die.

"Bugger it all." Her voice cracked as she set her coffee cup down on the small table beside her chair. "I'm not going anywhere. I'll not leave you, not unless you take me back to London and dump me there, Magnus. I belong here."

The oak wolves stared back from the wood panel with a silent offer of agreement.

"Too right," she said forcing herself to relax. "I agreed to stay with him and I will. He'll just have to get accustomed to a female being around all the time. I'm going nowhere."

"Had you planned on going somewhere?" he asked, toweling his dark hair as he walked in from the wet room.

"No, I was giving myself a bit of a pep talk." She sucked in the sight of his broad shoulders, the ripples of muscle on his chest. Her gaze moved down to the towel he'd draped around his middle, clinging snug to the damp curve of his ass. Rising from the chair, she hurried to him, wrapped her arms around his waist, and laid her head on his smooth damp shoulder. Her previous experiences had been nothing like this compulsive need for Magnus. When she was nineteen, she'd had a bit of a glow about one boyfriend, but it was a timid kind of affection, rather like standing under a warm shower. With Magnus, she swam in an ocean of unfamiliar sensations, and though some might be scary, she didn't want them to stop. She wouldn't stand by silent if Magnus tried to end their relationship because of his guilt for who and what he was, even if he thought it would be good for her.

He laced his fingers through her hair and cupped her skull with his palm so he could tilt her head back until she stared up into the depths of his gaze. He angled his head to take her lips with his. After so many days with no contact, not even in their dreams, their kiss dragged her into a whirlpool of desire. Her heart raced fast. He rubbed his freshly shaved jaw against her chin. Smooth like a coil of moist silk, his tongue rolled with hers, twined, twisted, teased. She moaned.

Fighting for breath, she lifted her lips from his and pulled back. "Not now, not yet," she whispered.

"I know. Allow me to dress. I think it is best we deal with this situation by distancing ourselves from it."

A rush of determination hit. The same way she'd once dealt with Franklyn's mercurial moods, she prepared to counter whatever arguments Magnus might have for her to leave. "I'm not going back to London. Not on my own. I swear to you, I'll find my way back here. I'll home, just like the pigeon on a ship that crossed the Atlantic. It still got back to where it belonged. I will, too. You want me to stay, I know it."

"If you go to London, I promise I will be with you." A smile followed his words, tender, needy, and half-amused, lifting his former gloom to the expression she'd become more familiar with, the one that so touched her heart.

"I meant merely to suggest," he said, "we might leave the house today, perhaps go to a public place where…" The gleam in his gray eyes met her gaze, sending a torrent of need for him pounding through her.

"I want you, right this second."

Magnus shook his head. "I know. I'm afraid the consequences might be to neither of our liking. As long as you don't have to work on the preparations for the film shoot today we will go out. We can visit"—he gazed up to the ceiling—"anywhere you like in a twenty mile radius."

She couldn't still the smile or stop the tingle in her nipples. When she first visited to check the house out for the *Timeless* shoot, he'd been a total recluse for more years than she'd been alive. He might look like a man in his early thirties but his true age was far older. That he would suggest a trip out of the house today thrilled her, despite the cause for his suggestion. A journey away from what had nearly become his tomb showed a kind a trust she'd wondered if she'd ever get.

She offered him a smile. "Well," she said, pressing a kiss to his smooth chest, "as it happens, everyone thinks I am out of contact until tomorrow. No details about the full moon being the reason, of course, but I had to tell them I'd not be available. I can't do anything to move the project on until I get a few e-mails back in answer to questions I've asked. I also need Richard's fresh response to my running order. Therefore, I have time on my hands that I can devote all to you. So, yes, we can go out. I'd best do something with my hair. After that, I'll get the local attractions leaflet printed out."

Magnus cupped her chin with his palm, then brushed his lips over hers. "An excellent idea." A single judder on contact told her how he forced control over his baser urges. She was still struggling with hers.

* * * *

"This house feels so homey, so comfortable," she whispered.

"I agree. Hatfield has magic in the air."

"Have you visited here before?"

"Yes, I've visited once or twice, but not for some time."

She darted a glance to him. "Not for some time" might mean fifty years, two hundred years, or perhaps longer. Not a topic they could discuss in such a public place. She held the questions inside and stared at *The Rainbow Portrait* of Elizabeth I. "I think this image is magical." She was conscious others in the wood-paneled Great Hall wished to have their own moment of rapport with the daring virgin queen, yet she lingered for another second of admiration.

"It's one of the best pieces of propaganda produced in the period," Magnus said, when she took a pace away from the portrait.

"Propaganda? But it's beautiful."

"We'll go to get coffee now." He ushered her along toward the doors at the back of the hall.

"Propaganda is a strong word to use. Explain what you mean about the picture?"

As ever, his smile moderated his gaunt air. "The sweet virgin queen was in her fifties when *The Rainbow Portrait* was made, an age when many women of the era were already dead or contemplating their demise."

"But she looks so beautiful, so... Oh, Magnus, was she?"

"No. Queen Elizabeth made sure her portrait painters worked to her specifications. If their work didn't fit her desired image, the paintings were never made public, thus preserving the goddess myth." He squeezed her half-gloved fingers tight as he gave a low chuckle. "As far as I am aware, none of my genus has ever taken a place on the British throne." "Hmm. I still think she must have been very beautiful. The way she manipulated the media of her day was awesome. Clever." She linked her arm through his, glanced up to once again admire his profile, the set of his jaw, his sensual lips, the strong cheekbones, each lured her the same way today as they had the morning they met. No man could compare with this one. He was all hers, at least for now, and she'd do her damndest to make sure it stayed that way.

They entered the coffee shop. She took a seat at a table looking out onto autumnal gardens and he went to the counter. Several female heads turned as he passed. She couldn't fault the women for their admiration, and he didn't seem to notice their interest.

Magnus joined her, placing the tray with coffee and slices of walnut cake on the table. He set out the cups. She added cream and sugar. "I'm glad we came here. I like it," she said, sipping her coffee. "There are some fabulous places for a still camera shoot."

"I don't know about that, but I'm glad we came here, too. The grounds are magnificent."

"There's a kind of permanency to it."

"No," he murmured. "I can't feel such a quality here. We'd need to travel a little farther to find such a thing."

"Farther? Could we?"

Magnus stared across the table at her, his expression guarded as he set the cake fork down. "Yes, we could, but not today. We'll visit the chapel. You'll like it, I'm sure. The stained glass is exquisite."

He'd distanced himself again. After finishing her coffee, she left him at the table for a few moments. Attending to herself in the ladies' lavatory, she understood the reason for his intent focus on the grounds. In his effort to ignore her menstruation, he had pinpointed a laser beam of concentration to their surroundings instead. Perhaps another day or so, but goodness, how she longed for this month's period to finish.

Magnus, wearing a light colored mackintosh that emphasized his height over the other visitors, waited for her in front of the large window at the entrance to the café. His smile of greeting dissolved her, sending her senses reeling.

"Sorry if I kept you waiting. Chapel now?"

"Yes. You'll enjoy it. After, we'll take a walk to find the oaks. I need a reminder of their power."

A reminder? What did he mean?

The chapel proved as beautiful as he'd said. The exquisite stained glass captivated her. The delicacy the craftsmen of a distant age had created spoke of eternally relevant emotions, hopes, and fears.

"Are you ready to go?" she finally asked after they'd stood to admire the windows.

He took her hand in his to lead her out into the autumnal sunlight. She stretched her paces as he hurried her down the path. A fitful breeze swirled leaves, creating a flurry of shadow dancers in the afternoon light.

She breathed fast in the effort to match his swift long stride. "Is there a reason to hurry?"

"No, I wanted to wake myself up a little." He slowed his steps. His eyes gleamed as he turned to her. "It's good to taste the fresh air."

A shiver raced down her spine. Somehow, his mood had changed. She fought off the desire to run, to sprint off toward the distant trees, offering him the challenge to catch her. The last time she'd felt like this they'd shared the kind of lovemaking she'd thought just fantasy. "Magnus?"

"No," he replied. "I want you to see the trees. Once you have, we'll talk about permanence."

"Are you sure?"

"Yes. You know why." His gaze fixed on hers. "Help me, please, don't tease. It's not a good idea, not today."

She longed to roll with him in the bed of leaves, but the image in her mind closed under the shutter of his words. Another time. Another day. She focused on the trees, all of them beautiful in the last phase of this year's leaf. "I've never seen such magnificent colors or such shapes."

"These are probably the oldest oak trees in the grounds. They've had lots of time to grow in the way they wish." Tucking her hand through the crook of his arm, he smiled. "Some of these are century's old, one or two may be more ancient still."

Looking up to his smile, she nodded. His need to feel a part of time should be fed. Perhaps she might find a way. Now he'd mentioned it, she'd work hard to try to arrange a visit to Egypt for them. He'd traveled in his youth and could again. Surely, in Egypt he'd have a sense of time greater than his own.

"Yes, that would be an adventure we both might enjoy." He strode on beside her.

"You heard my thought?"

"Did I?"

"Yes, I didn't say anything aloud, yet you answered me."

He nodded. "I did tell you our link would deepen."

"Yes." She stifled the new rash of concerns this brought. "So you did."

Chapter 3

Heartbeat pounding, he raced over the mossy grass toward the slender figure who headed into the dense thicket of trees. Pale like moonlight, her slim legs moved fast as quicksilver. How he'd delight in stroking the satin smooth flesh of her thighs, teasing in between when he caught her. And catch her he would. When he did, she'd plead for his forgiveness, promise she'd never run again. He'd believe her, of course, until the next time.

The widening gaze, her eyes shining bright as she glanced over her shoulder before taking her first step into the shadows, increased his expectations. She filled him with determination. This tempting minx would howl for him.

How her dreams thrilled him. This one was proving as delightful as the others she'd gifted to him and allowed him to share. Full of life, vitality, and Sian, always Sian, no other woman had ever, or could ever, torment him in the delicious way she did.

The close-knit trees, with thick shadowy undergrowth, slowed his rapid paces to match hers.

A gentle breath, one not his own, told him where she hid. Less than an arm's length from him he caught a flash of the pale dress. He ducked down into the undergrowth at the base of a tall chestnut tree. Amber, ochre, rust, and orange, the autumn woodland colors complimented his mate's pure beauty. Her brandy wine, corkscrew curls cascaded over her shoulders. The rich, creamy lace gown clung tight to her slender waist, molded to her rounded buttocks. She clutched a frothy curdle at the front of the ankle length skirt up above her knees to lessen the impediment of her dress in her barefoot attempt to escape him. All of her image sent his blood rolling in eager excitement. He took a deep breath to force himself to calm. Sian knew him well enough to provoke his desire with ease. This little fantasy lured him toward the culmination hot and hard.

Her calves formed solid muscles as she stood on tiptoe. She took a step, then two more as she hiked the skirt higher. Her slender thighs elongated with her movement, sent a shiver of desire through him.

She glanced from side to side, taking a slow examination of her surroundings. Her breasts moved in the rapid rhythm of quarry at bay. His palms itched to soothe her torment, to tease her nipples until she whimpered. He smiled, for she seemed to have no idea he crouched so near. Her arousing aroma reached him, quickening his pulse. A tiny stir in the air from her body heat alerted him when she took a step closer.

The snap of a twig, as he moved his weight onto his front foot, sent her into flight like a hind from the hunter. She dashed off with a low cry. He paced after her, for memory told him the name and fame of this place. Strange that the woods of Symonds Yat would appear in her dream. She must have a memory of this famous beauty spot. He smiled again.

The escarpment's edge was bounded by a wide swath of forest. Below the top ledge were several more levels in hefty graduated steps, each set with more woodland until the final outcrop offered the courageous a place to plunge into the deep river, carving its way through the valley. She'd left herself no room to maneuver. Run as she might, she would only find a descent she'd rather not make without wings.

She'd flown, but in a machine. Might she fly in their dreams? What a thought. He increased his pace as he followed her, more eager than ever to see what she might do. The autumnal sun still held heat. He scanned the bracken-trimmed cliff top.

"Magnus!"

The cry sped him onward. He dashed along the ledge in search for her.

"Help."

The call held no real distress or fear. Another feint from her. She had the delightful capacity to dissemble like any eighteenth century Venetian courtesan. He could do nothing more than love her—stealthy, clever, and provoking as she was.

At the next shriek, he paused to look down. There, some way below where he stood, Sian's white-knuckled hands clutched a thick tree root protruding from the black soil of the bank. He could also see a small ledge under her foot supporting her weight.

"Ah, so helpless," he said as he ambled along. "I have to say, there are times when I worry about your psyche." He crouched, reaching forward to grasp her.

"I slipped."

A smile to delight him curved her cheek as he caught her beneath the arms and hauled her up. Once she stood on solid ground, he covered her mouth with his and lowered his hands until her sweet rounded ass sat in his palms. With her caught fast in his embrace, he swept at the back of her skirt to brush off the dirt, until she squirmed and whimpered in their kiss.

"I'm afraid, sometimes your desire to be captive is too much for me to refuse," he explained before he gave her a hearty swat.

Green diamond bright, her widened gaze met his. Her lips parted with a gasp of surprise. The trees took on a hazy hue; the leaves falling to the forest floor became mere smudges of brown such as a child might paint. "Do you wish me to take control of the dream?" he asked before he kissed the warmth of her neck.

"No."

She angled her head, caught his lips, and took them captive with hers. The delight of her kiss swept away any need for further words. Abandoning their kiss, he hoisted her in his embrace, stepping away from the ledge. Her small feet scrambled in the leaf litter, as he backed her fast into the smooth bulk of an ash tree's trunk. He hauled the delicate lace gown up as he pinned her in place. He wedged one thigh between hers, nudging and rolling against her pussy. His cock swelled solid in four heartbeats, eager for her. He molded his palm to her breast, enjoying the rigid lump of her nipple. "Now or later?"

She gave a small groan.

Answer enough for him.

His blood sang in his ears, for she wore no knickers. She hooked her thigh high and tight around his, clutched him closer. He needed no more encouragement. Fingers working quickly, he unlaced the hide breeches to free his erection to seek its warm, moist quarry.

"Oh, God." She stilled as he sought her entrance. "Magnus, there, oh, yes."

He held back for a second.

"Now, please. Oh, please." She tilted her hips to try to guide him inside.

Triumph warmed his chest at her pitiful whimper. "Are you sorry you ran?" he asked, before he smothered her mouth with his, drowning her attempt at a reply. He shoved his erection deep into her with one smooth lurch forward.

Sian clasped his shoulders with her fingers digging deep. Her sweet pussy welcomed him inside. She gave a low throaty moan.

Pleasure.

Hot delight.

Perfect.

Wonderful.

He pulled back from her. "You are all mine," he said, holding on as she arched back against the tree, grinding her hips to his. The swift pulses inside her took him hard and fast. Orgasm raged, stole consciousness, breath, so everything dissolved in pleasure. He clung to the light with one fingertip as his body powered into hers to give her everything he could.

Together, they sank down from the smooth ash tree onto the bed of silky grass.

* * * *

Clasping his face between her palms, Sian kissed him. Still locked together, they rolled on the rumpled bed. "Magnus," she gasped. She relaxed in his arms, the sensual pleasure of the dream rolling though her until she closed her drowsy eyes.

"Reality challenges our dreams. I need you."

His erection swelled inside her. The thick hardness engorged to make her catch her breath. Lifting himself up onto his arms, he eased in and out of her. He probed. His eyes glittered. The spark she found in his gaze added to the tingles. She reached up to caress the firm muscles of his shoulders before she wrapped her arms around his neck. His first deep thrust made her eager for more. He took up a rapid pounding pace that forced her down into the mattress with each reentry.

He'd never been like this before. His deliberate movements gave no allowance for her to dictate their pace. Tonight, she'd no choice but be receptive. He pummeled her, obliterated any thought she might have but him. She closed her eyes, her rapid breath racing with his.

Orgasm clenched her muscles so she clasped him tight inside her, to fight to hold his hot flood deep within. She dissolved into blissful perfection. "I adore you," she moaned. His flow slowed, and she eased her thighs clamped on his waist.

His heavy breaths hid any words she could recognize, but his satisfied groan filled her with pleasure. Closing her eyes, she drifted on a tide of satisfaction.

* * * *

Sian woke to light spilling in from between the wide curtains. Moving her stiff limbs, she spread her thighs so she could pull back to ease away from him. He mumbled in his sleep. Sighing, she sank down with a soft moan, and eased her aching muscles. Good God, she'd spent months doing yoga, but tonight it hadn't helped at all.

Was an all night lock with your partner wolfie or tantric? Who the heck knew? He'd sure made her wonder.

Her wish for a chase through the woods when they had visited Hatfield began all this. She'd enticed him in the dream she'd led, but perhaps she'd not repeat the scenario for a while. The low sound of her name spread contented warmth through her. Turning toward him, she hooked her leg over his and rested her arm about his waist. She sprawled onto her stomach to go back to sleep.

A fresh call of "*Sian*" pried into her peace. A shiver raced down her spine, but she fought off the enticement to another dream, because this one came from someone other than Magnus. The screechy voice was somehow familiar. It belonged to someone with glossy dark hair and cold eyes, a person who yelled so loud the noise grew to painful howls. Silly, it couldn't be Franklyn. He couldn't call to her, not from the rest home. Another shriek echoed but she ignored it.

As if she'd dream with a howler. Too tired to consider more about the interruption in her thoughts, she edged closer to Magnus's warmth.

He tightened his arm about her and sleep blotted out everything else.

Chapter 4

The tenth of November, the day for the film shoot, drew nearer, and although Sian's preparations for the event were impeccable, Magnus's concerns grew. His recollection of the day she first came to the house, all business, bold and sassy, regenerated. How he'd wanted her despite it, or because of her reaction when he faced her down. Courage like hers was rare. Heaven help him, he'd discovered more of its depths these last two months. Sian's bravery gave him hope, and he took a gamble on it. Faced with her sheer determination, he had tested fate and chanced she might leave him after he'd explained to her why he lived alone as he did. He remained uncertain if he should accept the joy of the love she offered. There were few people like Sian.

Each dawn, as the shoot-day approached, he dwelt on the need to find another place to spend his time during the days when the whole camera team, the musicians, dancers, sound crew, and all the many others she'd explained would be necessary for the film, came to the house. The prospect of so many disturbed his equilibrium. He'd not invited so many strangers into his home for more years than he cared to think about. Though he did his best to disguise his apprehension, without a doubt, Sian knew.

"Magnus, it will be fine. You can come to watch the filming if you want. Think of the event as if it were a step back through your vacation pictures. I promise the costumes will bring back happy memories."

He shook his head. "Thank you for the thought, but no, I'd rather not. Perhaps I'll spend the day researching decoration for the renovation of the conservatory."

"If you're sure. I'll keep the crew to the schedule. Everyone will be out of the house and off the grounds by six-thirty, no later, I promise. That way we can have dinner and the evening together." She offered him a smile filled with confidence.

"Wonderful, I'll look forward to dining with you."

"Hmm..." She stared at the letter she'd opened. "Here's some information you might want to look at, too."

He accepted the papers. "Green Girls?"

"Yes, in answer to my advert regarding the walled garden. It won't put itself to rights, and as much as I enjoy looking at it, I don't think we'll resurrect it alone. In my opinion, we need specialist help. I like the look of this group."

He assessed the business card, professional enough to be encouraging. Opening the sales literature, he gave it a quick glance. "Every employee is a descendant of a Land Army girl?"

"Yes, it's their advertising gimmick. They all had relatives in the Land Army in the war. You must know of the Land Army."

He nodded. A wave of helpless adoration hit him at this new example of her happy knack of finding his weak spots. If she'd been a tigress in another life, he'd not be surprised, because Sian sank her claws into him with loving relish, tearing into his open heart. "Yes, I have recollections of the Land Army, my dear. I was quite active during wartime. It was easier."

"Anyway, what do you think of their price list, their offers?" She nibbled at a piece of toast.

He shrugged his shoulders. "I've not much knowledge to make a comparison."

"Well, I think they're impressive. I thought it might be a good idea to contact the director, Martha Raynalds. I checked her resume on their website. It looks good."

"Very well." He flipped the pricing pamphlet over and caught a glimpse of the photograph of the director. "Dorothy Fowler?" he whispered.

"No, Magnus, Martha Raynalds." Sian got up from her seat at the breakfast table. "I have to do one final e-mail swoop of the team this morning. Then, once I get all the 'I'm so happy' replies, I'll know everything is ready for the shoot. I'm itching to get it over with."

He smiled in response to her enthusiasm because he wholeheartedly agreed. Once this music film was complete, he'd close the door on Gorsewell Productions and so would Sian. His concern with her taking over the arrangements for the filming remained. If, while he recovered at the rest home, Franklyn Gorsewell so much as squeaked in her dreams, he'd face a reckoning. After this film shoot ended, there should be no more reason for Sian to have any contact with the obnoxious lout.

Though she'd not said, not since the dreadful night when Franklyn had woken from the drug induced coma and the evil wretch had invaded her dream, he knew the jealous bastard still tried to lure her. Only yesterday Franklyn had called to her. Gorsewell was playing with the dream interactions. Magnus had sensed the slimy maggot's presence once or twice in the aftermath of the dreams he'd shared with her as he and Sian had slept.

The night he had sought vengeance and attacked Franklyn, he should have finished him off.

He closed his eyes at the image of the blood-splattered apartment. Such a powerful memory should have held a kernel of satisfaction, but it didn't, only a deep fear at what the beast's bite could do.

His initial gut instinct after Gorsewell attacked her in the dream, had been yes, here was one he would have to subdue. The visit to the hospital with Sian at the beginning of October had set him wondering at the possibilities. Franklyn suspected him for what he was—he'd sensed it. Hence, he'd given a sharp heads-up to a potential werewolf to know his place when in the presence of his creator.

When he returned home with Sian, along with easing her fears, he'd tried to dismiss his initial thoughts as an overreaction to the situation. So much medical interference, the drips, the drugs, the blood transfusions, surely they must mean Franklyn remained a man.

They must.

Perhaps he should do a little investigating the day the film crew was here when Sian was busy. He'd find out what Gorsewell was up to in the rest home where he recuperated from his injuries. The wish that he'd gnawed at Gorsewell's shoulder for longer nagged, an ever present concern. A huge sigh left him, for if Franklyn were to become a werewolf, his and Sian's life would never be the same.

The consequences of his carelessness would need time and effort to put right. He could not begin the process until, if Gorsewell were infected, the yob accepted the inevitable and came to his creator in deference. Somehow, he hoped that would never happen. Should Gorsewell change, then he would feel compelled to return here. Perhaps when he felt strong enough to challenge for Sian, he would.

A prickle of sensation lifted the hairs on his arms. If Gorsewell wanted a fight, he'd be overjoyed to oblige. No twenty-first century spiv, the perfect description of Gorsewell, a furtive, cheating, greedy bully, would take the woman he adored. He took a swig of tea and swallowed. Presently he must await Gorsewell's healing. He'd deal with the outcome when the first opportunity presented itself.

Once he'd finished his cup of Earl Grey, he glanced at the promotional pages Sian had left for him, Green Girls and their company director. He looked again, certain this image could be no one but Dorothy Fowler. A finger above six feet tall, with a physique to match, she was able to down a pint of the Highwayman's Rest's Best Bitter as fast as any man. Dorothy had also shared other appetites as demanding. So many years had passed since he last saw the woman he remembered. But the sweep of fair hair from this girl's wide forehead, the strong but attractive open features, he couldn't doubt his memory. Yet Dorothy would be old now, in her eighties or nineties, not youthful and full of vigor, nor capable of shoving a wheelbarrow full of vegetables. A sudden inkling gave him gooseflesh.

No, impossible.

Damn it, he'd call the gardening company this morning as soon as they opened to find out if his intuition was right.

* * * *

"Thank you, Mrs. Tyson. We'd be most pleased. Sian and I have enjoyed all the meals Cook has so far presented. Yes, of course, I understand. You have my thanks." He set the phone on its cradle before picking it up to call through to the study where Sian worked for much of each day to prepare for the filming. "Can we talk for a few moments?" he asked.

"Hi, Magnus, I'll just click this thing. There, yes, done. Now, you have my full attention."

"Mrs. Tyson has rung through to me. It would appear, since I'd not told her of other plans, Cook has taken it on herself to present us with a fine Bonfire Night meal tomorrow evening, including a Neapolitan Bombe for dessert."

"A what?"

"It's an amaretto-laced mousse."

"Oh, will you want fireworks, too, Magnus?"

"Good grief, no. We'll make our own." The low chuckle in response warmed his blood. "I do think I've discovered a surprise of my own to share with you. One I hope you'll understand."

"Of course, I will. I'll meet you for lunch. You can tell me all about it then. I'm afraid I have to go. The bass player in Dreams is having a bit of a meltdown. His girlfriend is in rehab and he doesn't want to be too far away from her for too long. I need to dole out a lot of reassurance."

"No doubt he will be grateful. You're so good at reassurance. I'll meet you in the dining room at one." He set the phone down. When focused on others in this way, her voice always made him smile. Part of his desire for her originated from her rare generosity of spirit. His confidence she would understand what he'd discovered this morning remained high.

Sian's passion for beauty encapsulated the needs of body and spirit as well as aesthetic pleasures. He'd never met another woman like her. Julia had demonstrated a similar ability to meet him in dreams, but she had possessed nothing like Sian's talents to control him, or the bountiful spirit to offer herself in such an unconditional way. Julia had never given herself in the same manner, despite her promises of love. When faced with the question of their marriage, Julia had obeyed the will of her father, who had thought him a wastrel, and she had declined. He shrugged his shoulders. The heartbreak from so long ago seemed as though it belonged to another person, yet at the time he'd thought her refusal permanently stole every hope of joy.

No, not that, for he had dreamed and hoped still, even when he reached Italy. Julia had dreamed with him. When those interactions ceased, he'd been full of fears for her. His return from the continent to find Julia dead shattered him.

Sian was something so much more than Julia had ever been, vibrant and stronger, too. His feelings for her were…like the first time he saw electric light in London in the late nineteenth century and understood what it meant. She was his true mate. He could taste it, feel it stronger inside with every day they shared.

The agony of the question plaguing him clenched an iron fist around his heart. To make her his forever, he must offer her the bite of the beast. A shiver rolled down his spine.

Not yet. She must be sure in her decision and…she was so much younger than him. Even though she thought herself ready, he doubted she understood all she would lose.

He gazed back down to the image of the Green Girl's director. Another cloud of concerns to mull over, but simple in comparison to the dilemma he and Sian faced. She would understand the circumstance regarding Dorothy. Perhaps she'd recognize his need to take things a step further so he could find out the truth.

The prospect of a living connection to his past warmed his heart. Bonfire Night tomorrow, the fifth. There would be fireworks in the village, though he never attended the pub display. He liked standing up on the roof walkway to watch, yet sometimes the thunder of noise brought back so many recollections of the war, he crept back into the house filled with sorrowful memories. Not of the second war when he'd known Dorothy Fowler, but the first when he'd known no one but servants and the lads who made up his company in the mud-bath trenches of Verdun and the Somme.

He shook his head and glanced at the computer. An age must have passed since he thought of the pals he'd led, encouraged, and marched with through the mire as they made their way from one battle to the next. Pursing his lips, he whistled the first few notes of "It's a Long Way to Tipperary," astonished he recalled the tune with such ease. He must be growing sentimental. He hit the touch screen to refresh his search and focused.

Artifacts for the conservatory should be his goal for the morning. Sian was always full of her morning's achievements when they met at lunch, and he must have something positive to tell her. After that, he'd share his other news.

* * * *

"What do you have there?"

"I printed this out. We could go tomorrow evening after dinner." Sian waved a piece of paper. "It's a Bonfire Night firework display, hosted by Stonewells Cricket Club, not more than three miles away. The display starts at nine-thirty. I think it looks like it would be great, as long as there's no rain. Can we go?" Her smile beamed her enthusiasm.

"Of course," he said. "You have found the perfect post-dining entertainment. I have to say dinner tomorrow evening will be *tres* chic. The staff are preparing an extravaganza between them."

"Sounds exciting." She sat, reached over for a plate, and passed one to him before she helped herself to sandwiches and a side salad.

He took a chicken portion and a little potato salad for himself. "Indeed, it seems Mrs. Tyson and Cook were rather concerned we were alone so much last week, thought perhaps we'd starved. Well, you more than I, or so I think. They've enlisted the help of the local Women's Institute to create a celebratory menu, apparently. I think half the village has been involved in planning this while the ladies have been away from the house."

Sian laughed. "I see. I'm looking forward to the results. So, shall we book a cab?"

"I think if I telephoned my mechanic Monty, he may be willing to drive us in one of the cars. We'll not take Bertha. I'd hate to get holes in her canvas roof from a stray firework. It's so hard to get replacements for vintage vehicles, and although Bentley are very good suppliers, I've had to have things custom made once or twice. Maybe one of the other cars would benefit from a spin. Do we need to book tickets for this event?"

Sian pushed the advert across the table to him. "No, it says they take a donation of five pounds on the gate."

"I see. The display seems interesting."

"Don't you go comparing this to the fireworks for the king or anything extravagant like that." Her gaze snapped with crackles of her own.

A wash of tenderness hit him. She spoke so readily of his longevity, as though it might be an ordinary part of their life together. "Of course not. I'm sure the display will be a most pleasant, simple entertainment." He broke the chicken leg in two. "Thank you, for finding the event. I shall look forward to it. I'll telephone Monty this afternoon. I'm sure he won't mind taking one of the cars out tomorrow evening."

"Now, what was it you wanted to tell me? I'm intrigued—you sounded so mysterious."

He took a deep breath. "A discovery I made regarding the horticultural company you found."

"Oh, yes, the Green Girls. "

"Indeed. It appears their sales pitch is no exaggeration. Martha Raynalds is, in fact, the descendant of a Land Girl who worked in this area in the 1940s."

Sian's eyebrows arched. "No. Did you know her ancestor?"

The link between them had deepened, as he'd suspected it would. Already, he must make an effort to keep information back from her. "Yes, I believe I did."

The delightful smile dissolved. Her brows drew together as she narrowed her eyes. "How did you know her?"

He gazed down at his plate for a second or two in an effort to gain time. Today, he'd made a grave mistake, one born of his stupid lack of emotional perception. Sian was special in so many ways, but she remained a young woman, with all the emotions of a young woman. She'd not had a couple of centuries to teach her the true depths of his callous selfishness. Cursing his foolishness, he looked at the wedge of tomato on his plate as if it were the latest art offering to the Tate Gallery.

Sian might be hurt if he told her his suspicions, yet he couldn't live his life refusing to share the truth with her. As time passed, it would destroy them. Due to their situation, they both had to accept unusual occurrences, some of them difficult. He looked up into eyes full of fire and ice. After a small cough he spoke. "Martha Raynalds's grandmother, a delightful woman, Dorothy Fowler, worked in this locality for some time. I, er…" He paused.

"You slept with her?" She set her half-eaten sandwich down.

"A very brief liaison."

"Did she know the truth about you?"

"No."

"Did you love her?"

He shook his head. He shouldn't have told her, should have kept the secret. "I was home on leave. We met at the Highwayman's Rest. The pub in Heathstoke. Dorothy was a marvelous darts player. I spent a little time with her during my leave."

Her gaze held his, searching, but she didn't speak.

"No, I didn't love her, Sian. I have only loved twice, you know that."

"Do I?"

"Yes, you do." He swiped the napkin over his fingers before he took her hand in his. "I have loved Julia and you. No other woman has touched me in the way you do. After Julia's death, I thought I would never love again. A creature such as I has little right to ask for love. I'd not offered to make Julia like me, therefore she had no protection as I do. I never wanted another cruel disease like smallpox to steal my loved one from me in such a bitter way again. My passion for Julia seems a pallid thing in comparison to my feelings for you. I never anticipated I might find you."

"So, why tell me of this woman Dorothy? Did you think your—" She shook her head. "It's no good, I don't understand, Magnus."

"You would have discovered it, either in the dreams or from my reactions to her granddaughter. You would have known, and I thought it worse for you to find out then, rather than now from me." He pressed a kiss to her palm.

She leaned back from the table. The napkin slipped from her other hand. "You've booked them?"

"Yes. They'll come to the house at the end of November. I've scheduled the visit to take place before the next full moon. From my conversation with Martha, as long as I'm agreeable to their terms and plans, once they've evaluated the garden, they'll work through part of December to clear and repair, do some minor decorative planting. After the initial work, they'll offer me more in-depth plans for spring."

"I see."

"I'm not sure you do, but I thought it important to tell you."

She narrowed her eyes. "There's more. I know it."

"It's an inkling I have. I won't know for definite until I meet Martha in person."

"You think she's a relative?"

He stared, not astonished she'd understood so quickly. Her pain radiated to him, but it was too late to do much to mend the situation. "It may be possible."

She removed her hand from where it topped his. The set of her shoulders squared. "Magnus, how could you?" She shifted her gaze from him to stare away across the dining room.

"I wanted you to know."

The gloss of tears shone in her eyes.

Guilt snapped through him. "Would you rather I'd not said?"

"No." She faced him again. Her sadness poured like a corrosive through his soul. "But I wish you could understand."

"I do."

"No, you've no idea. Since you told me the truth about you in September, I've spent hours longing for you to say we will be together always. That you'll allow me to be your love in truth, that one day we'll become a real couple and have children. Yet, each time we've spoken of it, you back off, tell me it's impossible, you won't inflict your malady on a child. Yet today, you sit here at lunch and tell me a woman gardener I found on the internet happens to be what you believe is your granddaughter!" She swiped at a tear. "How could you?" She pushed the chair back and stood. The thick weave of her curls swung when she shook her head. She turned on her heel to the door. "I need to think about this."

"Sian! It's not like that."

The heavy carved door slammed behind her. He buried his head in his hands. Sometimes the truth hurt more than anyone could imagine.

Chapter 5

Sian grabbed her jacket from the walk-in cupboard in the entrance hall. She shoved her arms in the sleeves as she headed out the front door and through the black and white tiled portico. Outside, her confusion didn't lessen as she'd hoped. She strode down the cinder path, her vision bleary with tears. She palmed them away, but more fell. What an arrogant, soulless, thoughtless bastard he could be.

No one in their right mind would welcome the news he'd just shared. The possibilities this discovery opened up were so disturbing she couldn't get her head around it. She'd not considered he might have had a child. This woman, who could be his granddaughter, might represent something she could scarce believe. Was this the only relative he had? Over the years, he might have fathered hundreds of children. He could have scattered infants throughout eighteenth century Europe in his youth. More since as he traveled. Though he'd explained his relationship with Julia, he couldn't have always lived like a monk since 1763.

She stood still where the cinder path forked, one side leading to the gateway to the rose garden, the other to the lake.

"How could you?" she yelled.

A wave of anger sent an adrenalin rush barreling through her body. She broke into a run, pounding down the path toward the lawn and lake.

No, not that way. She changed direction for she'd no wish to look at the pagoda or recall the golden autumnal day she and Magnus had first made love skin to skin. What a bloody fool she was. The steps to the terrace came into view. The early autumn day that had changed her life, all happened here. After the best sex she'd ever known, and with her shredded underwear in the bin, she came here to sit with Magnus for tea. Trust and truth, they'd spoken of both, but the conversation had delved into much more. Magnus hadn't pressed her, but she'd acknowledged there was no other man she wanted. She'd trusted him, but look at the truth he had offered her.

She wasn't good enough for him to make her his forever. Oh, no, she was just a one-lifetime screw. Not much more than a roll in the hay for a guy who was near immortal.

He'd refused to make her like him, point-blank. No way. Yet a girl he met in the pub had his child. "Selfish then. Just as bad now!"

Turning away, she ran off the path, over the slope of slippery grass, along the thicker, rough turf on the flat ground. She didn't slow the pace as she pushed herself hard on the track into the woods. She dodged to avoid fallen branches and rotting logs half-buried in the undergrowth. Despite the difficult ground, she raced on until her chest burned fiery with her efforts. No matter how fast she ran, she couldn't leave the pain behind.

Twiggy branches lashed her face as she dashed through the trees. One vicious hit caught her cheek a stinging blow that forced her to slow. A few paces on, she had to pause. She bent with her hands on her thighs. A muscle burn flamed. She must make the time to run more. Finally, her breathing slowed, her legs eased, and she sank down onto a mossy damp tree stump to think.

She'd never imagined he might have had a child, or dreamed the idea would hurt so much. Self-analysis proved hard. It wasn't the child, or in this case grandchild, who might appear in his life that bothered her most. It was the symbolism of what it might mean.

Magnus said he hadn't loved the woman. That, at least, was something.

She wiped her eyes with a tissue, and her nose with another, as she recalled his surprised expression at her reaction. He didn't expect her to be hurt or even upset because…he thought she wouldn't feel that way.

She shook her head trying to get into Magnus's mind. He thought he'd offered her something no one else had ever had from him. She stood and walked for a short way as an idea formed. No one else had ever gotten so close to him. Maybe she'd gotten more intimate than even Julia. Of course, Magnus offered Julia marriage, but she'd refused and they had parted, in the physical form at least.

They hadn't discussed marriage, but with contraception, there was no need these days. At least they had that freedom in their physical relationship. And, God, it was so good with him.

The complexities of life with Magnus needed a lot of mental agility. She swallowed past the ache in her throat, blinking her eyes to finish the tears.

Rain dripped from the branches, oozed through her hood, sneaked in cold rills down the back of her jacket. She ambled on, kicking dead wood out of her path with no real sense of direction. Did it really matter if she met a woman who could be his relative?

A huge sigh broke. It mattered all right. The news rocked her trust, shook up their insulated little world. That was part of the problem.

She must try to get him out of the house more. For twenty-four and a half days each month, he passed as an extremely attractive man. A dozen women checked him out in not so subtle a fashion the day they'd visited Hatfield. A fresh prickle raised gooseflesh. Never having been the jealous sort, the heart-thumping reaction to his news had surprised her as much as she might have shocked Magnus. She'd not permit jealousy to beat her. She'd squash the emotion before it took a hold.

For at least part of each month he could go out, meet people, socialize. They could even go to London. If she could persuade him to take a trip there, he could forget for a time the werewolf days. She would make sure they came back in time for the change.

She sniffed because her tissues sat balled in her hand, a sodden, crumpled mess. The raucous call of crows sweeping over the trees brought her back to the afternoon and where she stood. Wiping her nose on the back of her hand, she turned to head to the house, trying to work out the convoluted path she'd taken to get to this spot in the woods. She couldn't see the building through the trees. Slowly, she checked for any sign of the roof or chimneys. The gleam of one of the lights from the turrets shone through the pines. Magnus had repaired a large part of the house after the bomb damage in the war. A pity there wasn't more illumination on that section to show her a path back. Muddy and sodden as she was, she'd aim for the front door so she didn't trail dirt into the drawing room, or have to take the longer route around the house to the kitchen entrance. She walked toward the light, cradling her hurt like an infant to be soothed. Magnus was hers, and one day they would be together forever.

* * * *

Inside the glazed portico, she paused, flipped off her muddy shoes, and took off her wet jacket. She placed her hand on the house door and it opened at once. She took an involuntary step back, dealing with the staff here didn't come easy at times, and today the housekeeper seemed almost psychic.

"Miss Sian, what has happened?"

"Nothing dreadful. I got caught in the rain, Mrs. Tyson. I'm a bit wet that's all."

"I thought you'd gone out with Mr. Johansson."

"He's gone out?" She couldn't hide the astonishment.

"Yes, miss. Mr. Johansson took the car over two hours ago. I thought you were with him. I thought it a little odd he didn't say whether you'd be in to dine."

"Yes," she said, fighting off the catch in her throat. "It is a bit odd. I'm sure he'll be back and we'll…" She could hardly believe he'd gone out in the car. Would he be back this evening? "I'm going to take a hot shower. Would you please bring me a pot of tea upstairs?"

"Of course, miss."

"Thanks, Mrs. Tyson." Certain the housekeeper would be aware she'd been crying, she hurried into the main hallway to the stairs. Magnus never left the house. She had to give him reason to go out, or offer the lure of entertainments to persuade him to venture into the world beyond Darnwell. Every time they'd gone anywhere, she'd always found the venue. She thumped up the stairs.

Their room was spotless. The log fire burned steady, livid coals forming from the thick rack of wood. The hearth offered a comforting glow in the late afternoon gloom. Tyson would come up with her tea in a few minutes. The housekeeper would draw the drapes after she put down the tea tray, and then leave. The strangeness of having staff to wait on her, like in some kind of television drama, still struck her. Most days when Cook and Mrs. Tyson were here, there was at least one encounter when she waited for someone to call, "That's a wrap."

She glanced around at the sumptuous splendor. Soon, she'd be alone with nothing but the carved wolves at the foot of the bed for company. She sighed, tugging off her muddy jeans and damp socks. Clutching the wet bundle, she went into the bathroom where she stuffed the grubby clothes into a large laundry hamper.

The copper bath beckoned, offering her comfort and warmth. A long soak might make her feel better. She peeled off her shirt as the water ran. A shame he had no perfumed candles in here. At least she could have the lights a nice moody violet. She tipped some Ylang Ylang scented oil into the water.

The bedroom door slammed. Concerned Mrs. Tyson might struggle with a tray, she went through to the bedroom.

Magnus.

She froze, staring into the gray eyes that bored into her.

"Where did you go?" he asked, his voice clipped. His tone sent a shiver through her.

"To the woods. I needed to think."

"I looked for you." His voice grated like minced gravel.

"But you didn't find me."

The corner of his mouth twitched. "No. You were lost to me."

She swallowed hard, blinking back a hot teary sting in her eyes.

The tap at the door rang like a gunshot. Magnus snapped around to stare at the housekeeper.

"I've brought up the tea for you, Miss Sian. There are two cups. I saw Mr. Johansson park the car." Mrs. Tyson's voice faltered as she looked to them both. She placed the tray on the side table by the hearth. "I'll leave this here, sir. Do call down if there's anything else you need." Tyson backed away and whisked out the door.

Magnus reached out. He touched the curls at the side of her face. "Your hair's wet."

She shivered. "I know."

He rested his hand on her arm. "You're cold, too."

"Yes, Magnus. I'm wet, cold, and—" *God damn it.* She couldn't stop her lips clamping together as she grimaced, fighting tears. A fresh shiver chased the first.

"I didn't mean to hurt you." He slid his arm around her and urged her into his embrace. "Forgive me? Please?"

She didn't put her arms around him but remained motionless.

He held her for a long, bleak time.

"The bath's running," she eventually said.

"Go and bathe." He released her from his embrace. "I'll pour the tea. We'll talk when you're warm."

Right this second, though she ached for him, she couldn't make this easy or offer what he wanted—forgiveness.

"Sian, let me help you." He urged her toward the bathroom.

He'd said those words once before, the first day they made love in the flesh. She'd wilted with the power of his command that day. He'd robbed her of all the will she possessed. Today proved no different. He guided her with his hand on her shoulder. She moved as he wished until they both stood in the steamy warmth of the bathroom. Magnus flipped off the taps before he tested the temperature with his hand. He yanked off his shirt. The rest of his clothes followed, dumped on top of the chair in the corner.

Dazed, she stood—present, yet not. Awake, but unmoving. The mesmeric command he used was a deliberate control. She had neither the strength or the wish to fight it. The physical lure of him proved as powerful as ever. She feasted her gaze on his body. The need to touch him grew stronger, and she took a step forward.

He lifted her chin so she met his eyes. So much sorrow and concern filled his gaze. The combination brought a lump to her throat. She raised her arms so he could tug off the camisole top. He took the chain with the key to his wolf bonds from her neck and bent to ease her panties down her legs.

"Now, get into the water," he said.

She stepped into the bath. "Oh," she exclaimed when the heat contacted her chilled flesh.

He joined her, easing himself down at the taps end. A gentleman even though they'd quarreled. She lay back in the water until it warmed the base of her ears. It wasn't the kind of row many couples might have. Not a yell and shout fight. No.

This was worse. He'd hurt her and not understood how.

"I do understand. I can only plead for you to forgive me. I didn't think it through before I told you. I never meant to cause you pain. Believe me, all I want is to protect you from the horrors that can be caused by what I am."

The day dissolved with the touch of his palm on her leg, the way he smoothed her skin. He leaned forward. A tingle of sensation snapped her back to full consciousness as he placed his other hand on her thigh, rubbed with his fingertips until she breathed out on a long sigh.

"We need to talk."

His low voice soothed her more than the warmth of the water. A tremble shook her lip. They'd talked already, and she'd lost it in a way she'd never experienced before. She hooked her forefinger around his. "What do you want to say?"

"Will you listen to all of it?"

"Yes, Magnus."

"I want to tell you how much I need you and make you believe it. If you understood how important you are to me, then today you'd not have been so hurt."

She sat up. Her hair dripped over her shoulders. "You think I'd have been okay with you having a child with a woman you hardly knew, whereas, with me, you've said it can't happen. I don't understand the difference."

Magnus closed his eyes for a long moment. "The two things are not one and the same, not at all. One is an accidental event from long before you were born and many years before I met you. The other is your wish for something very different."

"So, if this girl is your granddaughter, she'll be like any other girl?"

"I didn't say that."

"Then I don't see the difference at all, at least not about the idea of a child. You say you didn't have a permanent relationship with her mother."

He leaned forward to cup her chin in his palm. "I know. But, please, believe me, there is a difference. For us to share our lives, for you to have the child you want, within a lasting relationship, we'd not merely make love. There is much more to consider."

"I see. So, in fact, we're back to our last conversation about this. You have to make me your mate, not your wife, not your live-in lover, but your mate."

He reached for her, put his arms about her and pulled her up from the warmth so she straddled his thighs. She closed her eyes as he took her mouth with his. He kissed her until she whimpered.

"Yes."

His thought powered through her, melted her bones and she relaxed against him. Desire smoldered in her skin, so her nipples hardened in anticipation of his caresses. She moved her mouth from his. "Then do it, Magnus. Please, I'll beg if I must. Do it. Make me your mate."

"Not yet." He moved her to lie over him in the water. "I know you think you are certain this is what you want, but I need you to have more time to think about all the possibilities, the dangers, the way of life you'd have to accept."

She sighed. Some, though not all of the pain, eased from her heart.

"Forgive me?" he asked. "I swear I'll not be so thoughtless again."

Everything she'd told herself in the woods, all the tears, the hurt, and the determination to do whatever she must to keep him, swept through her. His reasoning caught at her heart.

He tightened his embrace about her until she gave a small squeak.

"I'll not let you go unless you truly wish to leave. I will know if such bitterness is to be mine, Sian. I want you to stay so very much. Everything is right with you." He found her lips with his and kissed her until the water around them matched their body heat.

"I'll take you to bed now and show you how much you mean to me until dawn." He rose from the tub with her in his arms.

"You'd best tell the staff we won't be down for dinner," she murmured.

"You can telephone down to them while I dry you off in front of the hearth." His dark gaze held hers, full of promises to make her stomach roll with desire.

God help her, wolf curse or not, she loved him.

Chapter 6

Hunched from the pain, and clumsy in his efforts to open the door, Franklyn Gorsewell dropped the keys. He stooped in a welter of agony. He grunted like a hog as he fumbled around the moss-coated plant container beside the front step to find them. At last, the chilly metal met his fingers and he opened the door into his ground floor apartment. After kicking the pile of mail and assorted junk publications aside, he went down the short hallway. The fine hairs on the back of his neck rose as he walked into his darkened sitting room.

The place stank.

The unmistakable scent of urine, mixed with the metallic smell of blood, blended with a savage animal musk. The odor sent a shiver down his spine.

He flipped on the light. The arcing splatter of blood up the walls had spurted from an artery to create a huge pointillist curve on the ceiling. The boarded up window relieved the rusty brown pattern. Thank God, the neighbor found him when she did. The patio window glass had shattered the night of the attack. A welter of lethal shards still lay where they'd fallen, some stained with his blood. Many sat end up, buried in the thick carpet.

He'd bled so much, he should be dead.

The wide patch of dried blood appeared so much worse than he'd imagined. No wonder the ambulance crew and the doctors in the emergency room thought he could lose his arm from the horrific injuries.

A fresh memory of the creature with its snarling jaws tormented him. Instinctively, he drew back from the pain of its bite. He forced himself to look at the room. No monstrous beast salivated with hate in its eyes. He set his bag down by the door, as far from the glass fragments on the carpet as he could. No one would believe the truth if he tried to explain. It was better the medical staff had recorded that the glass caused his wounds.

His recovery, remarkable in itself, had given the medical team so much to ponder. The causes had faded from their interest, but he'd known. Hovering in a daze from the painkillers, he hung on to his sense of self by his fingertips. He'd understood when the torn skin, savaged muscle, and shattered bone healed at a stunning speed. Inside he'd changed. While he had recovered, he'd accepted the strange alteration to his senses, and he'd learned to dream.

A surge of excitement twitched through his cock. In his first dream after the attack, he'd found Sian, along with a sense of reality he'd never experienced before. The heated throbbing recalled how close he'd been to screwing her. He'd lunged between her wide-spread thighs, his cock oozing pre-cum, and he'd almost entered her pussy.

She'd been coy at first as they'd danced, typical Sian, but when she'd understood he wasn't going to take "no" for an answer that night, she'd kissed him. He had thrust his tongue down her throat as she gave in. He could still hear her enticing noises, feel her writhing beneath him on the smooth polished floor when he had peeled off her short dress, followed by the sexy bra. The little whimpers she'd made when he had sucked at her nipples and tugged down her tiny panties to strip her naked, had almost taken him over the edge.

He shook at the recollection of her luscious, smooth, round ass under his palms, her hot, hard nipples pressed tight against his chest when he moved to mount her. If only he'd managed to go all the way to get inside her that night.

His desire, checked by her youth and innocence when he'd first hired her, had built until he had to fight to control it whenever she was near. The wicked little temptress, she knew he wanted her. She tormented him. He'd thought it kind of cute the way she'd made so many efforts in her leather gear or rubber dress, all intended to appeal to him. He'd been on the verge of making a move when she had gone walk-about at the Darnwell Estate.

His sweet, sexy muse had no idea how many times, and in how many ways, he'd filled her pussy with his cum over the last four years. But, the strange dream he'd had the night he awoke in hospital, so powerful and strong, it took his need for her up another million notches. He'd tasted something better than the usual lust-filled explorations his imagination contrived. A kind of perfection he wanted every other fantasy of Sian to mimic.

He'd felt her warmth beneath him and needed it again. Like a drug, she fed his hunger. That night she'd been with him all the way, rubbing her silky mound with its little strip of curls against his hand, urging him on.

When he had parted her thighs, she'd made fantastic, gurgling pleasure noises. She had lifted her hips for him as he licked and sucked her rigid nipples and probed deep in her pussy with his fingers. The memory of the sensation blasted back through him.

Fabulous.

Tight, hot, wet, and magic. Until she had fled. She'd wriggled like a wanton little snake, had shaken her pretty tits in his face, before she had slipped from his grasp and run.

Damn her bloody tower.

She'd hidden inside the tall stone tower in the dream. Though he knew where she was, he couldn't penetrate the brambles to reach her. She had hidden inside until the dawn.

Franklyn eased the snakeskin jacket from his damaged shoulder. Most of the normal range of movement had returned but at the cost of exquisite pain. He'd also suffered the onset of referred trauma to his hip. He limped bad enough to use a stick. The specialist's promise that the torture would ease as time passed had yet to materialize. When it did, he'd be ready to take Sian and deal with the big threatening bastard she'd brought to the hospital to torment him.

Though he'd been so sick, near dying, Sian had turned up with the one responsible for his injuries. He had known the animal who'd attacked him. The one who had delighted in menacing him with veiled threats while he lay helpless in a hospital bed, and the horrific beast, they were the same.

He wouldn't always be defenseless. Every day he got stronger. Soon he'd be well. The arrogant creep she'd taken up with would find out Franklyn Gorsewell was no one's yes-man. He smiled.

Yes. Squaring up to that thing, even if it came in wolf form, would be a pleasure. The disconcerting sensation of constant aggression, his heightened hearing, the acute sense of smell, the shivery strangeness building inside him, it would pass or he'd find a way to deal with it.

No one and nothing would come between him and his treasured muse. From the first day he'd seen her, so vital and perfect, she'd been his "darling girl." The emerald-eyed, naive, little teenage minx the job center sent around had mesmerized him. He had hired her as his assistant on the spot. She was all his to adore, to teach, to entertain, the flawless unformed clay he could mold into the perfect woman.

Sian. His Sian.

Perhaps he'd indulged her too much. He'd sent her on a two-day-a-week training course for two years, had found her a decent place to live, and had gotten her out of the poxy bedsit she'd been in since she came down from Bath. Discovering she had lived alone since her mother had died, he'd never been stern with her, always sought to ease her worries and fears, had done so much to make her smile. He understood his mistake now. All the indulgence had turned her into a spoiled brat. He'd been so busy this past year, and she'd rocketed out of control. The last few months she'd turned uppity, and had lacked his guidance while she was at Darnwell. She'd even forced him to threaten to fire her.

He should have had her sooner and made her his.

If he'd been sensible about things rather than quite so caring, he'd have put his foot down about boyfriends when she had first taken one. He should have fucked her silly little brains out on a daily basis as soon as she'd hit her eighteenth birthday, not left it to some other lucky bastard to claim her virginity. He recalled the disappointment when he had discovered what she'd done. That was the opportunity to show her who was really the boss, but he hadn't taken it. Being a thoughtful gentleman didn't always bring its rewards. The regrets didn't do much to help his mood, but a new wave of determination squashed them. He'd make up for the three years he'd lost since he'd bought her the silver eighteen badge.

The first chance he got, his cute Little Missy Armstrong would be bouncing her sweet cheeks in his bed or on his office chair. Whenever and wherever he wanted her, she'd be willing. Once he'd schooled her wild side, they'd be married before next year was out. He smiled at the image of Sian, naked and sweaty, her pert little tits jiggling as she pounded out her long-standing dues by grinding on his cock. How sweet she'd look. He massaged his swollen erection as it strained up toward the waistband of his tracksuit trousers. Sian would grunt and groan for him, too, her tight pussy stretched and slippery hot as he filled it. She would moan her pleasure.

Later.

He'd finish a long wank with her in mind, later. He had things to do first.

Heading into the kitchen, he faced the lure of the half-empty Scotch bottle. It was only mid-morning, but he could do with a belt. The alcohol's interaction with the painkillers might prove enough to finish him, though. The Scotch would have to wait for another day. He filled the coffee machine, then waited, tapping at the counter until it produced the brew he needed. The milk in the plastic bottle had blue veining like ripe Stilton cheese. There was no need to open the top to take a whiff. He binned the milk and two monstrous hairy things, which might have been tomatoes. He carried his mug of black coffee through to the desecrated lounge where he sat facing away from the worst of the damage. Before he took a mouthful of coffee, he opened his laptop. While the log-on took an age, fourteen lots of updates to download, he drank the first decent cup of coffee since the attack, but the taste wasn't quite right. Maybe the coffee had gone off while he was away. Once he got in, e-mails jammed his in-box, but he ignored them.

First thing was to get this place cleaned up. He'd book into a hotel for the rest of the month while repairs and redecorating went on here. Scrolling, he dismissed his usual hotel haunts. He'd stay in a quiet place where he'd be able to sleep in peace, somewhere he could dream. Soon he'd be at the stage he wouldn't need the mind numbing drugs to help him sleep. He punched in the credit card details as he booked a room. His muse—she better look out. He'd find her in the dreams, haunt her every moment until she opened her legs for him, and when she did, he'd make sure she entertained his cock majestically.

He'd start by giving her fantasy nights so she'd wake up wet because of him. That would do until he got to fuck her for real. His cock gave another throb as he stroked it.

Oh, yes, she'd love it all. Maybe he could manage more than once or twice if he flipped the dream sequences.

When she was back in the office, where she should be, he'd stifle any excuses, hold her tight in his arms and kiss her before he gave her pussy the kind of workout she'd never forget. Maybe he'd lift her shirt, stroke over her tits, or put his hand up her skirt to massage her ass, before he sent the other girls out of the office for a break. Either way, he'd make sure he did something to give Evie and Jess a good idea of just what Sian was about to get. She could babble as much as she liked about their relationship being solely business, but she'd never be able to deny he'd fucked her after the other girls saw her tits in his hands. Each single member of the Gorsewell production team would know she'd given him everything he wanted.

Perhaps if he timed things perfectly for their first fuck, when the other girls got back from their break, Sian would have her long legs hooked up over his shoulders. He'd be humping her ass on the desk. She'd come hot and hard, yelping and screeching her delight. She'd beg him to fill her. Fabulous.

His muse was going to wail like a she-cat when she came. He could hear the delightful sounds she'd make as he enjoyed a full recompense for all the fucks they'd missed the last three years. His breathing snapped to a faster rhythm. He dumped the laptop on the small table. He was ready for her so he eased his trousers down. He closed his eyes as he laced his fingers about his cock, pictured Sian, her face contorted in orgasmic pleasure while she rode him, naked, with her pretty tits bouncing. She'd hump like a bitch.

A fresh surge of blissful throbs pulsed the length of his cock in response to her trembling pleasure cries in his office. He'd have her legs spread so wide they'd straddle the arms of his chair to make a bold offering of her pussy for his pleasure. How she'd howl. "Ohh! Ooo! Ohh! You're the best, Franklyn! Ooo. Ohh. Ohh. Yes! Franklyn, you're the bessst!"

Tension swelled through him. He pumped hard at his cock, beating the meat as the up-swell of spunk burbled in his balls. He'd fuck her so she passed out, so she screamed in pleasure, so she came as hard and fast as he…. The cry of orgasm burned his throat. Hot, wet jets spurted through his fingers.

Even as a wank, she was perfect. He had to have her, he must, no one could match her. He wiped his wet and sticky palm on a wad of tissue and cleaned his stomach, loving her for the fabulous fuck she was.

As for the current hulk of a boyfriend, he may well wind up dead. Franklyn Gorsewell had friends, lots of them, useful friends who didn't ask too many questions, and he always got what he wanted.

Chapter 7

Dressing for their Bonfire Night dinner on the 5th of November seemed an activity both familiar, yet also recalled from the distant past. Tonight, Magnus discovered his trouser waistband was a little loose. No doubt he needed a new dinner suit. He glanced to the jacket on the hanger. The lining, too, didn't please him. The lime green satin, patterned with brown circles, no longer spoke of sophistication. He should go back into the local town to pick up the new jacket he'd ordered. In fact, he might order a complete new wardrobe.

Sian would forgive him his lack of current fashion sense as she had forgiven him in matters far more complex. She hadn't fled at his confession of what he was, and even though she'd not hidden her natural fears at the prospect of facing "the beast," she'd listened and accepted him.

Since that day, he'd done all he could to convince Sian that no matter what, she was and would always be his love.

Now there was the problem in a nutshell.

His reflection wavered in the ancient mirror as he tweaked to straighten his bow tie, and once more, he examined the options concerning Sian. He couldn't give her up, such a course was impossible, but nor could he yet face taking the step to make her like him for eternity. She deserved choices, needed the time to experience more of the world, of life as a young woman without the burden of centuries to consider, and the trials of transforming to wolf-form with all the needs the creature demanded, satisfied once a month. She must have the chance to leave him, if she wished.

No experience had yet stolen her faith in the future. He'd not be the one to inflict that loss on her.

"I'm afraid you'll have to accept my word for now and have a little patience for what you think you desire." Her reaction would be familiar if he said those words to her tonight. The involuntary expression she was unaware she made and her wide appealing gaze would caress him. If he didn't take care, she'd wheedle a promise of further discussions on the subject.

He no longer smiled as he set the silk cummerbund around his waist. By making her wait, he risked losing Sian forever. He had to accept the possibility. The thought of her loss chilled his heart, but he had no right to demand more of her. Though she might believe she'd be willing to give him everything, he'd no wish to live with her bitter recriminations a hundred years hence if it turned out she wasn't. They had years until the decision might become imperative to slow her aging. Somehow, when the filming was completed, he would take her mind from the worries that belonged in the future.

He pulled on his dinner jacket and shrugged his shoulders to make sure there were no wrinkles in the fabric.

No wonder Sian seemed tense at present. What with the discovery of his possible relationship to Martha Raynalds, the vile intrusion of Gorsewell into her dream, and all the preparations for the filming, she'd a lot on her mind. Her understanding of him as the wolf must also take a toll. Not many individuals could assimilate such knowledge without it twisting their opinion of him. Experience had taught him that much.

Tonight's entertainment would take her mind from some of her concerns, perhaps. When they retired this evening, he'd do his damndest to use pleasure to blot everything from her thoughts. He pulled on his wristwatch, six-forty. There'd be time for a glass of sherry before dinner. The door to her tiny dressing room remained closed, and he'd no doubt she'd stay in there until he left their room.

"I'll meet you in the yellow drawing room," he called before he made his way out to the stairs.

* * * *

Sian squinted into the mirror, trailing her eyeliner along one lid. She double-checked, then swapped closed eyelids and did the other. The effect hit the spot she wanted. She'd not worn her evening face while she'd been at the house with Magnus. They'd both preferred to dine casually each evening. What with the preparation she'd done for the first transformation, and then the second, along with their discussions about the ongoing renovations to the house, the search for suitable antiques, there always seemed something to occupy them. Dressing in her best for dinner tonight would be a fun alternative. Even if she'd have to swap her heels for Wellington's when they went to the firework display.

The gown she'd picked hung on a hanger on the door. Nothing too glitzy, nor her favorite leather dress, were right this evening. Tonight she wanted feminine with a bit of *umph* behind it. Too much time sloping around the house in jeans and T-Shirts, so easy to fall into that trap. Magnus, when she first called at the house, had worn flannels and his brass-buttoned blazer with a crisp white shirt and a cravat. A retro look she loved, but he'd succumbed to her influence with the jeans. Once this week was over, she'd talk to him about it. He didn't have to wear jeans to convince her of anything.

She smiled. One of the funniest things had been the day she came back here for the second time. After the glances he'd given her tutu and leggings on her first visit, a week later for their next appointment she'd worn her best cashmere business suit in an effort to impress. But when he opened the door, he'd been wearing jeans. A softness warmed through her, followed by the glow of desire at the recollections. Her business suit hadn't lasted long. The extremely expensive trousers ended up on the floor of the pagoda along with his jeans. That day, the dreams lived.

God, they had been good together right from the start. She smeared on some lip-gloss and grimaced to make sure it hadn't gravitated to her front teeth.

They needed to talk about so many issues. With the big problem of his longevity and her wish to become like him looming over them, their day-to-day conversations didn't focus on small points. Slipping into the dress, she hooked up the front of the corseted bodice. Cost a darn fortune, this dress, from one of her favorite designers, but it was worth it, because it made the most of her assets. She'd worn it to the award ceremony in January and turned heads, not bad in A-list company.

She stepped into her heels. Though Magnus hadn't said, she'd picked up he liked them. Each time she'd worn the crimson patent stilettos, he'd spent a great deal of time focused on her footwear. Tonight's gift for him, her heels, was a starter, at least. Somehow, she'd say sorry properly for being a bit crazy the other day about the Martha Raynalds revelation. She shouldn't have jumped to the usual conclusions. There wasn't anything to be jealous about in him having a brief relationship with someone seventy years gone.

He hadn't cheated on her.

The hurt came because she wanted him, not just wanted to screw him. Though she'd be happy to treat him to a weekend of love-making in her flat in London, she wanted so much more.

Tonight she'd apologize, tell him she forgave him for dropping his bombshell of news, and she'd do enough to make certain the only woman on his mind was her. She hoped.

Bonfire Night was special, had always been a night to look forward to when she was little, before her mother got ill. Every year they'd gone to Bonfire Night parties or to the big displays in the parks in Bath. Once she'd moved to London, the parties and the displays got bigger and better.

A piece of normality for her and a reminder for Magnus of the fun activities the year offered. She clipped on the pearl earrings that had been her gran's. The creamy gems gleamed with a fabulous richness.

One last glance in the mirror. Yeah, she looked good. Maybe later, after the fancy dinner, she'd convince Magnus it was all going to be okay. Somehow, she had to do that more than anything else.

She made her way down to the drawing room and paused at the small portrait of his parents, as she did each time she walked the long corridor. The proud faces, the medieval pose and demeanor, made her wonder if she might have ever connected with this couple. Why did they leave their son alone when he wasn't much more than a boy? Magnus had never said, but he'd needed them. Surely, times were different back then in a way people wouldn't understand now. She certainly didn't. "Not giving any secrets away tonight, are you?"

The pair remained as inscrutable as ever.

She strolled on and into the drawing room. "Oh, my, you look wonderful."

"Thank you. A stunning gown. You are beautiful."

She smiled and moved across the room to join him. "I'm glad you like the dress."

"Sherry?"

"Please."

He poured her a glass from the decanter on the sideboard and handed it over. "It's not the dress—it's you who are beautiful."

She sipped from the small nineteenth century glass before giving him a light kiss on the jaw. The lippy didn't mark his cologne-scented skin. "I'm looking forward to dinner tonight. From what I gather, it will be a sumptuous meal."

"I believe so. I don't understand what has prompted the culinary experimentation, but I'm sure we shall be the beneficiaries of all the work."

She laughed. "Perhaps the ladies want to show off a little."

"Yes." The haunted look flashed in his eyes. "I rarely give them the opportunity to do that."

"Exactly. So tonight we shall enjoy a wonderful meal."

"Do you think they mind?" he asked.

"Mind cooking?"

"No. Do you think it disturbs them that I don't have guests?"

She shook her head. "I doubt they've thought about it before now. It's always been that way. Me being here has kind of shaken things up a bit." She flashed him a smile.

Magnus slipped his arm around her waist. "I am most thankful for your presence."

She slid her arm about his hip and squeezed. "I'm glad about that." She glanced to the clock. "It's just seven. They will be waiting for us, so I suggest we go, but before we do, I want to say sorry."

"Sorry?"

"Yes, I was an absolute—" She puffed out a breath. "Yea, I was stupid to react the way I did about your news. I'm sorry."

"I was clumsy. It won't happen again."

She shook her head, sidling closer to him. "No, it was my fault. You see, I sometimes forget the timescale you work on. Next time I'm about to have a hissy fit, I'll make myself count to a thousand."

His lips moved in the start of the smile she loved. It grew like warmth when the sun appeared from behind a gray cloud and rose up to light his eyes. "Would it help if I promised to kiss you until you reached your count of a thousand?"

"Maybe."

"We shall forgive each other and be gentler with our love."

"Agreed." She took another sip of sherry. "But not too tender, Magnus. There has to be a little bite."

His expression froze, and he gave a quick shake of his head as though disturbed by her words.

"What's wrong?"

"Forgive me, my thoughts quite escaped me."

Uncertain if she'd understood him, she looked into his soul-drinking eyes. Though his skin was firm and lined little, his eyes betrayed the depths of his experiences. They showed a wealth of sorrows. Yet as the gray pools sucked her in, they changed so they looked like mountain water streaking over pebbles.

"Sometimes you manage to take me quite far away," he said.

"Good. You need to get out of the house more."

He laughed and linked his arm through hers. "Shall we dine?"

Chapter 8

Languid after their extensive meal, they nestled in the back of the car on the short drive to the cricket club. Magnus, his arm around Sian, caught a few smiles in the rearview mirror from the taciturn mechanic, Monty.

Perhaps he should speak with his few staff regarding their speculation. They appeared to have become a group of romantics. He smiled as he helped Sian out of the car.

"There's the gate. Here, I'll pay the entrance fee tonight," Sian said.

"If you so wish." He glanced at the tall bonfire, and after she paid the donation, accepted her arm laced through his.

"We can get a glass of mulled wine, sweet toffee popcorn if you want. The fireworks are due to begin in about five minutes."

Her infectious excitement raised his smile. "I haven't tasted mulled wine in an age."

Sian led him through the scent of wood smoke from the bonfire. Beyond the fire, the aroma from the hot dog van grew stronger, the smell of fried onions, too, and farther on, a stall selling cinnamon doughnuts laced the air with toasted sugar.

"Oh, Magnus, look. Candy floss." Sian pointed to a stall where the bright pink confection on sticks shuddered in the breeze.

"Would you like some?"

Her smile curved her cheeks. "Please. Don't you like it?"

He shook his head. "I'd prefer to buy it for you. We'll get some in a bag, rather than on a stick, so it doesn't blow away, and then we'll find a spot to stand to get a good view of the fireworks."

They did. Ten minutes later, as Sian finished the last of the fluffy, pink candy, and he sipped a glass of warm mulled wine, the first rocket soared into a clear, dark night sky as though it wanted to reach the farthest stars.

The small crowd of on-lookers responded to each element of the display, children yelled and their parents exclaimed. Sian stood with her back pressed against him, close in his embrace. He rested his chin on her shoulder. A contentment of sharing this experience with her mellowed his usual concerns at being at such a public event.

The other people offered no sidelong glances and asked no questions. Here, no one knew or guessed his name and lineage. Perhaps Sian was right, and he should take the opportunity to leave the house more frequently. The world had changed a great deal. Rumor of what he was might no longer provoke a threatening mob as it had in his youth.

He relaxed. Together, he and Sian stood in the same way many couples did, cuddled close, arms entwined, their heads together as the fireworks crackled into the cold night. He'd no doubt the couples around them loved, old or young, newly-wed, or those who'd been together for years. They loved with the knowledge they were free to do so.

A freedom denied to him and the woman he wanted. He could offer her a snip of happiness, followed by the bitter taste of increasing loneliness if she became like him. Any attempt at an ordinary existence could only be doomed to failure. If he did as she wanted and shared the werewolf curse with her, he would condemn her to days as a she-wolf. Such an existence would hurt her, destroy her joy in life, and it would all be his fault. If she accepted an eternity with him, her friends and colleagues would age, fade and die, but she would remain untouched by the years. Yet each month, she'd suffer the torment of the moon's savage spell. How could he offer her such a thing?

He inhaled Sian's subtle fragrance. A fierce need for her bloomed, not just for this night, or the next, but for all the nights there were or could ever be. This was his woman, his mate. He squeezed her tighter and met her gaze as she tilted her head.

The whoosh of a large rocket drew her attention. "Look!" She caught her breath. A chest-thumping roar shook him at the explosion of thousands of tiny blue sparkles that dissolved into bright cerise blooms.

"So beautiful," she said as the last floated down.

He nodded. For the first time since they'd met, he'd discovered her true power over his body and soul. She believed in him as a person. To Sian, he wasn't the beast, or a rich man in need of sensual body satisfaction. He'd known admiration for his strength, for his wealth, for his home, for his prowess, and even Julia's sweet gifts had offered him tenderness, but Sian eclipsed them all. The light of her love warmed him and wouldn't let him hide. For her, he must be more man than he'd ever been before. While they were here, there could be no room for such meanderings of the mind though, since her ability to pick up his thoughts was growing daily. This night, he would concentrate on the present alone. They would love like the couples around them, bound by this simple experience to remember.

The last of the colors faded into swirls of smoky mist. "I'm so glad we came tonight," she whispered, her breath warm against his throat.

"Yes," he said, aware of how she'd chipped away another chunk of his disguise built with such care over so long. At its simplest, Sian wished for them to live in the same way as those who stood around them tonight. A fresh batch of fireworks erupted, screaming into the night. Sian lifted her gaze to the sky. Incandescent streams of silver and gold, shot through with brilliant blue, wove a path to hide the stars.

She tilted her head so she faced him. He brushed a stray strand of hair from across her lip and placed a gentle kiss there as the magnificent display ended. Together, like others around them, they slowly moved in the misty, gunpowder-scented night. He linked his arm through hers. They ambled back to where Monty stood by the car. Magnus helped Sian into the back seat. He joined her and gave a nod to Monty.

Sian rested her head on his shoulder, relaxed and quiet. He gazed out the window as the dark countryside slipped by. If he had any courage at all, he ought to return her to the life she knew before they met. No other course was humane or compassionate.

"Magnus," she whispered. She angled her face so her lips could press against his.

"Yes?"

"You do understand, even if you send me away, I'll want to come back to you?" Her words caressed his jaw.

He sucked in a breath. Private thought might have become a thing of the past, certainly when they were physically close, but that didn't stop him cursing his stupidity for allowing his thoughts to dwell on their future. The perfection of her in his embrace, the sensation of hope, the prospect of harmony and peace together, he couldn't bear it. He edged back from her. "You accept I have lived a long life?"

"Yes."

"You accept I am different from others?"

She nodded, smiled.

He glanced to the driver, glad Monty's presence made further discussion difficult. "Then, please forgive my musings?"

Her smile grew, and she kissed him again, her lips soft as a moth's wing on his skin. "Of course, Magnus, at least until we are home."

* * * *

Monty stopped the car by the front door. "Good evening, sir, miss," he said, a little gruff as always. He held the door for them as if he'd been a chauffeur his life-long.

"Thank you, Monty, I'm grateful."

"You are most welcome, sir." A twinkle lit the watery blue eyes.

He led Sian into the portico, swept her up in his embrace, and held her there so the green Wellingtons could slip off. Still holding her tight in his arms, he carried her indoors where he set her down to remove her coat. He took off his own as she pulled off her scarf.

"Thank you for a wonderful evening, Magnus."

"I should thank you. I'd never have thought of going to Stonewells for the firework display. See how you brighten my life?"

She laughed.

"I'm serious," he said, catching her around the waist. "You have no notion how much you mean to me."

"Really?" she whispered, as he pulled her a little closer.

"I swear on all you may believe to be holy."

"Show me," she whispered.

He sucked in a deep breath. "You have my promise I will, every moment from now until dawn, if you'll allow me." He swept her up into his arms.

"Please, Magnus." She put her arms around his neck.

He took the stairs one at a time, enjoying the light glowing in her eyes, the softness of her gaze, and his anticipation of her skin against his. In their bedroom, he placed her on the bed, turned to the hearth, and in no haste, started to strip off his clothes. He looked over his shoulder at a creak from the bed. "No. Wait. Please, let me help you. I'll undress you."

The pupils of her eyes dilated fast, and he smiled. Tonight, he wanted her to enjoy him, all of him. Each pleasure he could give would delight her. By using his control, her lassitude would give him all the time he needed.

Naked, he lay down beside her, kissed her silken lips, and listened to her gentle breath in response. She lay languid in his embrace in a way he'd not seen before. He slid the pearl clip from her hair, then placed it on the bedside cabinet. Her gaze followed his every movement as he moved down the bed to smooth his fingertips over her feet, her ankles, and up to her knees. Silky hosiery. He smiled as he touched the warmth of her skin above the stockings, never tights. Should he leave them on? Or not? He moved his hands back down her leg, pleased by the little tremors in her muscles. "Sit up for a moment. I'd hate to spoil your gown."

She complied.

With the care of a lady's maid, he unclipped the corseted bodice. He slipped the dress from her shoulders down to her waist. All the time her gaze stayed on him. "Lie down now," he said.

She lay back down and careful not to tug the delicate fabric he slid the gown from her.

Her underwear tonight, pearl white, accented with two tiny pink flowers, was so virginal, yet her nipples peeked from the half-cup bra, demanding his attention. He stroked his tongue in the valley between her breasts. Her small whimper encouraged him. Pushing the silky fabric down with his thumbs, he revealed the puckered areola and proud nipple of one breast. He unclipped her bra as he nuzzled closer to take it between his lips. Sian sighed as he caressed her smooth skin. He stroked her hip and thigh as he licked, sucked, and nibbled, awaiting her first moan of pleasure.

She pushed up to press harder against his fingers when he stroked the damp silk fabric of her panties.

"Oh, yes."

He smiled at the needy whimper, then moved across to her other nipple. He took it into his mouth and sucked so hard she groaned.

Wonderful.

Sian lifted her hips farther from the bed in an effort to chase his hand. He returned to caress the tender skin above her stocking tops, but didn't as much as graze the fabric of her underwear.

Her breathing quickened in response to him suckling and stroking. The rise and fall of her murmurs told him the level of her arousal, but he wanted more from her, a lot more. He released her nipple and lifted up to look into her eyes. "I want you to relax for me. Close your eyes."

She lowered her lashes. Her long sigh warmed his cheek. He slipped his arms around her and drew her closer still. Electric sparks of delight flittered on his skin at her touch. *Exquisite.* Angling his head, he pressed his mouth to hers, then teased with his tongue until she opened her lips to suck his inside the moist heat of her own.

Tonight, he would share an experience with her beyond the here and now. They would dream together. He held her close, allowing his consciousness to waver from the room. They lay on the bed, but stood elsewhere, too. The sensation of presence flittered back and forth. The embroidered silk coverlet, Sian, fragrant and warm in his arms, and yet music drifted nearby, the sweetness of violas beckoned. Sian remained enfolded in his embrace as he moved toward the call of violins.

A waterfall of satin encased her, silk shirt and breeches him. Her lips warm on his still, he opened his eyes.

The ballroom wavered for a moment before each mirror, each glimmering candle-laden chandelier, stilled and solidified to a reality of sorts. Sian broke their kiss. "Magnus?"

"Stay with me?"

"Forever. For as long as you want me to."

He smiled and the music swelled as if in response. "So beautiful," he said and placed a kiss on the pale skin of her inner wrist. "Dance with me?"

"Of course."

Snowy white rosebuds nestled in her hair. Tiny ringlet curls wavered, and the thick brandy-shaded strands made intricate twirls. A tiny lace choker graced her neck, and the square neckline of her gown, also trimmed with lace, enhanced her décolletage. A heavy satin skirt flowed to her ankles. Her satin shoes matched the roses in her hair. He led her in the elaborate, slow steps of a minuet. Faultless, she moved with him. Each graceful line of her arm, the arch of her neck—a dream-enhanced perfection to please the eye.

Their reflections twirled with them, seeming to fill the room with other dancers, each version of Sian a beauty who would steal his soul.

Ah, my soul. Will I keep any vestige of it once this night is done?

Together they danced; a couple alone, yet surrounded by themselves. Starlight beckoned through the open doors so he led her onto the terrace. The crescent moon shone on the lake. He took her into his arms, pressing a kiss to the coral-rouged lips.

Reality slipped again. Skin to skin, they lay together, limbs wrapped warm around each other. "You are perfect," he whispered, tracing his fingertip over the rise of one of her breasts. He cupped the firm, smooth round, and tweaking hard enough to make her moan, he rolled her nipple under his thumb. She shifted beneath him, whimpered, and molded her loins to his. One wisp of fabric barred him from heaven. A breath of her warm fragrance stoked his need as he inched off her underwear. As soon as he freed her from the panties, she parted her legs so he could lie between them. He pressed a kiss on the curls at their apex. She gave a small gasp when he palmed her legs wider. "I want all of you, Sian. Give me all of you?"

Her hips juddered, her flesh warm under his hands. He moved to raise her to his lips. He nuzzled her clit, captured the small bead of flesh, and sucked the tender morsel.

"Magnus!" Her cry echoed throughout the room.

Slow, each movement deliberate and lingering, he pleasured her, tasted her salt and lapped at the flow of her nectar. She wound her fingers in his hair, grasped, and released with rhythmic panted breaths. He maneuvered her so her hips moved in time with her moans. The tension in her muscles increased, and he slowed the pace, flicking his tongue with the lightest of strokes to keep her hovering on the edge of orgasm. He glanced up to her face. She'd arched her neck, lay open-mouthed gasping, her eyes closed as she trembled. His cock throbbed, hardened to granite, but he'd take her over the edge now before he enjoyed the delight of burying himself inside her.

He breathed hot on her moistened clit. She locked her thighs around his head. Open mouthed, he sucked, flickering his tongue faster at her wild cry of delight. She ground herself against him, gasped, and twisted beneath him. Her pleasure pulsed so strong, he almost broke and hit the peak with her.

But no, tonight he'd offer her as much as he could. Backing off, he pushed her knees wider apart, slid up the bed, and moved to nestle his cock in the entrance of her pussy.

"Yes, now," she mouthed against his shoulder. "I want you."

"You are all mine." He drove forward and reveled in her silken heat as she took him. She clutched him tight. He thrust into her again.

"I live for you," she moaned.

Her body blended with his. They moved in a harmonic synchronization. Sian wrapped her thighs around his waist, adding momentum to their joining. Her mouth against his throat, she matched his rhythmic gasps. Together they pushed toward the peak.

Sian cried out and gripped him tight inside her. Her pleasure forced him over the edge. He let go into a final tumult of movement. Orgasm thrummed through him as he kissed her. "My love. My life."

Chapter 9

The morning of the tenth dawned misty wet. Rain pattered rather than pelted, but its incessant thrum did nothing to soothe his mood. He and Sian breakfasted early in the dining room where she could look out for the first arrivals. Twitchy like a busy sparrow, she finished a slice of toast. Though his apprehension about today remained heavy, he couldn't deny the spark of excitement in her eyes or the flash of color in her cheek.

"After today, we will have the world to ourselves," she said as she got up from her seat. She bent and swept a kiss on his cheek. "Don't forget you can join us for the filming. You could watch from the sidelines if you wish."

He shook his head. "No, I think not."

The whoosh of air-breaks shook the windows.

"Good grief. What's all that?" he asked.

Her impish smile appeared. "Kit, lots of it. I must go. Have a wonderful day." She bounded out the door, the rubber soles of her Nike's squeaking on the polished floor. He sighed as he glanced to the window where the side of the massive lorry obliterated the usual view.

Two days, she'd promised, no more than three if things didn't go well today, and all this would be finished. Even with so much disruption to the house, he had no regrets. He should be glad he'd agreed to them filming, for if he hadn't, Sian wouldn't be part of his life. How dreary his existence had been, for so long, before she walked in to light his world with her incandescent presence.

He placed the breakfast dishes on a tray and took them down to the kitchen where he set them in the dishwasher. Both the house staff would be off until the filming had finished. Until then, he and Sian must look after themselves.

Tonight he would surprise her. He'd make dinner. Perhaps an Italian style meal would please her. Yes, a good selection of antipasti accompanied by a nice bright wine. That would be perfect to help her relax after today. Somewhere in the cellar, he'd find the very thing. It might take him a while to locate the wine, but he'd the whole day to look. After turning the dishwasher on, he made his way down the short corridor off the kitchen.

The unmistakable smell of the subterranean storeroom gave him pause. Tiny goose bumps prickled his arms. The light overhead flickered, casting shadows. The electricity supply down here had always been fitful. A flashlight stood on a shelf by the door. The staff, well experienced with the problems, always left a heavy-duty torch by the entrance. He picked it up and headed along a walkway.

Floor to ceiling wine racks and larger wine bins, some of them stacked high, others with half a dozen bottles, stretched the length of the room into the shadows. So many memories swept over him at the sight of the well-stored bottles.

In his youth, he'd favored white wine and stocked a great deal of sack, along with a sufficiency of port for guests. He recalled little of the first months after his return from Europe in the summer of 1763 and the bitter discovery of Julia's death. The wine merchant visited monthly, at his order. The heavy drinking went on into the following year…or perhaps the year after. His memory remained hazy.

He shook his head. It had taken him a few more years to discover the overwhelming powers of opium.

Such had been his drunken excesses, even his physique had suffered, and he'd grown careless. One full moon he had killed a worker on the estate, which would have horrified his father had he known, but his parents weren't present. They'd left long before he met Julia. The upshot of his grief-laden folly led to the villager's attempts to kill him and his flight to London.

Sian had experienced some of his worst memories, running barefoot beside him over the stubbled field. In his eighteenth century reality, he'd fled. In their dream, he had carried Sian with him into the drainage ditch. They'd escaped the man wielding an axe. Thank God, he'd managed to wake her at that point. He'd been glad she'd seen no more.

Sian would be appalled at the way London had offered him sanctuary during the rest of the eighteenth century. A place where he'd hidden from the world in plain sight, killed with a savagery to shame him now, and roistered with the worst of humanity.

He sighed and made his way down to the next rack of bottles. "Ah, claret."

By the mid-eighteen hundreds, when he'd returned from his sojourn in London, claret had been his first drink of choice, and he'd restocked the cellar again. As he traveled the globe during the later part of the nineteenth century, he'd developed a taste for gin. Several crates of the green bottles still stood in an alcove. In the early twentieth century, brandy had been his preferred tipple, and later during the twenties and thirties, cocktails entertained him. Each taste preference was marked here as he'd made all the necessary additions to his stock.

The wine cellar should be a pleasure to contemplate, but his enforced imprisonment down here in the past wiped the gloss off such thoughts. Sian's presence meant he no longer must dwell here in the darkness during each month's full moon. He paused, picked up a bottle, and wiped off a layer of dust.

A low electrical hum came from overhead, the usual sign the electric was about to go. He set the bottle down and looked up. The strip light seemed steady enough.

Noise!

Crackling whines, whistles, and electrical feedback echoed around him. He'd not heard anything so loud since…the last war.

The blare of sound ceased. He picked up a bottle of white wine and headed back to the door. Thank heavens he'd sold off the horses in the sixties. They'd have been terrified by the noise today. He placed the wine on a shelf in the kitchen out of the sunlight. Later, he'd return to put it to chill for the evening. The wagon remained parked outside, a looming reminder of all the strangers milling about in the house. He'd find no peace even if he went up to the library.

Strange, from his earliest boyhood, this house rarely offered him a sense of refuge in any way. He wasn't foolish enough to think it might give him sanctuary today.

Out.

He'd go out in one of the cars. Take a drive to the Downs, maybe get lunch at one of the pubs en route. Without Sian to accompany him, the outing wouldn't be as great a pleasure, but she had given him a tremendous gift, one she little realized. Since meeting her, he'd lost some of the wariness of being away from the house. He'd rediscovered he could venture into the world outside.

He raced up to their bedroom. No Mrs. Tyson today, so he quickly made the bed. He tossed the counterpane over the top. Not anywhere as neat as when the housekeeper did the job, but it would do.

The long leather coat from the forties hung on a back rack in one of his wardrobes. He'd not worn it for several years. He donned the supple brown leather. The result wasn't right, not if he compared it to what he'd seen men wear in recent films. Perhaps he should order a new one, something more up to date. A ridiculous sense of planning an adventure hit him, as if he were preparing for a safari or a trek in the Patagonian forests. Sian was right—he should get out of the house more often. That's what he'd do today. He'd go shopping, even if he had to do it alone. He'd take a good amount of money with him and visit the tailors. He strode down to the study.

Post-it Notes and print outs from the computer lay scattered like large confetti all over his roll top desk Sian had used for the last couple of weeks. He crossed the room to open a small block section of books on the bookcase. They fronted one of the safes that he had installed in the sixties. Several others, much older, were hidden in places around the house. One, in an earlier age, had been his father's strong room. He'd not entered there since he sailed to the continent in the autumn of 1760.

In truth, he'd been nothing more than a heartsick boy when he left for France at the start of his journey through Europe after Julia refused to marry him. Sian showed him a different kind of relationship, one built on his trust in her, and her selfless faith in him. She had lifted him from the kind of imprisonment no felon knew in this age. He'd never find the way to thank her.

But he could try. He'd find a little token for her. On High Street, where his tailor's shop sat between a bakery and a shoe shop, an independent jeweler stood opposite. He'd take a peek at their current offerings. Two birds with one stone: a new waxed coat, green, like those he'd seen some other men wearing at the firework display, and then something for his… The word wife hovered, but he daren't use it, not even to himself. If he called her that, the next step became inevitable. He selected the keys he wanted from the small rack in the safe, tossed them up in his hand, caught them, and hurried out of the study.

At the bottom of the main staircase, he ignored the glances from a pair of men carrying large silver cases and the assessing gaze of two young women who'd have passed as interesting strumpets in his youth. The urge to escape couldn't be denied. He had to get out. He strode fast toward the door. The last person he saw, a lean man with a limp, garbed in a long gray raincoat with a dark fedora shadowing his features, could pass a message to Sian. All these people here must know her. "Tell Miss Armstrong that Magnus will meet her after the filming, would you?"

"Yes, Mr. Johansson."

He strode quickly to the garage with the wide, green, double doors. Inside, he walked down the row looking for a car Monty had recently serviced, one with an orange card tied to the wiper blade. The black Mark II Jaguar deserved an outing as much as he did. He removed the card, opened the door, and inhaled. The sweet smell of clean engine oil and leather polish lingered.

The Jaguar purred into life as he turned the ignition key. He headed out, driving slow past another lorry, no doubt containing more of what Sian described as "kit." He turned left at the gates with a rare sense of pleasure. Enjoying the moment, he accelerated down the country road.

* * * *

"Sian, you're looking well." Richard offered Sian an embrace as they met outside the portico.

"Thanks. I'm fine, honest." She gave him a quick hug, took a step back, and nodded toward the three men waiting for the lorry's tailgate to descend. "Everything okay so far?"

"Yes, we should have all the equipment in situ well before lunch time. The sound desk is already up, of course."

"Good. If the weather improves, as the forecast said, we can get all the outdoor shots done today, a smidge past mid morning, I think." She glanced up at the heavy clouds. "It's supposed to clear by then."

"Gary," Richard called out. "The generators need to go to the three sites you've got on your plan. You'll need tarps ready, too."

"I'll leave you to it, Richard. I'll go inside. I don't want any damage at all, and I know they've begun walk-throughs with the dancers." She hurried back into the house and headed up the corridor to the ballroom to double check all the furniture had been moved. As she entered, one look at the expressions of the dancers soothed her fears. They might smoke or sup vodka as they practiced plies, but they understood beauty.

"Sian, this place is so cool. It's awesome."

She nodded to the girl in the luminous pink leg warmers, and smiling, moved through the room to step out onto the terrace. Her initial panic had settled. Things seemed to be going according to schedule. The mobile kitchen offering food for the crew and cast had started to serve coffee. She counted the band members as they stood next to the truck with steaming mugs in their hands. They'd better use the ashtrays provided. If she found one butt where it shouldn't be, she'd kick someone's ass for sure.

A light breeze promised no rain despite the wretched weather forecast.

"Sian, come look at this, will you?" Jerry beckoned.

She followed him out into the long corridor, entered the music room, and was pleased to see Jerry had covered the worst part of the damaged walls with his big mirrors. This room, where so much beauty was spoiled by damage from the fire in the house, always brought a sigh. As to the wrecked conservatory beyond, she could only guess how much Magnus wanted that renovated next year. "Right, what's the problem?"

"Our lead ballerina has put on pounds since the fitting. One twirl and she'll pop the seams. I think she'll look like a split saveloy roll in this frock if she tries to perform in it. I want to put her in a green gown I have on the rail."

"Show me the gown, Jerry." Sian crossed the room to him. "Why has Tanya put on so much weight?" she whispered.

He smirked and cocked his head toward the dancer. "Nature's bounty. She's three months gone."

"Oh, God."

The elfin-blond ballerina in a short robe sat waiting with a worried expression.

"Should I say congratulations, Tanya?" Sian asked.

The girl smiled. "Oh, yes. This is my last job this year. When this one is finished, I go home to Shropshire and Carl. We are going to grow spuds, keep chickens, and have a beautiful baby."

Sian leaned forward and gave Tanya a hug. "Jerry's got another dress he thinks will be right for you. Shall we take a look and try it?"

"Thanks. I didn't want to let you down, but I never thought I'd get this big so soon."

"Big?" The girl looked ethereal slender. "It's not a problem as long as this dress fits. Will you be okay with the arabesques? What about the lifts?"

"Sure. Robbie could lift a brick privy. He's got a lot of inner body strength. He won't drop me."

Jerry held up a sheaf of ivy green chiffon, the bodice decorated with jet and silver spangles. "This is the dress. What do you think?"

"Perfect. Try it on, Tanya," Sian said. "We've got the shoes to match, yes?" she asked Jerry.

The blond-haired girl beamed. "I carry a lot of spare shoes in the car. I've got flats and blocks—silver, black, emerald, and bottle green."

"Silver with it. Jerry, get the makeup girl to put a silver spray on her hair, green ribbons, maybe feathers, anything floaty." She turned to the dancer. "That okay with you?"

"Great, I was so scared you'd send me home."

"No, I think you've done us a favor, too. This green is going to look so much better, more dramatic than all the pale stuff the other dancers are wearing." Sian gave Jerry a hug. "And as for you, well, what can I say?" He beamed back.

"Sian, I've set up the bedroom with the props you wanted. You want to come up stairs and check?" One of the property girls called from the doorway.

She turned from the wardrobe master. "Sure, Jo. I'm itching to see how the design we made has worked out." She followed the young woman up the stairs.

"I hope you like it. I think it's great." Jo opened the double doors to the guest suite.

"Wow! It's fabulous. I knew the colors would work. Those blinds you suggested make all the difference. It was a good idea to get them. Do you think the camera crew will be happy with the light level?"

Jo nodded. "I dragged one of them up here earlier. He seemed happy enough."

"Really?" Sian smiled.

"Nothing like that, at all times professional."

"Good. I'd best go down. The guys from the band must have drunk enough caffeine to rouse them by now. Maybe we can get together at lunch time."

"Sure, see you about half-twelve."

Sian made her way down the corridor to the stairs. A sense of connection with reality hit her. This was the life she'd lived and loved. The last two months with Magnus seemed more like a sexual fantasy, where she'd tasted the fulfillment of so much desire. Somehow, she must convince him to make her his mate. Only then, would things stay the same between them. She didn't want to think what might happen if he continued to refuse her wish. She'd never thought of herself as being vain, but the prospect of growing old while he remained as he was frightened her. No way would she want him to see her in old age. Couples aging together was something different.

He had to make her like him.

She descended the stairs, pleased to hear the screeching chords of an electric guitar. The guys must be getting ready. That they'd agreed to play live thrilled her. The effect would be much better for the whole shoot.

"Oh, wow. You look so authentic." She stared at the two lead dancers in their eighteenth century costumes. The white wigs, the lace and satin, the heavy makeup—all of it just as she'd seen in the paintings Magnus showed her. "Amazing."

"Thanks, chuck. I can't wait to murder this one, she's been moaning all morning about the skirts."

The girl snapped a glance to her partner. "You try going for a pee in this thing."

"No real murder, hey? Remember, you two are supposed to be passionately in love."

"Yeah, yeah," the girl said as she grabbed his silk clad arm. "Come on, Romeo. We'll go through the lift sequence again."

They strode off toward the ballroom. Sian's sense of presence shifted back to the exquisite experience she'd shared with Magnus last night. No one could wish for anything more beautiful. She couldn't be without him. She would be a shell and nothing more.

Chapter 10

Franklyn limped to the courtyard where the food wagon stood, got a coffee, and with his hat dipped low on his brow, parked in a shadowy corner to drink it. Astonishing how a gray raincoat and a fedora, combined with a black walking stick, turned him into an invisible man. Best solution all considered. No matter what, there was no way he'd have missed this shoot. From the little he'd seen so far, things looked well organized, typical Sian. He'd taught her well. She'd sure been eager to learn. They'd shared breakfast meetings in the park that dragged through to dinner in the evening. Days, weekends, he'd given her both so he could talk her through each task when setting up a job, introduce her to the musicians, artists, and technicians who were important to his world. All the time and effort he'd spent meant she had learned fast until she had developed much of the skill of an expert in her field with the panache of a young woman about town.

What a bloody fool he'd been. So many people had told him how good they looked together. No one once asked if he truly was her uncle. He shouldn't have waited.

He inhaled and winced. The scent of hot coffee and fried onions couldn't mask the underlying smell here.

Prickles of gooseflesh pebbled his skin. A reaction to the odor of this place he couldn't control. Something familiar in the mix of scents goaded his senses, raised his need to leave a mark of himself here so Johansson would know he'd been present today.

The lusty scream of a tormented electric guitar blasted into the morning. The wails echoed around the courtyard. Sound, raw and hot, thrummed through his veins.

He had to hand it to Sian. She'd worked her little ass hard, quite literally, to make sure the *Timeless* film happened here. Once he got her back to

London where she belonged, he'd find a way to express his pleasure at the results of her work.

The coffee revolted his stomach. Since the attack, things he used to relish the taste of didn't satisfy in the same way. None of the doctors offered reasons for the changes. They fobbed him off with the usual line; it could be the medication.

He didn't need their excuses or platitudes. He'd a better idea what was happening. Being here today reinforced his suspicions.

The creature that attacked him wasn't an animal. It was something more. A stirring in his gut told him the beast came from this place. He'd hunted once on safari. This morning his blood sang in the same way as he drove to Darnwell. He'd trailed his quarry. As soon as he set foot out of the car, his body tingled. He loved the edgy sharpness still powering through him.

The sight of the big bastard that Sian was screwing sealed the deal. Johansson was behind all this. He was both attacker and prey.

When the over-muscled owner of the house spoke to him in the corridor, he'd reeled in astonishment. Couldn't get his head together fast enough to say what he should have. Who the fuck did this guy think he was issuing orders to a total stranger?

Franklyn barked out a laugh. The last thing he'd any intention of doing was telling Sian "lover boy" would meet her after the shoot. If he had his way, he'd be driving her down the motorway to his hotel.

The music splintered his thoughts. Leaning heavily on the stick, he walked over to drop his polystyrene cup in the bin. Despite the reek, he'd take a look inside the house, maybe see the amazing mirrored room Sian had sent him pictures of when he agreed to hire the place. If he managed to get in to see the room, he'd take a wander round the grounds after, and then call Sian's phone.

Sian. Surely he would find her here. He breathed deep and discovered the exquisite aroma he knew so well. Sian. A beautiful scent in direct contrast to the beast smell that soured the day. She was close, might even have walked this courtyard less than an hour ago. He followed the lure of her around the corner onto a terrace overlooking a lawn.

Two of the dancers he knew, both in full makeup, costume, and debating loudly, stalked past. He hunched his shoulders so they wouldn't recognize him.

"I told you on the third beat be ready for the lift. Where were you?" the male dancer asked.

"Concentrating on not falling arse over tit because of the flower pot thing. You're such a pain," his partner replied.

Franklyn grinned. Nothing changed. They'd used this pair of married dancers a couple of times. How those two lived together, he'd no idea, because they fought constantly. Yet on screen, they exuded a magic chemistry. They always came across as passionate lovers.

Once Sian saw sense, she'd be the same with him. They might disagree about a few minor matters; he knew she disapproved of his little treats, like how much he drank, or the occasional snort, and the work trips to the US, but everyone would know they were right together.

An unusual half-door that stood open offered him a quick entrance to the house. Her lingering scent beckoned him. He ducked inside, stepped into a lemon yellow room with sofas and tables, big vases with the kind of oriental designs he loathed. The place was a mausoleum. How the hell did someone as electrifying as Sian live with all this? Sian was neon, bold and bright. She didn't belong in this house of the dead. His Rosebud needed the energy of the city, the glitz she enjoyed, a night at a good dance club before a long slow fuck when he got her home.

He walked through into a portrait-hung corridor and made his way along, side-stepping the spaghetti lengths of black cables running down the passageway. Two large guys, both dressed in dark blue sweats and T-shirts, hulked by the door, but neither challenged him.

Useless security. He'd change the company they used after this shoot. Anyone could get in here. Limping along, he eyed the portraits.

A fresh waft of her scent hit him. There she stood.

Instant arousal gave him a yardstick hard-on. He ducked into an alcove along the side of the wall, but could still see her. Today, her jeans fit like a second skin. The little white T-shirt clung, outlining her breasts. Her sweet, pointy little nipples beckoned him to suck.

Computer notebook in hand, Sian strolled down the corridor toward him with Richard, deep in conversation.

How he longed to seize a hank of her gleaming curls to drag her over here. She'd not run like she had in the dreams. It was time she understood the truth. She'd played around here, but now she needed to come home and face the consequences. He wanted to make her sorry for all the suffering she'd inflicted. He'd never hurt her, not really. But he wanted to see some penitence. By the time he'd finished with her, that juicy bottom lip would quiver. He might just kiss it better. No, he wanted some tears spilling down those porcelain cheeks. He'd make sure she'd be very sorry before he forgave her.

Not now. He needed to get her out of here before he could think about anything else.

Richard led Sian into a room off the corridor. One of them closed the door behind them, shutting him out.

A new crackle of guitar strains wavered for a minute, but silence snapped it off. He moved from the alcove, strolled the way Sian and Richard had come toward the pair of double doors standing open at the end of the corridor. He winced at a sudden screech of feedback. The sound engineer must have screwed up somewhere.

Fucking hell!

Dancers milled around but didn't detract from the magnificence of the room. The band, on a raised platform at one end, didn't hide the plasterwork moldings. The lights and equipment were multiplied a hundred times by the extravagant mirrors. The chandeliers gleamed like brilliant cut gems.

Everyone bustled about, each one of them focused on their task. Not a smidge of gossip to eavesdrop on as he passed. In fact, no one spoke. The initial fear he'd be recognized by one of the crew or the band faded. He moved like a ghost among them all. Certain the cameras weren't filming yet, he strolled across the room, suddenly eager to escape his tormentors lair.

He stepped out of the open French windows onto another terrace overlooking the grounds. Bile stung the back of his throat. Along with the stink of his enemy, he smelled money. A lot of it. Johansson must have a fortune to keep this place going. He couldn't understand why such a recluse agreed for the filming here. The guy could be in no serious need of cash. That must be how he'd managed to get into Sian's knickers. Capital, enough of it, anything and anyone could be yours.

A wave of disappointment crashed through him. Johansson, the bastard, had bought her. It didn't seem possible Sian could be a whore to wealth. He swept a glance over the terrace with its stone ornamentation, the well-tended acre of lawn and mature trees. Money, old money, all spoke to him from the view.

There was even a fucking lake. He narrowed his eyes and headed down the steps toward a building at the end of a causeway. No wonder Johansson enthralled her. An apartment in Knightsbridge didn't compare with a country estate like this. He should have realized. Sian, intelligent and sharp, still had vulnerabilities, a susceptibility to beauty and wealth part of them. He should have protected her from herself.

She must feel like the lady of the manor here.

No wonder she'd decided to stay, but once the shoot finished she'd head back to the city. No! During their disagreement at the roadside, before the monster had attacked him, Sian had said she'd stay with Johansson for good.

Off balance, as he had been since he left the nursing home, he thumped the stick into the turf with each step. Bitterness swept through him when the house filled the view from where he stood at the top of the grassy bank. He couldn't lose her like this. Not to some rich recluse who would use her and dump her once he got bored. He had to get her back.

He gripped the stick so tight his knuckles cracked. Damn it, he should never have agreed to go to Chicago back in August. He could have sent one of the others to the meeting. That way he could have dealt with Johansson himself. The guy frightened Sian. After her first visit here, she had said as much, but he had made the damn trip across the pond anyway and left her to come back here alone. She had needed him, but he'd made a joke about it.

A groan tore from his throat.

Slow as an old man, he hobbled down the slope to the jetty. The wind whipped across the gray lake, chilling him. Another layer of disgust made him gag when he breathed in a massive dose of the stink that pervaded the whole estate. Someone should take a bucket of bleach to the place.

The wooden boards of the causeway looked solid enough. He made his way across to the oriental building with faded red paint.

A fucking pagoda!

He paused at the end of the causeway, coughed, and choked on the rank smell. A crazy urge gripped him, weird and strange, like so many others he'd experienced since he woke in the hospital. The desire to pee and mark the place with his scent became an urgent demand. He glanced about.

Not a soul stood at the edge of the lake. He saw no one across in the woods. If he had a clumsy spray slash here, who would know? Chuckling, he stepped onto the decking. He'd give the place a good dosing inside and out.

A few minutes later, laughing, he checked his shoes as he re-zipped his fly. He'd sure sweetened the air here. The house at the top of the rise loomed as though it disapproved, but he didn't give a fuck. Rosebud, his baby girl, was a captive there. Held by the lure of a rich guy. This was the first step to rescue her.

Don't you worry, sweet-cheeks. Uncle Franklyn's coming to save you and bring you home.

Chapter 11

Magnus studied the three pieces the attendant in the jeweler's shop had presented. He discounted the ring right away. Too much could be read into the gift of a ring. Besides, when he did give Sian a ring, it wouldn't be something as gaudy as this ruby and emerald confection. The string of pearls attracted him. They were long enough for her to wear as a single or double loop but not matronly like the triple sets.

Memories of another time shouldn't interfere with the present, but they did. So many sets of pearls, their appeal for women seemed eternal. Sian deserved something more. He set the necklace down on the black velvet square.

The last piece, an art deco platinum bracelet, set with square diamonds and emeralds in a Greek key pattern, held a certain charm. The emeralds weren't quite as bright, or the same perfect shade as her eyes, but he liked the piece. He held the bracelet to the light, using the assistant's loop to examine the stones. The diamonds were good. He nodded to the young woman behind the counter. "The very thing I was looking for. Can you gift wrap it for me?"

"Of course, sir. May I ask how you wish to pay?"

"Cash. I don't use cards."

"Very well, sir. If you'd like to take a seat, I'll wrap the item for you."

He sat on the leather sofa opposite the counter. While he waited for her to return, he counted out money from his wallet. The bank notes entertained him. Their size and style had changed so much over the years. One of his safes held a great deal of paper currency, which in today's world would no longer be legal, but the aged notes might be worth something to collectors. Maybe he should look to find out what was in the old strong room. A pity the days of paying in gold guineas were long gone. There had always been a satisfaction in a weighty bag of coin. At some point soon, he would contact the accountant and check the funds available for his renovations on the house.

The young blonde returned with an small, elegant parcel wrapped in silver with gold ribbon trimmings. He went to the counter and handed over the correct sum. The girl wrote him a receipt itemizing the bracelet.

"Thank you, sir," the girl said handing over the document. "Do call in again soon."

"I may well do that." He picked up the small package, waiting a moment for her to finish checking the notes before he slipped it into his pocket. As soon as she smiled and placed the money in the cash register, he left. One day he would call back here no doubt, but should he ever want a ring for Sian, a special ring, he knew of somewhere offering a higher quality of stones and workmanship, along with a range of other special enhancements.

Might an engagement ring be enough to help Sian understand how much she meant to him? A solid reminder on her hand would be a constant token of how much he cared.

He strode the few paces to his tailor's, where he collected the jacket he'd ordered in September and bought a long, green, waxed topcoat off the peg. While waiting for them to parcel it up, he decided he liked his brown leather one better. Perhaps he'd get used to the new one. From today, he'd make an assessment of his wardrobe. He didn't want Sian thinking he looked as antique as some of the furniture in the house.

Along with the coat, he added an order for a new full dinner suit with waistcoat, black and gray, and arranged a date to come back for a fitting, and picked up a couple of casual shirts. With that done, he made his way back to the car. He stowed the carrier bags in the boot, before he settled in to drive to the South Downs to grab lunch at the pub.

Autumn had swept through the county this last week. Today the trees could hold onto the last of their leaves no longer. Soon it would grow colder still. The wonderful prospect of long winter evenings in front of a warm hearth with Sian raised his smile.

This year they could celebrate Christmas, too, as the full moon occurred after the day. He couldn't remember the last time he'd made anything of such seasonal festivities. How much he had changed in the brief time Sian had been in his life. Five, no, four months ago, his only thoughts for December would have been a bonus for the staff. He must take care not to become complacent, nor take Sian for granted. She was a treasure, and he must convince her he cherished her above all else.

At the pub he checked the day's lunch specials, written in the glass case outside the door, before he went inside. Mid-week the bar was quiet. He ordered a pint of bitter and a steak sandwich. Drink in hand, he walked across to sit at the table he'd shared with Sian the last time they were here. If he narrowed his eyes against the light, he could see her opposite him, as she'd been that day, pale and full of trepidation.

He'd tried to give her confidence in the task she'd agreed to perform. Before he transformed the night of the full moon, she would chain him to the floor rings in the small white room he'd had built in the 1920s. Once she bound him, she had to slide across the metal bars to secure him inside. If she had wished, she could meet him in the dreams. He sighed, for he'd not done much to help her with her concerns, not as much as he should have.

"Your sandwich, sir."

Startled out of his introspection, he glanced at the girl holding a plate. "Thank you."

He moved his keys so the girl could place the plate on the table. He lifted the wedge of bread and steak to take a bite. Lunch without Sian's company wasn't the same. He found little savor in the food.

He left the pub having only drunk half his pint. Most of his meal remained on the plate.

The clock on the dash showed three-thirty. He had time to take a stroll over the hills for an hour before he drove back in the lowering dusk. When he returned, Sian would be waiting, and the house would be quiet.

* * * *

Appalled to find the two big trucks and several cars still parked outside the house when he returned, he drove around to the garage, parked the car, and made his way into the house through the staff entrance. He flipped lights on as he walked through the corridors, surprised by so much darkness. In the main central corridor, he found the sound of voices coming from the den. Sian had promised the crew would be gone by six-thirty. He checked his watch; it was almost that.

How ridiculous he should be apprehensive about entering the room. He waited in the corridor outside the den, uncertain whether to cross the threshold and face them, or go upstairs and wait until they left. He counted the different voices: Sian, light, amused and laughing, Richard, the technical manager, another female voice, too, and a deep-voiced man.

Damn it. He strode through with what he hoped was a convincing smile. "Good evening." He took off his coat and slung it on the back of one of the bucket seat chairs.

Sian got up from her seat. She embraced him. "Magnus, I'm sorry, the time has vanished today. Let me introduce you to everyone. I'm sure you remember Richard Astle, our tech wizard."

He nodded. "Yes, I recall meeting you earlier in the year, Mr. Astle."

"This is Tanya, a solo ballerina. She's leaving us today to go home to her partner. They are having a baby."

"I'm pleased to meet you, Tanya. Accept my congratulations."

"This is Jerry Finch, our costume manager."

"A pleasure to meet you, Mr. Finch." He took in the offered smiles, a light of interest in the wide eyes of the delicate girl. "I hope they haven't worked you too hard, Tanya."

"No, sir. Today is my last shoot until…" She shrugged her shoulders. "Sian invited me to have a goodbye drink, though mine is healthy juice."

He nodded. "I see. Perhaps I can join you and wish you happiness."

"Of course, Magnus. Here." Sian poured him a glass.

"All best wishes to you, Tanya." He tilted his glass, pleased the others joined the toast to the silver-haired girl. He took a sip. Champagne, but not from his cellar.

Sian stood beside him. He slipped his arm around her waist, uncaring if these people should see. "Did your day go as you might have wished?"

"Oh, yes! We got the still shots done, and the dancing, too." Her glance turned from him to Tanya. "All credit to this lady here. She sure made her last day with us a spectacular one."

He raised his glass again to the young woman who smiled in return. "Then it would seem today was a good day."

"Yes, Mr. Johansson," Richard said. "We'll be done here by mid-afternoon tomorrow for certain."

"Thank you, Mr. Astle. It is a pleasure to find your timing will be so impeccable."

"Just like I said." Sian held his glance for a few seconds. "You don't mind us celebrating Tanya's leaving, do you?"

He shook his head and pressed a kiss to Sian's cheek. "No, of course not."

"That is very kind of you, Mr. Johansson," Tanya said as she rose from her seat. "But I do need to get back to town tonight. Tomorrow I have to drive up to Shropshire, and I still have to pack." She turned to Richard who had risen, too, and offered him a kiss. She reached across to give Jerry a peck on the cheek as well before coming over to give Sian a hug. "Thanks so much. I'll post about how I'm doing down on the farm. It'll all be on my Facebook page." She kissed Sian's cheek. "Bye," she said. "Oh, Lord, here I go again." She brushed at her eyes.

Sian handed over a tissue. "Travel safe."

The others called their good-byes, too, as Tanya headed to the door.

"I didn't mean to break up the party," Magnus said.

"No, don't worry about it. We've all got to either drive back to the city or the hotel tonight." Richard set down his glass.

"I see."

"Yes. The band are schlepping back and forth from London, but that's their choice. Like most of the crew I'm staying at a local hotel."

Sian slipped her arm around him and squeezed his hip. "So, I'll see you guys tomorrow morning about seven, okay?

Jerry nodded, rising from the leather sofa. "Have a good evening."

"Bye, see you tomorrow," Richard called from the doorway.

Sian turned in toward him to accept his embrace and a kiss.

He studied her face. Her eyes shone with an animated spark showing how involved she'd been with making something happen. He swallowed before he hugged her against him. "I have a surprise for you. An Italian meal ready in about half an hour, we can eat in here. You can watch TV and…" He thought for a second. "Cabbage out?"

Sian giggled. "Veg out is what you mean."

"Yes."

She hugged him close and planted a kiss on his lips. "I am so proud of you."

"Why?"

"Because you came in to say hello."

"Hmm. I'll go to get dinner ready. You've time to shower and change into something more comfortable if you wish."

"Thank you, Magnus. You are so thoughtful."

He turned away to head downstairs. Indeed, tonight he was thoughtful. She'd no idea how much.

As he set the wine in a cooler of ice and laid out the antipasti on a tray, he considered the magnitude of what he'd asked of Sian. More than ever, tonight's brief meeting with her colleagues and her air of satisfaction in the day told him her loss to this world would be a sadness. He'd no doubt she didn't recognize it at present, but she would at some time in the future. Should he make the point to her now? A part of his soul shriveled at the thought, for she may agree. Fresh from today's triumphs, she might very well decide she wished to return to the life she'd enjoyed before they met.

He folded two napkins, watching the little clock on the stove as he waited for the bread rolls to warm.

The notion of her loss stung him, twisted his heart until he could scarce think straight. The oven timer pinged, breaking his thoughts. He bent to take the tray of rolls from the oven and set them to cool.

Some might call it cowardice but his fear took control. Tonight, he'd say nothing to her about returning to her work, to her world. Instead, he'd relish her rare beauty of body and spirit, and give her the gift he'd bought for her.

Shall I keep her chained to me with diamonds?

He loaded up the tray, made his way out of the kitchen, and up the stairs to the den. A sense of guilt rolled through him. After a day or two, a week at most, he'd remind her she could, if she wished, return to work in the city. Not with Gorsewell, though, not with Gorsewell Productions.

Chapter 12

Sian rubbed a dollop of scented lotion into her arm and studied the raw purple scar with its slashed edges. The wound had sealed. She hoped the thin scar would grow less colorful in time. She slathered on some more lotion before teasing the comb through her wet hair. The day had left her tired in a good way, not wired or tense, but content with how the shoot had gone. Truth be told, she'd enjoyed seeing things come together, even troubleshooting had been pleasant. Overall, the day's results proved more than satisfactory.

Her reflection smiled back as she stroked moisturizer into her skin, and after she rinsed her mouth with mouthwash, she looked again. For the most part, she'd always been dispassionate about her looks, but tonight she wondered how many wrinkles she might have to get before Magnus did as she wanted.

She hoped he wouldn't leave it too long. She'd rather not be a gray wolf.

She swiped on a little lip-gloss and spritzed on a dash of her favorite perfume. Weird, but Magnus wasn't like an ordinary wolf. His thick pelt was honey and apricot with darker shades that enhanced his features. He stunned her. He was so amazing. His gold-flecked eyes could suck her soul from her body. When he held her gaze in wolf-form, she got lost in his eyes. Each time he had looked at her, she had told herself to look away. The connection was much worse on their second full moon together and she'd needed all her will to force her gaze from his.

What decided the color of a werewolf? Might it be genetic? Magnus had dark hair as a man so it couldn't be hair color. She twirled a curl with her finger. What color wolf might she become? She shook her head. Tonight her mind had hit strangeness, indeed. Shoving her feet into her slippers, she wrapped herself in a big fluffy robe before heading down to the room Magnus had filled with all kinds of boy's toys and gadgets over the years.

Tonight it would be good to "veg out" as he'd said. She chuckled again. *Cabbage out?* That might be a new one to use. She opened the door and smiled at the view.

He always managed to give her just what she needed.

A log in the hearth had taken. Yellow flames flickered with a comforting glow. Several lamps were lit, and a candelabrum stood on the low table by the long sofa. She met his gaze. A rise of pleasure warmed her at his expression.

"Wine?" He came to hug her and placed a kiss on her cheek.

"Please. What's all the food on the tray?"

"Antipasti. Parma ham, Bresola, olives, artichokes, sun dried tomato, a little cheese, some olive oil, and rolls. I hope you like the idea."

"Yes." She accepted the glass and took a sip of chilled white wine. "You've been planning this evening for some time."

"I thought after all your efforts today you'd need some relaxation and a treat." He slid his arm around her.

A fresh appreciation of his care for her pricked her conscience. Her doubts regarding the past held no substance.

"Come and sit down. You must be exhausted. Relax for a while before we eat."

She curled up on the sofa with her feet tucked under her. Leaning across to the small table he'd placed nearby, she set her glass down.

"Would you like to watch TV?" He sat beside her.

"Not now, tell me about your day?" She nodded toward the tray he'd prepared. "Did you spend the day in the kitchen?"

Magnus laughed.

Few people would understand what a precious sound his laughter was to her, or how the laugh lines around his eyes didn't truly reflect age or experience. "You look so happy," she whispered, reaching out to touch his cheek with her forefinger.

"I am happy. You make me so. No, I didn't spend the day in the kitchen. I went out to visit my tailor."

"Again?"

"Yes, but I also went shopping for something else. Wait a moment and I will show you." He crossed to where he'd slung his coat earlier. He picked the garment up and rummaged through the pockets until he drew out something small with ribbons. "Here it is."

The dainty, silver-wrapped parcel in his hand set alarm bells ringing in her head. Small and pretty, she'd lay her life that whatever the gift wrapping hid was expensive. Very.

"I wanted to give you something to show you how much you mean to me. I didn't find the right thing to do that, but this is a small token of my—"

"Don't, Magnus."

He shook his head. "It is a small gift. Please, accept it." He pressed the box into her palm and closed his larger one over hers.

She blinked. "You don't need to give me things," she whispered, lost in his dark gaze. "I'm not here because of—"

"Please, indulge me. Permit me the pleasure of offering you the trinkets I wish to give you."

A flash of the gilded ribbons shone in the firelight. "When you put it like that. What is it? I've not had a trinket since my Gran sent me a pack of building block pieces."

He laughed as he moved his hand from hers. "Open it. I'm afraid I have to say my gift doesn't have the intellectual charm or challenge of building blocks."

Careful not to tug, she eased the ribbons away so she could open the silver paper. Inside she found a leather box, embossed with the jeweler's name, obvious. Her stomach flipped. Lifting her gaze to his, she gave a small shake of her head.

She opened the lid of the box and caught her breath. Diamonds and emeralds sparkled in the candlelight. A moment of disbelief hit. This bracelet screamed class. She flashed a glance to him.

He smiled, but not in any expectant way. He didn't appear to anticipate her shock, awe, or anything. "Put it on. Please?"

"It's so beautiful. It's not the kind of thing I'd normally wear with a bath robe," she whispered, taking the bracelet from the velvet inner. Exquisite, flawless, utterly gorgeous, and too damned expensive for her to even think about, she slipped the cool links over her wrist like a bangle, having no need to open the catch. The gems were smooth as she stroked over them.

"May I see?" He lifted her wrist so he could tweak at the safety chain. "Wear it for a day or two. If it seems too loose I can take it back so they can adjust it."

She shook her head. "No. It's perfect."

"Sian, look at me?"

The depth of his gray gaze sucked her in.

"These are pretty stones, rocks if you will. They have an intrinsic value because of what they are. They are nothing in comparison to you. I want you to remember that."

His words swept her away, as so often he did. She lifted her arms around his neck and pressed a kiss to his lips. "Make love to me, Magnus. Now, please."

He laid her back against the sofa and opened her robe. "No gem could ever sparkle like you in firelight."

A heady rush of desire swept though her, instant arousal from his lightest touch. She groaned as he kissed down her throat. Time meant nothing as he touched her, licked and sucked her nipples until they tingled, heating to firm beads. She burned like the hearth, smoking white-hot. Her aching need drove her to touch him. She clasped his shoulders beneath his shirt and smoothed her palms over his muscles. His caresses pushed her on to gain more contact and she reached around his waist to open the button and zip on his jeans.

His groan sounded as she stroked the length of his erection.

The demand for him inside ramped up to another level. She moved her hand from him, and clasping his ass, shoved the jeans down until she felt his skin against her open thighs.

He kicked the jeans off. She shifted her body to nestle tight against his, eager for all he could give her. "Now, Magnus."

He parted her thighs shamelessly wide. She arched up to him. Tantalizing her responses, he filled her, inch by inch. His gaze never left hers until he lay lodged as deep as he'd ever been inside her.

"Oh, God."

"I want to show you how much I need you."

The words fired her passion. She hooked her thighs high round his waist. "Yes."

The initial sweet rhythm between them became a gallop. One swift breath after another, she kept pace with him.

She rubbed her nipples against his chest, and clinging tight cried out, "Magnus!"

A blistering flash.

Delight.

"Yes. Give me all of you."

Strung out like the stars in the cosmos, she didn't breathe.

He tilted her head back, clasping her hair in his fingers. "You're mine."

Eyes closed, she inhaled his scent, relishing his weight above her, not yet willing to move to separate them. His embrace cocooned her from everything else.

A log in the hearth hissed.

She opened her eyes, astonished to find she still lay with him on the long sofa in the den, the firelight shadow dancing on the ceiling. Never before had it felt this right. Tilting her cheek against his, she met his gaze as he lifted his head. "Magnus," she whispered, doubtful words were enough.

"You are my woman, forever, for all time. I will cease to be whole without you."

Inching away, she shifted position, relaxing her legs around his waist. She struggled to hold back tears of completion. Caressing his hair, his shoulders and back, she shifted again as he withdrew, and gathered him into her embrace. She cradled him until he pressed a kiss to her cheek and moved from her arms. He stood, dragged on his jeans, and adjusted his clothing. The soulful expression in his gaze melted her. They had no need for more words. She wrapped the robe around herself, certain tonight the bond between them had deepened to become more solid.

Magnus stroked his fingers through her disheveled damp hair. "Would you care to eat now?"

She nodded, suddenly ravenous, and took a sip of wine from her glass. "Please."

He filled a plate for her and passed it with a napkin and fork. The bracelet glinted in the firelight. She wondered if she'd ever get used to wearing it. He sat beside her with his own plate. "Do you truly think the film shoot will be complete by tomorrow evening?" he asked.

"I think things went so well today that if they go as well tomorrow, everything will be wrapped up by lunch time."

"Amazing."

She popped an olive in her mouth, nodded, then swallowed. "Yes, it's the way things can be when everything gels."

"You have organized it down to the last detail, so I'm not surprised it has been a great success."

"I know, it's one of the reasons I did so much preparation," she said and smiled. "Everyone knows exactly what's expected of them so it makes it easy. I think you'll love the film. I'll see if I can snaffle a copy for us tomorrow. I'm certain they'll be able to burn a disc for me. We could watch it tomorrow evening if you like."

"Really? It's so easy?"

"Of course it will be a raw, unedited copy, but you'll be able to see what all the fuss was about."

"I'd like a copy as a keepsake for us."

"You would?"

"Yes, so we have a record of what lay behind our first meeting."

"Then, I'll make sure Richard doesn't leave the house until I have a copy in my hand."

Chapter 13

Franklyn sat in the warmth of his hired car with his phone in his hand. Sian twinkled back from the screen, eyes sparkling full of excitement, her glossy red lips open as she laughed. The image didn't please him half as much as it once had. Today, it only added to his sense of self-loathing.

For three hours, he'd tried to gather the courage to hit the number to call her. He'd paced the grounds at Darnwell where the very air seemed to press in on him, crushing his hopes to doubts. The closer he got to calling her, the worse the sensation became. The place carried some kind of energy to thwart him. Since when did anyone or anything intimidate Franklyn Gorsewell? The sour taste of his visit wouldn't go away.

The longer he'd stayed on the grounds of the house, the more his anger robbed him of everything but the need to get out of there. He had, and after speeding out of the gates, thundering along the country lanes, he had pulled onto the motorway. Two junctions farther, he parked in a lay-by on the way into London. He battled with his thoughts on the morning. The sheer foulness of the place clung about him like a wet Mackintosh. An overwhelming sense of defeat rolled over him again. He must get a grip. Make some decisions and soon.

He'd sell the apartment any way. Once it was tarted up, he'd sell the place.

The prospect of returning to the scene of the attack rolled in a bitter wave each time he thought of home. His hotel was impersonal and untainted. No one knew him. There was something to be said for that.

Sian taunted him again from the phone.

He could send a text.

Coward. A text just meant he didn't have to hear the dismissal in her voice.

He found Sian's number and a fresh image, one from two years gone. Oh, God.

He'd insisted some guy at the party take the picture of them together. Sian, the muse. Sian, the perfect nymph in a gauzy pale robe she'd worn for the fancy dress party they'd attended at some TV celeb's house. She had her hand on his arm, her other hand caressed the laurel wreath he'd worn. Her smile for him still held the same impact. The nymph and Zeus. She had danced with him most of the night.

The ache for her soured his gut and set his senses reeling.

Careful to avoid any challenge, or offer her anything but a handover meeting, he set up a message for her. He stared at the words. Surely, Sian couldn't read any motive but business into that.

She had told him she would leave the company after the shoot. He hadn't believed her and he still didn't. With him in hospital, she'd stepped in and taken over immediately, but she'd not kept him in the loop. The doctors had said it would take him months to recover. They were wrong.

No way could she think he'd simply pass all future control of the company over to her on a permanent basis. She had to know he'd be back.

He tortured himself again as his thumb hovered over the send button. She'd have to respond to his message. She'd never yet ignored one of his texts in all their years together. If he opened the line of communication, she'd have to meet with him to hand control of the company back. Face to face, at least he stood a chance to remind her where she belonged.

What the fuck was wrong with him?

He hit the send button. His fingers shook, but he'd done it. He set the phone down, checked the rear view mirror, then pulled out into the slow lane. The little hired car tootled along, windows rattling. Another layer of exasperation wrapped around him like a blanket. By the end of the month, he'd be driving the Porsche. At least he could be sure of one thing in his life.

The small dining room at the hotel had closed by the time he'd arrived. All he could do was order yet another room service blue steak. Rare.

Once in his room, he picked up the remote and put on the TV, its volume muted. He rang down to order dinner, then as he sat waiting for his meal, his gaze kept returning to his phone on the coffee table. Unable to believe she'd ignored him, he twice checked the thing hadn't somehow turned itself off. Each time he put the phone back on the table, a new level of frustration topped the last.

A rap at the door announced dinner. He crossed the room, opened the door, and lifted the silver cover from the plate before letting the waiter in. Blood pooled on the white glaze. Satisfied the chef had cooked this one right, he nodded and stood back so the waiter could enter to set the tray down.

"Anything else, sir?"

"No. Thanks."

He inhaled the ripe fragrance as he lifted the silver lid again, but even the compelling scent of a blue steak couldn't completely distract him from the phone. Slashing hunks of bloody flesh, he ate fast, wolfing the meat down with his phone sitting in front of him.

Nothing. No reply, not a voicemail or even a text. Sian lived with her phone beside her. Even in bed, her phone always nestled close by. He knew it. He'd called her early more than once just to hear her sultry tones as he roused her from sleep. Her husky voice was sexy enough to drive him to lust-filled thoughts.

She had to have the phone with her.

Unless she was busy with the boyfriend.

He flipped the TV to a different station, then another and another, but it didn't matter what came up on the screen because his attention kept gravitating to the phone and over to the bottle of tablets he'd left on the edge of the dresser. He'd missed two doses already today. He should take one of the powerful tablets now.

No.

The phone stayed silent.

He opened the mini bar. Perfect. He pulled out the two small bottles of Scotch whisky. There would be enough for one hearty belt to help him sleep.

The ice cubes rattled as he tossed a couple in the glass. He twisted the tops off the bottles, each snapping with a little crack. The familiar smell brought a moment of normality into the day's madness. Aching for more, he poured the rich amber liquid over the ice, then sat and sipped.

The fiery brew made a warm pathway to his gut.

No more tablets. He'd begin the process of getting back to being himself.

By the end of the month, he'd return to the office, maybe sooner. The alcohol hit. He took another swig from the glass. He'd welcome anything to quiet his senses and help put his head together so he could work out how to get Sian back. The kidnap plan today had been a bit crazy. He could do better than that.

The fucking mausoleum got the better of him. He needed to focus and get a realistic plan together, maybe set a little bait of his own to bring her back where she belonged. Johansson hadn't been challenged while he was away in the U.S., nor when he got back. It was time he made a move to show he wouldn't let his sweet pea go without repercussions.

He glanced to the silent phone again as he sipped from the glass. A prickle raced over his body. He caught a waft of her beside him, so rare and beautiful, even if illusory, he could taste her, not the drink.

Maybe he could search for her in the dreams. She'd been there once last week, but had vanished as soon as he'd caught her. Tonight, he would try again.

Chapter 14

Sian, still asleep, rolled into the space of his body heat. Magnus bent to press a kiss to her cheek. He smoothed one long spiral tress from where it threatened to fall over her face.

"I'll be back before breakfast, sweetheart. I need to run." The last word came out like a growl. Gooseflesh lifted the hairs on his arms. At least twice a week he ran circuits of the lake, but today the need to beat the bounds blasted through him with an urgency he'd never experienced as a man. Something he couldn't identify prompted his need to race across the pathways, to circle the grounds.

Quickly he donned a T-shirt, sports trousers, and running shoes. He took one last peek at the beauty in his bed before he made his way downstairs. The quickest exit was through the door in the drawing room. He ducked as he bent to go through.

The chilly morning smelled damp, mossy, and mushroomy, like the loam had chosen this dawn to awake from a long dry sleep. Another scent curled in the air. The hair on the back of his neck prickled. He set the timer on his watch and headed down the cinder path with the intention of circling the lake. This run usually took a little over an hour. He'd be back well in time before the camera crew and musicians returned to finish their work.

Mist hovered over the surface of the lake. He breathed deep when he reached the base of the grassy slope by the causeway to the pagoda. A wash of foul odor shook him. He paused to inhale again, hardly crediting what he'd discovered.

Disgusting.

His muscles bunched in tension.

He knew this reek and the one responsible for it. The arrogant bastard had been here!

Sian!

He looked back to the house, suddenly full of fears. Not merely for her safety in the dream world they shared, but in reality, too. Heart thumping, he raced back up the slope, ignored the slippery grass, and hit the cinder path fast. Cranking the speed, he dashed up to the terrace.

As he glanced to the ornate clock on entering the drawing room, he'd beaten his usual time for such a short run by half again. Long ago as a boy, he'd experienced a similar change in his body and its abilities. At first, the change had made him faster, but the later alterations had overwhelmed him in sensations. Could it be possible the impact of the bite on Gorsewell might have repercussions in his body, too? An alpha male ready to mate had to be at his strongest, fastest, and most protective of his chosen partner. Was the vile stink he'd discovered in the Pagoda the final proof he couldn't dismiss?

He tugged off the muddy running shoes before he trod on the fine-weave silk rug and crossed the room with them in hand. He slowed for the polish of the mahogany boards, then hurried down the hallway, up the stairs, and to the master bedroom.

He took the time to control his breathing for several repetitions. Quiet so as not to worry her, he turned the door handle. Light spilled in through the half open drapes. A beam of gold hit the end of the bed.

Angel.

She slept. Her hair a beacon on the pillow.

Not truly angelic, she stirred his sensuality far too deeply for that.

A wave of fear clutched him. The image of her the night Franklyn got into her dreams, the glassy-eyed fear, her cries before he had finally woke her, pierced him like a red hot needle.

Magnus shoved a hand through his sweaty hair. He took another look where she lay in their bed. If he must, he would kill Gorswell before the brute harmed her body or mind. The contact from him couldn't be allowed to escalate further. He must be stopped.

Carelessness on his part created the problem and he had to deal with it.

Another glance at Sian reassured him for now. He'd leave her to sleep a while longer. Still considering his apprehension, he stripped and walked into the wet room where he turned on the shower. The cold jets shocked him to silent agony. But his mind roared a discovery too savage to be borne. The next full moon Franklyn would turn!

Teeth clenched, Magnus edged the temperature control a notch hotter, then another, until the chill warmed.

Gorsewell would become wolf and need to kill. He must be developing fast if he felt confident enough to come and leave a scent mark here.

There was no way to prevent the full moon transformation, only a hope if he came here as a new wolf, he could be managed.

The new made werewolf would return to the house. That much was obvious. He would come to try to claim his place and Sian, too. Did Franklyn fully realize what was happening or why? Perhaps he might.

Even after so many years since the event, he recalled his own development in exquisite detail. The memory of the final process of his first transformation remained a bitter pain. Though his father had tried to prepare him, he had been terrified. The fear had never truly gone. So many years had passed until he found that his rage freed him to gain some control.

Like the opium he had used for a while, the drugs in the hospital must have prevented Franklyn turning in the last full moon. This next, the process would become unmanageable.

Franklyn would kill without compunction.

All he knew of Sian's boss promised the man would revel in the physicality of a new and powerful form. He'd kill. He would delight in it, and once he had, he would want to satisfy another need. The need to mate.

That's why he came here yesterday. Why he left a scent imprint of himself.

He grasped the shower bar.

Franklyn believes he can take Sian from me. I am changing because of him!

Alpha status would bring more speed and strength. Both would be welcome, but he would concentrate his hardest to develop the other additional skills he'd need to protect his mate. He would fight with everything he had to keep her safe.

A tremble shook through his cheek, his hand, and his fingers, followed by a surge of energy. He could hardly hold back the growl forming in his throat. His vision clouded.

He shook his head. Not now. It was morning. There would be no point.

He couldn't feel the water lashing his skin and a fresh rush of wolf energy raced around his body.

He would master this, accept the strength of the wolf, and take command.

The need to give in burned from within.

Not yet. Hold it. Stop it. Bear it!

The fizzing blood pulsed with less intensity through his veins. His vision cleared to normal in the steam.

Methodically he washed with the blue shower gel, his hair, too, yet still he could scent the vile stink wafting across the lake from the pagoda. All the time he stood under the powerful jets of the shower, he restrained the need in his blood. By allowing the active agent to filter in drip by drip, it dispersed before compelling his transformation. This, too, must be part of the changes within him since he bit Franklyn. He'd never had this amount of power to influence when he might take the wolf form. If only he'd realized the true magnitude of his mistake.

Too late now to harbor regrets for his clumsiness and folly at not killing Franklyn outright. He must deal with something worse—a new wolf, one hungry for its place, its power in a pack, and worst of all, greedy for Sian.

I must accept the role of Alpha. I made him what he will be. He owes me deference. One way or another, I will take it from him. If he's not willing to give it, I'll see him whine for his life!

* * * *

"Thank you," Sian sat up in bed, yawning as she accepted the coffee cup. "You must have been up for a while." She touched his damp hair. "You've showered already?"

He nodded.

"Are you all right? You're not worried about the crew coming in today are you?"

"No. I'll spend the morning in the library."

She sipped the coffee. "Then what's troubling you? I can see something is—feel it."

"Nothing to worry you. We'll talk about it later today after the film crew has departed."

"Is it important?" She set her cup down on the bedside table and pushed back the sheet. "Should I be worried?"

He gave a quick shake of his head. "No, not this morning. You concentrate on what you need to do to see the filming completed. I'll go down to make us some breakfast while you shower and dress. Scrambled egg and toast in the kitchen?"

"Sounds great."

Magnus got up from where he sat on the edge of the bed. Every line in his torso spoke of his tension. Her concern grew. She took her coffee cup into the wet room, drank some more as she cleaned her face, then stepped into the shower.

The scent of toast met her in the kitchen. Magnus sat staring out of the window. He didn't turn to meet her as she entered the room. Her certainty that something disturbed him deeply grew. "Is this for me?" she asked sitting opposite him across the table.

"Yes." He lifted the silver cover.

"Thanks." She sloshed a dollop of ketchup on her plate, then picked up her knife and fork. "Everything will be over by lunch. I promise I'll do all I can to make sure the filming is complete."

He gave a small clipped smile. "I know you will."

"There won't be any problems, I'm certain." She set her knife down and patted her pocket. "Oh, heck, my phone is upstairs. I'd better go fetch it. There could be all kinds of messages."

"Finish your breakfast. I'll fetch it for you. Where did you leave it?" He stood.

"Thanks, I think it's on the small chest of drawers in my boudoir. I can't believe I forgot it."

"I think you were a little distracted last night. I'll go and get it for you." He strode out.

She ate another mouthful and took a sip of coffee, all the time wishing she could get to the heart of whatever worried him. The clock showed almost seven. The crew would turn up soon; she'd not have time to discuss anything with Magnus until they left. After today, there would be little to do for Gorsewell Productions since the next big project was some months away. Evie could handle most of the queries that might come up.

There would be time for Magnus. They could settle back to planning for the conservatory restoration and the resurrection of the walled garden. She sighed. The prospect of meeting the director of Green Girls still concerned her.

So many complications.

"Here you are." Magnus offered her the phone.

"Thanks so much." She took it to check the messages. One stood out like a beacon.

Franklyn. What did he want?

She glanced up with a smile. "All's well," she said, hoping Magnus didn't see the lie in her eyes or hear it in her voice.

The last thing she wanted to do was to open the message with him clearing the table. She'd look at it upstairs. "Thanks for breakfast. I'd better go up to see if anyone's arrived yet. I'll come to find you in the library when the house is clear of everyone. We'll have a late lunch then. Yes?"

He nodded. "I think you would say 'that's a plan.'"

Pocketing the phone, she laughed as she hurried out of the kitchen. She dashed up the staircase and into the long corridor heading down to the ballroom.

The fabulous room, ready for the rest of the shoot today, was still and quiet, a sharp contrast from the music and dancing filmed yesterday. She went to stand by one of the long French windows overlooking the terrace. Here, with plenty of light to see, she opened the message from Franklyn.

Shit.

The message on the phone screen glowed.

Hope the Timeless *production goes well, my Rosebud. Am back in town as of today. Will be in the office by the end of the month. Will call next week to set up a time for handover. We need to meet.*

Her gut rolled, souring breakfast. The last thing she wanted was to meet with him. There wasn't the need. She could do a handover via e-mail. One of her palms tingled. Fear at his violence came back with a punch, the revulsion of finding him in her dreams, of evading his efforts to…

God, if what he'd done the last couple of weeks had been in the flesh, it would be attempted rape.

How darn typical of Franklyn to send a message like that. Like nothing had happened between them. Vile bastard.

Even the word *Rosebud* sickened her. He'd called her that for years, from her earliest days at the office, when he'd been so attentive. All the time he helped build her career, she'd been Rosebud. At first, she'd been pleased with the little nickname, but not now. Never again. *I'm not your Rosebud, Franklyn.* She'd come to understand that the unease she had felt with his petty bullying, his demands for the kind of clothes she wore when working, the lascivious comments, and the way he always attempted to touch her, was justified. All the things he did; they weren't right.

True, she owed him a lot. Without him, she'd probably have struggled like so many other seventeen-year-olds who didn't live with parents. Even so, no matter how much he'd helped her, it didn't give him the right to treat her like he owned her.

She checked the time the message came in. Late yesterday evening. He'd be wondering where her reply was. In the past, she always responded straight away to his texts even when he woke her at four in the morning. But now that she'd discovered what a manipulative swine Franklyn truly was, he could go to hell.

"Morning, Sian."

She spun around. Richard stood across the room. "Good morning. Everything okay?"

"Sure. Have you got a minute?"

"Yes." Slipping the phone into her pocket, she strolled across the room.

"Good, I want to show you something I found last night when I was going through the stills I've been sent so far. It's weird, and I think you should see it." He opened the lid of his iPad. "Take a look at this."

"Is he doing what I think he's doing?"

Richard gave a small nod. "I think so. Crazy, hey?"

"Disgusting. Was it one of the crew?"

"No, not as far as I can recall. I didn't see anyone in a fedora yesterday."

"Who took the shot?"

"One of the photographers working in the grounds with a long lens. He took a rash of pictures. He was trying to get some good background images of the lake and the woods. Along with them he also got this." Richard closed the image down. "When security arrives we need to have words with them."

She nodded. "Yes. How awful. I daren't tell Magnus some stranger in the grounds peed up the pagoda wall like a stray hound."

Richard nodded. "I agree. Mr. Johansson would not be pleased."

"You bet your life. I can't believe this, I really can't. I'd best go get my clipboard and notes for the day. I need to calm down a bit so when I see the security guys I can control the anger so it bites them, not me. We pay that security firm a small fortune, but their staff don't stop something like this happening."

"Before you go, Sian, I have to tell you, the really weird thing is I think I know the physique. Something about the angular shape of the shoulders, the size of him, he looks familiar."

"Who do you think it is?"

"Well, it might seem crazy, especially with him being in the rest home after the accident, but I'd lay a fifty pound bet that's a picture of Franklyn."

Her stomach dropped. A lump formed in her throat. "Let me look at the photo again." She yanked the iPad from Richard and opened the image. "Oh, my god. I think you're right."

Chapter 15

"I want everyone checked this morning. Understood?" Sian eyed both the security guards. "The evidence is incontrovertible. Yesterday, one of our photographers got a picture of someone not on the list. A stranger made it past you both. You know I expect better. I'll not have my people left to the mercy of stalkers or other assorted odd-bods. You can think yourself lucky I don't report you so you forfeit the fee for this assignment. Any more shoddy messing about, and I will do just that. Am I making myself clear?"

The larger of the two no longer met her gaze but answered. "Yes, totally."

"Good. You both have a comprehensive register with every person who should be here on it, from the girl in the chow van to the members of the band. I want to see you've checked everyone today. If you discover anyone who isn't on the list, I need to know immediately so I can decide whether we call the police or not."

"Yes, Ms. Armstrong."

She sucked in a deep breath as she handed over another two copies of the list she'd made. "In case you've mislaid the originals. I'll meet with you both at eight-thirty when you will have the results I need. Thank you, gentlemen."

They both turned and left the room without a murmur.

"Sian, you're awesome when someone riles you," Richard said.

She shook her head. "Richard, that is a cliché of the worst possible kind. Let's get this morning underway. Please keep things tight to the schedule for me. I want the house cleared no later than two, okay?"

"Yes, ma'am. I suggest we keep the information about yesterday between us. I don't think this pair will volunteer they dropped a bollock. It's maybe best no one else knows. You know how edgy the band can be. Do you have time for a coffee?"

"No, I'll be prowling the place until I'm certain they've done their job. You've got my phone number. Any problems at all, call me." Taking her phone from her pocket, she strode out of the drawing room.

The crew had arrived in the courtyard, along with the security pair. Several stood in line to get coffee from the food truck. She gave the security guards a curt nod as they stood ticking people off the list.

Farther on, out on the terrace, the choreographer stood chatting with one of the continuity girls. Nothing untoward there.

She headed into the ballroom. The sound engineers and two photographers, all of whom she knew by sight, were at work with their kit. Still a sense of unease rattled her, along with the desire to send Franklyn the kind of text he'd never forget.

She should tell Magnus. He had the right to know. But something had worried him earlier, and she didn't want to make things worse. He couldn't possibly know about this already.

Franklyn could stew waiting for her reply.

The shriek of an electric guitar wailed down the corridor from the open doors of the ballroom. Recording of the three final tracks off the album had begun. She glanced to her wristwatch. They were doing well with the timing.

Not wanting to disturb the filming in the ballroom, Sian made her way back to the drawing room before going out onto the terrace to walk the short way around to the other courtyard at the back by the rose garden. One of the security guards stood at the end of the terrace. Much better than yesterday, at least they weren't wandering around in a pair. She glanced across to the lake and the pagoda.

A fresh sense of disgust hit her. Filthy yob!

She'd not forget the image Richard had showed her, not for a long time.

A man in a set of old-fashioned green overalls, carrying a steaming bucket and a broom, headed toward the path down to the lake. That was Monty. She'd best let security know he belonged on the estate. The photographers, too, just in case they need a few extra shots.

Oh, my God. Magnus knew! He must have contacted Monty to clean up. That's what had upset Magnus so much this morning. He knew Franklyn had been here and what he'd done. Oh, why hadn't he said?

She called the guard from her phone. "It's okay. I know the old boy down by the lake. He's one of Mr. Johansson's people." She could hardly call Monty a servant. "He's been sent down there by Mr. Johansson."

"We've checked everyone, Ms. Armstrong, everyone is accounted for," the guard said.

"Excellent. By my estimation, the crew will be ready to leave by one, the band before then. I want them all checked out as they leave the grounds. You call me when the kit and props are loaded onto the wagon because I want to personally see everyone is off-site."

"Yes, Ms. Armstrong."

In the meantime, she'd inspect the rooms used yesterday for even a nick in the paintwork, and try to work out a way to explain to Magnus what had happened. Only once she'd done that, would she contact Franklyn.

The haunting first chords of her favorite song from the *Timeless* album met her as she entered the long corridor to go along to the music room. For some crazy reason, tears stung her eyes. The strength of love to last eons, to right all manner of wrongs, and most of all, to protect the one you cared for.

She nodded at the last sobbing note of the guitar. The certainty grew. She'd give anything to protect Magnus from his fears, as well as the nuisance Franklyn made of himself.

All she had to do was hold it together and be strong. Somehow she would do it.

* * * *

Sian waved the last lorry off at two-twenty-five precisely. She clutched the disc Richard had given her. All her memories of the morning and yesterday were ready to watch. Richard had proved his worth today. He'd even seen that the bins provided for the crew were taken away before he left. She slid the disc in her back pocket. Perhaps she and Magnus might look at it later this evening. Closing the door behind her, she hurried upstairs to the library. He must have heard the equipment loaded into the trucks, so he would know the shoot had finished.

They'd so much to talk about. Her hope to keep Franklyn's appearance here a secret had dissolved as soon as she realized Magnus had asked Monty to clean up the pagoda. She paused at the top of the stairs where she undid the clip keeping her hair back. She ran her fingers through the long strands, then rubbed at the back of her neck to ease the tension. She took a deep breath and opened the door into the library.

Magnus sat at the computer. He turned to her as she stepped into the room. "All complete?"

She nodded. "Yes. It was an epic shoot. They did so well. I've got a copy of it from Richard."

He stood from his chair and greeted her with a hug. "You are obviously satisfied with the event."

"Yes, I am. Though, there were a few issues." She held his dark gaze. "You know of the most important one."

"I do?"

She could pretend she knew nothing about Franklyn's visit and disgusting behavior, but a lie would do neither of them any good. She curled her arms around his neck with a sigh. "Yes. We need to talk about it."

He twirled one finger through a curl. "I see," he said. "Yes, we must talk, but I suggest we have lunch before we do."

"If you want to, that's fine. I'll go make us some sandwiches. Do you want to eat up here or down in the kitchen?"

"We'll eat in the den. We can come back up here after. Sandwiches are perfect. Shall I come and assist?"

She laughed. "No. Why don't you call or e-mail Cook and Mrs. Tyson to tell them they can return tomorrow? Coffee, and cheese and pickle?" She pressed a kiss to his cheek.

"Sumptuous. I'll telephone the ladies."

She left him and made her way to the kitchen, full of concerns about their forthcoming discussion. There had to be more to it than merely Franklyn's visit but she couldn't think of anything else.

Events of the last couple of months played through her thoughts. Ever since Franklyn's accident, Magnus had seemed more concerned about her boss than she'd thought he would be. His explanation the night that Franklyn had first appeared in her dream, that it was a one-off occasion, had proved wrong. The experiences had happened several times, the dreams almost as deep as those she shared with Magnus, though each grew more horrific than the last. She needed to tell him.

But he would be so hurt to think Franklyn could threaten her in such a way. She made the sandwiches and coffee, and carried it all up to the den. Magnus had left the door open for her. She found him bent, lighting a fresh stack of kindling beneath a fat log.

"Here we are," she said setting the tray down. "Would you like coffee?"

"Thank you, yes. This will be ablaze in ten minutes."

When flames licked greedily around one of the logs, he came over to her, and she handed him his mug. They sat together, and for some time, ate in silence. Staring into the fire, she wondered again at his choice of rooms for their discussion.

This room had always been a place where they'd relaxed, but this wouldn't be a comfortable chat. She placed her empty plate and mug back on the tray, then stretched to iron out the kinks in her shoulders, before rejoining him on the sofa.

"Are you too tired to talk now?" he asked.

"No, I don't want to put this off. I'll tell you what happened yesterday, even though I know you know some of it."

Magnus walked across to set his plate and cup on the tray, then turned back to her with sorrowful eyes. "Tell me."

"I found out this morning, from a picture one of the photographers took, Franklyn came here. He was on the grounds yesterday."

He nodded. "Yes, when I ran this morning, I discovered he'd been here."

"I'd guessed you knew before I did. Tell me how?"

He reached for her hand, urged her to sit closer as he settled beside her, and slid an arm around her when she did. "You understand sometimes I can sense things?"

"Yes."

"When I ran this morning, I smelled his presence. I knew he'd been here."

"Smelled him?"

"Yes. He'd left a little message for me."

"He peed up the wall of the pagoda! I saw the picture of him doing it."

"You are correct. That's why I asked a favor from Monty."

"I saw him going down there with a bucket and a brush."

Magnus smiled. "Yes, I've no doubt Monty's been very thorough. I told him I thought a fox had got in there."

"You were right in one way. Though a weasel is more apt to describe Franklyn." She wound her arms around him, inhaling the fragrance of his cologne. "I'm so sorry he managed to get on site when I was in charge. I can't tell you how upset I was when Richard showed me the picture."

He squeezed her so tight she gave a squeak. "You mustn't be frightened of Franklyn. I will make sure he never comes anywhere near you."

Why should he say that? She peered into his dark eyes. "I refuse to be frightened of Franklyn."

"Then, I have to say, I think, at present, you should be careful of him."

The bleak tone shook her. "Why?"

Chapter 16

The trust in her eyes raked over him as if his hopes and dreams were coals already alight in a burner. Today might see the end of any chance of keeping her love. The urge to hold his thoughts to himself tempted him, but he couldn't shirk his guilt in this cruel circumstance. She needed to know.

A log in the hearth hissed.

"Please, Magnus, tell me why you think I should be afraid of Franklyn."

He cupped her chin with his palm, tilted her head, and kissed her. An offering of peace he didn't feel, an oath of all he held so dear and was about to risk for the sake of a vile wretch who should have died. Gently, he released her before he moved back on the sofa. "I have made a grave mistake."

Sian's eyes widened, the pupils dilating to dark wells in which he could drown. She shook her head. "No, we're not a mistake. Everything I do is to show you how much I care about you. I try so hard. You are my world."

"Ah, I didn't mean us. We aren't a mistake. I meant something else. I fear you'll be angry when I tell you. I swear I didn't intend for this to happen. As ever, unexpected consequences can be the most savage to endure."

"What's happened?"

The moment returned and raised his blood. How helpless he'd found himself while she shook in pain, wept in his embrace on her return from the accidental meeting with Gorsewell.

She'd bled as he had treated her hands, had cried when he dug out chunks of gravel buried in the fleshy parts of her palms. Each little whimper as he'd yanked at her damaged skin ripped at his heart. Franklyn had caused her suffering. "I want you to think back to how you felt when Gorsewell assaulted you."

"Yes. I was very frightened that day."

"You came back here, injured, so afraid, and I ached for your pain because I hadn't been there to help you when you needed me most."

She shook her head. "You weren't to blame for anything. You couldn't have known Franklyn would flip, or that I'd meet him on the hard shoulder in his new Porsche. It wasn't your fault he had the opportunity to shove me around."

"As you said yourself, he could have killed you." He held her gaze again, allowed a little of the savage fury he'd experienced to rise. "I wanted to kill him, Sian."

"You did?"

"Ah, if only you knew. The entire time I fed you brandy while we took the gravel from your hands, I raged inside. When at last you slept…" He swallowed deeply, and her eyes widened.

"No," she whispered.

Understanding crept into the surprised expression. She guessed, or had read his thought, and somehow that made the rest of the telling easier. He sighed, recalling the moment his fury set him free, and welcomed another level of her trust. She would understand.

"For the first time in my life, I changed at will. Like an adult might."

"Like an adult?"

"Yes. For"—he raised her hand and kissed her palm—"many, many years I've lived in the state of omega. I willingly gave up any notion of a pack such as my father would have had me create. I thought living, or should I say existing, alone was the most honorable alternative I had. I avoided the change I might make, except when the moon robbed me of control. With the knowledge of how Franklyn had harmed you, hurt you, I discovered my fury gave me a new kind of power. I reached maturity that night."

"You grew up?"

Offering her a small smile, he nodded. "You could put it in such a way. The experience stunned me once it was over."

"What happened?"

"While you slept, I tracked Franklyn. In the wolf-form, I found his home."

She clutched his hand. "You." She gave a small gulp. "You tried to…"

He closed his eyes in an effort to avoid seeing her disgust. This beautiful woman he adored, all he ever seemed to do was cause her anguish. How much could she bear before she did the one thing she could to save herself? Surely, after tonight or tonight itself, she'd abandon him, leave, and his existence would become meaningless. She took her hand from his and left him bereft. Her lightest fingertip caress on his upper lip made him flinch.

A gloss of tears shone in her eyes when he opened his.

"You tried to kill him."

"Yes, I did. Somehow you called me from him before I'd..." He had not been able to resist her command. He'd heard her soothing voice, and the wolf, bound to her, too, had returned. As dawn lightened the sky, exhausted by the run, but triumphant in his vengeance, he'd again changed at will.

His moment of elation was lost as he looked into her tear-filled eyes. "Forgive me?"

He slid from alongside her. Sank onto his knees on the floor, knelt in front of where she sat on the sofa. "I beg you, please, say you forgive me."

She clutched her face with her long slender fingers and shook her head. "I didn't know. I didn't guess it was you who hurt Franklyn like that." She sniffed, swiped at her eyes. "God..."

Reaching out, he took one of her hands and offered her a folded handkerchief from his pocket. "Here."

Tears rolled down her face. Each shimmering drop rang a death knell for their love. She shook out the handkerchief and used it slowly to wipe her eyes. All the time he ached to hold her, to plead with her to care for him still, monstrous as he was. Her complexion had paled. He hung his head. How could he torture her like this? She deserved so much joy and delight. All he could offer her was the wretched world of the wolf, and if he explained his fears, the bitterest truth of all might destroy her.

"Magnus," she whispered.

He looked up,

"Hold me? Please."

Joy quashed the fear in his gut. He moved to sit beside her, took her in his arms, and smoothed his hand over her hair, stroked her as he held her close. For now, for this moment, she'd allow him to love her. Soon, she might think again. "You have to know I am not sorry I bit Franklyn. I wish I'd finished the job."

Sian shook in his embrace.

"You know I have killed in the past." He stroked her hair again.

"Yes, but this."

"I wanted to protect you from him. I still do."

She gave a tiny nod against his shoulder. "I know. But it was a mistake. You said you thought it was a mistake."

"Look at me."

Emeralds from the bottom of a pool, the wavering brilliance of her eyes, searched and probed. He caressed her face and prayed she would understand.

"The error I made was to leave before he laid dead. By doing so, I have created something to haunt us both." The shudders running through her transferred to him as she clung tight.

She sniffed, swiped at her eyes again with the handkerchief. Tears tracked from the corners. "Tell me," she whispered.

"I hoped, because of all the blood transfusions and medication Franklyn had when in the hospital, this wouldn't happen. I watched and waited. Even when he came to you in the dream state, I tried to convince myself it wasn't true."

"Franklyn's got into my dreams several times since."

He groaned at the news. "You should have told me. There can be no doubt my fears are justified." He kissed her damp cheek, her lips, and her eyelids. "Gorsewell wants you."

She stiffened in his embrace. Her small chin firmed as she opened glittering eyes. The determined young woman, who had captured his heart with ease, shook her head. "Wanting isn't getting. He can go to hell."

"I heartily concur. Believe me, by the end of the month he might think he has."

"You bit him."

The thought process flitted across her face. He watched the realization hit her. There was no need to try to reach into her thoughts or to keep his from her. She understood and blanched paler still. He could scarce breathe.

"Magnus, he'll become like you. Oh, my God! Franklyn will be like you."

"Sian! Look at me." He held her tight in his embrace, cuddled her closer, yet still she shook. "You need to listen so you understand."

The wait for her response tested his faith.

After more minutes than he cared to think on, she whispered, "He'll kill me if I don't—"

"No, he won't. You have to listen very carefully to what I'm going to say, and please try to understand. We need to talk and think in the way of the wolf. It is a path I can no longer shun. My body is making changes of its own to compensate for my mistake and give me the chance to deal with what will come. Franklyn's condition makes it imperative I accept all the new wolf energy and take control of the situation."

Sian curled up in his lap, laying her head against his shoulder. "Tell me."

He wound his fingers through her hair, coiled a palm full of the twirled strands, and gave a gentle tug to urge her to look up. "You know a little about me, about this house and my ancestry."

She nodded. He pressed a kiss to her lips.

"You know the curse that afflicts me. You have seen the thing I become."

Again, she nodded, but this time she leaned forward to press her lips to his.

Eager for a taste of her, he allowed their kiss to bloom until he tasted her passion. Then he eased away. "This is the important part. You know my bite in the wolf form can alter a person?"

"Yes."

The low-voiced word and her tense expression gave him pause. "This has nothing to do with love, desire, or the need I feel for you. It is a biological reaction. The process has always been a way for my kind to repopulate a broken pack."

"Pack?"

Her scent provoked his need for another taste of her lips. "Yes. Lone wolves such as I, we are a rarity. Few can tolerate such isolation brought by the state of omega. The werewolf is meant to live in a pack, with a leading male and female, as wolves do."

"The alpha male and female," she whispered.

"Indeed. Along with the alpha couple, there should be other members of the pack. A hunting pack needs more than a couple." He smiled. "No matter how much they care for each other."

"There should be beta members?"

"Yes, and others, too."

"Magnus, are you saying Franklyn will be a part of your pack?"

Words swirled in his mind for a few minutes. A pack of his own, and established with such a creature as Gorsewell in it, was a nightmarish prospect. He would never trust Franklyn. Even if it took decades for him to gain the courage, Franklyn would try in every way to lure Sian to him in dreams or reality, coerce her, or frighten her. Magnus shook his head. "The only way I will accept Gorsewell is with his profound understanding I am the leader of this pack and that you are mine. By the time I transform again I will be ready to protect my—" The need to say mate almost overwhelmed him. Sian was, and would always be, the mate he desired.

"I want to be yours, Magnus. I want you to do whatever it takes to make me yours, eternally. Forever, I want to be yours."

She lay curled in his embrace, fragrant, beautiful, and so very, very willing. He loved her, and she offered herself to him with so little concern. If his moral scruples allowed, he'd have made her his days, weeks ago. Thankful he retained some vestige of the principles he had learned as a boy, he sighed. "Yes, I know."

Sian held his gaze, hers fixed, brilliant but sharp. "You will have to make up your mind at some point. I want it to be soon. Otherwise, I will be in danger all the time."

"Don't say that. Franklyn is just a troublesome bully. I'll put paid to his appalling behavior soon enough once the full moon brings him here."

"What about the dreams?"

"You should have said. Together we are strong enough to send him running." He caressed her hair, teased at the ripples on her shoulders. "Please permit me to help you if he appears again in your dreams."

"He keeps saying terrible things. I didn't want to tell you what he said he'd do."

The hiss in his blood returned. A tremor juddered through his hand holding hers. "From tonight, there will be no more of his interruptions. All you need to do is call me. I will come to you immediately in your dreams. You can hide in your tower if you wish, or you can watch me teach him some very important lessons."

"I don't want to see him at all."

"Then you shall sleep like Rapunzel in her beautiful tower. While I eat my way through anything the thorn bushes around your tower might hide."

Thank God. She laughed.

Sian stretched in his embrace. She reached up to set her arms around his neck and looked into his eyes. "You will have to make me your mate for real." There was determination in her gaze. "If you don't, then Franklyn will sneak around or worm his way into my dreams and continue to do what he does."

"Can we wait until the end of this month? When the moon makes of him what it will, I will have answers, and we can discuss our situation further. I'll know much more when he comes here, because come here he will. He must."

"To this house?"

"Yes, as a new wolf he must come to the home of his maker, to take up his place as the lowest pack member."

She shook her head so the ringlets spun. "Not here, Magnus. I couldn't bear it."

"Yes. Please, don't be afraid. When he comes, I'll make sure he leaves as a very different individual, one who understands and accepts his lowly place if he wishes to live. He will not return thereafter, not until I call him to do so."

"But he'll be free to kill outside the house?"

"We all have to eat, and he will need to eat, in quantity at first. I'll not deny him the opportunity. A starving wolf is one who becomes reckless and is dangerous to all."

She lifted her palms to cover her eyes. "Please no more, not now. I can't imagine Franklyn like that." A huge sigh followed.

"I'm so sorry to have burdened you with this. I am at fault. You shouldn't have to worry about these things." He caressed her cheek, waited until she moved her hands. "Forgive me," he said. "I'd no wish to spoil your triumph today, but you had to know."

She clutched his shirtfront. "There is something else. I didn't want to tell you, but I must. Franklyn wants to see me, officially, to do a handover from my control of the company since he's been ill. He sent me a text, and I must reply soon."

He nodded. "I'm not surprised by his method to try to lure you to meet with him. Franklyn is a manipulative creature. What do you want to do?"

"I don't want to see him. There is no way I ever want to be alone in a room with Franklyn again. I can give him all the information he needs in an e-mail. I couldn't stand to meet him in person. "

"Then send him a message to say that is exactly what you will do. Tell him I am taking you away to recover from the strain of running his damn company, and you won't be available to meet him. Like it or lump it, he'll have to accept what you say."

"Away, Magnus? Really?"

There was no reason why not, and every reason to take her to the mountains. He could remove her from the situation with Gorsewell and give her peace for a few days. Together they could prepare for what she wanted. At some point, she'd have to challenge the summit. "Yes, we could go this evening."

They'd have to return here come the full moon, in fact a few days before, but in the meantime, he could take her somewhere peaceful, protective, and treasured by his family for generations. A part of his past that carried the hope of his future. "There is a small cottage we could visit in Wales. The accountant's office has a property manager who usually rents it out for me over the summer months. I've not been there for a very long time. I'll call him. We'll go there. Would going away to a secret address help you to feel safe and out of Gorsewell's reach?"

"Please. The more distance we can put between Franklyn and us the better. I can fight him off in the dreams if I don't have to worry about him turning up here, or forcing me to meet with him."

His heart flipped, for her strength of mind shook him. The understanding Sian still allowed him into her life, when she might have fought him, added a further depth to his appreciation. "Then it shall be so. I'll make the call to the accountant's office now. I want you to relax and unwind for a while. When I've made all the arrangements, we'll pack. We can travel to the cottage tonight."

"Isn't it a bit short notice for the people who manage the property?"

He laughed. "No. If I want to go there, I assure you they will see the place is ready for me. We'll leave a note for Mrs. Tyson and Cook. I'll tell them to do a spring-cleaning while we're away."

"But, Magnus, it's November."

"Then an autumn clean. I only want to give them something to do so I can pay them."

The tenderness he yearned to see appeared in her eyes.

"You are amazing," she whispered.

He couldn't answer for he'd no way to find the right words. Later, he'd try to show her in some small measure how much she meant to him.

As he walked to the study, one thought blasted through his head. If Sian were to leave him, he'd not wish to live. If he took her to the mountains, she'd be safe from Gorsewell. In addition, she'd be in the right place to learn some of what she'd need to know as his mate.

I have to make her mine. If I wait too long there are so many dangers to her and to us. I can procrastinate no longer.

His newly discovered mature persona demanded an alpha female. He would defend her in both body and dreams. Sian would be his cofounder of a new pack. She was his perfect mate. He'd do everything he could to keep her, and Gorsewell would be damned to a living hell if he tried to touch her.

Chapter 17

Sian couldn't relax. Their discussion kept repeating in her head, fueling a muddle of fear and hope. Along with the rest raced the nagging threat of a Franklyn who might be so much worse than she'd ever known before. What might a werewolf in a low depressive mood be like? What could happen if he had one of his high "master of the universe" flips? No one was going to calm that down with a cinnamon dolce latte. What if he changed after he'd indulged in his little white powder habit? The thought of a creature as powerful as Magnus in wolf form, perhaps speeding, filled with all that crazy energy, shook her. She could scarce sit still on the long, leather sofa.

Prioritize. She'd learned a lot about doing that, and she'd start this minute.

She'd deal with Franklyn first, then she'd be free to think on the other things. The magnitude of her conversation with Magnus rolled in her gut. Though he'd not said the words, she sensed either the threat to her, or the circumstances, had pushed him to decide their future. Grabbing her phone, she opened the text from Franklyn. Slow and careful, she constructed a reply to build a wall against Franklyn's request to see her. No need to tell him where she would be or give him any clues.

She didn't like putting Evie in the spotlight, even if the blond receptionist made doe-eyes at Franklyn every time he walked in the office, but everything Franklyn needed sat in the files Evie had on her computer.

She wouldn't lie and wish him well. Not now. Not ever. Text sent she could deal with the rest. At present, knowing Franklyn had come here and what he'd done, her sense of security in the house had been rattled. She didn't want Magnus to nursemaid her all the time. It wouldn't be right if he did. She had to work out a way of dealing with Franklyn's vileness herself.

She'd make sure Franklyn couldn't intrude in their physical world. Though she'd not done so since the day she bought it, she turned the phone off. She'd send him the e-mail from her iPad one day this week. Darn it, she should feel the weight of Franklyn's threats gone, but she didn't. He clung to her like the stink from some of the sleazier nightclubs he'd taken her to when she was younger.

Eager for something to take her mind off those memories and any others involving Franklyn, she went up to their room to pack some clothes to take to the cottage. Warm things would probably be best. Perhaps, there would be the chance for her to pick up some walking boots while they were away.

She hauled her vacation bag from the armoire and took it back into the bedroom. They'd be away for several days so she'd pack a mix of things she could layer. By the time Magnus came into the bedroom, she'd several outfits in the bag.

"All will be ready when we arrive. Make sure you pack a waterproof jacket."

"I have, and a lot of warm things."

He smiled. "There is heating in the cottage, but yes, warm clothes will be good for when we go into the hills."

She embraced him. "I thought so. I'll need some walking boots. I don't have anything suitable for winter hill-walking."

Magnus brushed his lips across her cheek. "We'll call in at the local town. They have an excellent mountaineering shop with all the best equipment." He glanced to his wristwatch. "It will take us about four hours to drive to the cottage, longer if we stop for something to eat on the way. I'll get my things. I think we should leave by four if possible."

"I'll be ready. Oh, will I be able to get a Wi-Fi signal?"

He shook his head. "No."

"Oh, I suppose we could pick up a hotspot somewhere so I could send Franklyn his wretched handover e-mail."

"Yes, I expect we could, and perhaps will. There is nothing urgent he needs from you, is there?"

"Not really. The next major shoot isn't for several months. The rest of the stuff is small fry. His request for a handover is a poor excuse to try to get me to go see him. "

"Then, we'll not mention him again today."

She grinned. The sense of escape powered through her. "You're right. I'll not say another word about him. On the way, you can tell me all about this cottage."

He caressed her cheek. "Indeed I will, but we both have to finish packing first."

"Right. I'll race you!" She turned from him and began stuffing several pairs of thick socks into the corners of her bag.

Magnus went into room where the armoires and tallboys held their clothes. He had far more garments to choose from than she did. She didn't doubt for a minute she'd win the race to finish packing first. Her jaw fell when a few seconds later Magnus came back carrying a large army style holdall.

"You can't have packed already!"

He smiled. "In one sense you're right. I didn't pack. This bag was packed some time ago."

She caught the unhappiness in his stance, a flash of it in his eyes, too. "Who packed the bag? Why does the thought sadden you?"

"Until quite recently, I had a valet." He smiled again. "I can hide nothing from you. Nathaniel Broomfield was a gentleman of considerable wisdom and charm. I was saddened to lose him, but couldn't ask him to continue to work. He'd gone well beyond retirement age in my service. His grandson wrote to inform me Nathaniel died a few short months after he left here."

"I think I understand." She crossed the room to put her arms around him. "This is one of the things you hate most isn't it?"

He drew a deep breath. "Indeed. I have always found the loss of those who I like and enjoy a wicked part of my condition. After Nathaniel, I told myself there would be no more." He bowed his head until his forehead rested heavy on hers.

"I think we make a pact, Magnus. I'm not going to mention the manipulative ex-boss,"—she angled her head so she could look into his eyes—"and you aren't going to tell me anymore horrible things about who and what you are."

He raised his head. "Am I as bad as that?"

She nodded. "Sometimes."

"I didn't realize."

"I know. I think it's because you've never really spoken about it to anyone. Or not for a long time, at least. Now you can't stop."

"Whoo." He blew out a long breath. "Your wisdom astonishes me. I accept your pact. I'll not mention any negatives again, no matter the provocation."

She clutched him and squeezed. "We'll have some days where we can be us, just us."

He clasped her tight, tugging her closer against him, covering her lips with his. Closing her eyes, she lost herself in his kiss, pressed her body hard against him to relish the way he could overturn any thoughts but those of making love.

He pressed small warm kisses along her jaw until he reached her ear. "I promise, while we are in Wales, we will speak of us, the future, and love."

A thrill shook through her with the warmth of his whisper. She looked up, met the tenderness in his glance, and suddenly nothing else in the world mattered.

"The sooner we leave, the better."

She nodded. She ached for him and could think of nothing else. Until the physical need was satiated, everything else could wait.

* * * *

The utter blackness of the November night kept her eyes focused on the beam from the Range Rover's headlights. Magnus stroked her inner thigh, as the automatic gears didn't need his help. The tender caresses sensitized her skin. She wished she'd not worn leggings. If he didn't stop soon, she'd demand he pull over to soothe her potent desire for his touch. The car climbed the road into the mountains. Hopeful she didn't appear too anxious for more of him, she murmured, "Is there much farther to go?"

His smile caged her heart and sent a flash of palpitations through to her loins.

"A little longer, half an hour maybe, perhaps a little more," he said, as they rounded a sharp bend in the road. He glanced to her with a wry smile. "I'd prefer to use manual from here on in, so you'll have to wait for me."

No other person ever read her mood, mind, and thoughts the way he did. She would wait for him for however long it took. Nothing but Magnus mattered. She traced a finger over the links and gems following the Greek key design. Magnus and she were like the bracelet, intertwined, bound beyond separation. She raised her glance to him but kept the words inside. He might hear the thought anyway.

His profile, as he studied the dark road ahead, brought the images of castle towers and knights of old to mind. She smiled at the sheer folly of such romancing. Their relationship had its own dragons to deal with, or creatures like Franklyn, in man or wolf-form.

She shuffled in her seat, adjusted the belt, concentrated on the darkness outside the windows and the branches of trees lit briefly by the headlights as the car passed. There must be something, other than the rash of worries, to focus on during their journey.

"Oh," she whispered when Magnus slowed the car and pulled into a tree-lined driveway. "You said the place was a cottage."

He glanced across with a grin. "My father always referred to this as 'the cottage,' and the name stuck."

A round tower loomed ahead. The massive construction of stone and mortar had a crenellated top. Several small vertical windows were lit by the car's headlights. "But, Magnus, this is a castle."

"No, this is what is known as a castellated tower. The Welsh borders have many of them. The people who lived during the era when the tower was erected preferred the protection of good solid walls." He turned the ignition off, leaned across, and kissed her.

Sian cupped his jaw with her palms, unwilling to allow this kiss to be a short and simple affair. Her heart took up a quickened beat, her nipples throbbing as he stroked down her back. She ached for more of his caresses.

"Soon."

The thought echoed in her mind as Magnus lifted his mouth from hers. "It's cold out here. We'll be warmer indoors."

He got out of the Range Rover, walked to her side, and opened her door. She stepped out into his embrace.

"I hope you enjoy this place."

Something in his glance to the tower showed her the importance of being here. "You'll need to tell me the story behind the cottage."

"I will, but not now. We'll go in. I'll fetch the bags." He released her and opened the car to take out their luggage. "The key will be under the blue flowerpot. Could you get it?"

She walked across the dark flagstones, and in the dim light from a lamp above the door, lifted a small blue flowerpot filled with winter heather. A key, the like of which she'd never seen, sat there as he'd said. The enormous lump of iron she picked up weighed heavy in her palm. "Wow. This must be handmade."

Magnus nodded as he set the bags down in the porch and accepted the key from her. "Yes, I've never thought about it, but you're right. I think it probably dates back to sometime in the sixteenth century."

"That old?"

He smiled so the crinkles at the corners of his eyes deepened. "Yes, that old." He bent, angling his head, and kissed her. A hundred thoughts spun away from the age of the place when his lips teased hers.

"Was this place home to your parents?"

He shook his head. "Not home, a retreat if you will. They used it as a hunting lodge for some time."

"Hunting?"

"Yes." He turned the key in the lock and pushed the nail-studded slab of oak open. "Come in."

She held his dark gaze for what seemed like an age. The invitation to enter here held a special kind of magic, something she sensed deep inside her. "Happily."

Magnus flipped on a light switch. She entered a circular room and inhaled the scent of polish and flowers, both mingling with the mysterious fragrance of aged oak. Dark wood paneling covered the lower half of the walls. A wide stone hearth with a curved fire back contained logs arranged above kindling in the fire basket. Nearby stood a large brass, banded bucket contained more. Red drapes hung at the small windows and at two doorways set in arches, recessed in the wall.

"Roses." She stepped across the rug to an ebony table where she reached out to caress one of the velvety, blood-red blooms in a cut crystal vase.

He set their bags down with a smile. "Yes, there should be wine cooling, too, perhaps in the kitchen. I'll go and check." He crossed the room to go through a door.

As she unzipped her jacket, the distinctive pop of a champagne cork came from another room. The impression of a special occasion thrilled her, and a spark of excitement gave way to a wedge of anticipation. There was more to being here than just an escape from Franklyn, or taking a few days to relax. He hadn't told her everything, and she'd not felt his thoughts since she crossed the threshold.

Magnus returned carrying a tray, loaded with ice bucket, and two champagne glasses. He set the tray on the table, poured, and handed her a glass. A moment later he lifted his in salute. "To you."

She sipped a mouthful of the heady fizz. "Thank you."

"You have no need to thank me. I'll light the fire." He set his glass back on the tray and moved to the hearth. The scratch of matches was followed by small bright flames that crept up along the kindling to play on the first of the piled logs.

She breathed a sigh as the firelight warmed the room with its glow. The tangy scent of pine smoke reached her. "This is an incredible place."

Magnus turned to her from the hearth. "I had hoped you would find it so."

His eyes, for the briefest second, appeared as she'd seen them in his wolf-form, and a rush of emotion hit her full-on, so she swayed, reaching for the solid table. This place was linked to them becoming a permanent couple. "I want to be your mate."

He held her gaze. One of the logs crackled. "I know."

Chapter 18

Franklyn reread the text from Sian, and the brutality of it punched into his gut again. Despite the drink, he'd dreamed about the words last night until he roused sweating. He'd forced himself to calm down and go back to sleep. When he woke to bright light pouring through the drapes, he'd half hoped the message might be part of his nightmare, but no. The screen proclaimed it true.

Unable to meet in person. I will be away.
I'll send you an e-mail with all the details you'll need regarding the completed Timeless *film. Evie has all other necessary information for you. Richard will have a copy to you ASAP.*
I'll take it my contract with you is complete.
Sian.

He closed the text. She'd burned her bridges and left him with ashes. The sheer audacity of the girl! Being madam at Darnwell had gone to her head completely. Damn waiting another week to return to work—he'd go to the office today to find out what damage she'd done in the time he'd been ill.

How much did she expect him to take? Disbelief rolled through him that she could leave him in such a way after all he'd done for her. He'd never realized until now how selfish and thoughtless she could be. For years, he'd treasured her, cosseted her, but all the time he'd cared, she'd given nothing back. His illness had led to more than one discovery.

The desire for her would never vanish, but it didn't matter anymore. He'd lived with it so long, the need felt like a piece of jewelry he always wore, its weight a part of himself. Today, she'd broken the chains binding him to her. Still, he'd fuck her stupid given the chance, any chance at all, in the dreams or reality. But she wouldn't be the only one he'd want from today. Never again.

When Johansson dumped her, which no doubt he would as soon as he'd gotten bored, she'd come running back to the city. She would beg to return to Gorsewell Productions. But she'd have to wait her turn for his attention and be on her best behavior to get anything except the lowest filing job. Somehow, he'd force himself to stay away from her no matter how sorry she seemed.

A fresh wave of anger savaged him at the heartless text. She would never make a fool of him again. If she was too dumb to see what she could have had, instead of burying herself in the country with a thug, it wasn't his fault. She had the chance for the kind of relationship most women screamed for, and turned it down in favor of a reclusive freak with more personality problems than a psych ward.

Thumping the stick with each step, he paced back and forth in his hotel room as though in a cage. The need to move, a demand to be active, raced through him despite the limp. He wanted the taste of fresh air. Though each time he'd ventured out, he could hardly call the air fresh. The thick soup of scents tantalized him. Every breath brought all kinds of information he'd never known existed. Like a boy with his first taste of girl flesh, he wanted more. The impact of Sian's message galvanized his need.

He'd get a cab over to the office, call in and say hi to Evie. Yes, he would go now.

Grabbing his jacket, keys, wallet, and phone, he hurried out of his hotel room. He took the elevator down to the lobby where the concierge beckoned to a waiting taxi.

The cab driver eyed him through the rear view mirror as the taxi made its way through late lunchtime traffic to the office. Admittedly, most of the cabbie's clients wouldn't sit with the window all the way down, but he couldn't resist taking repeated gulps of the odor-laden air. He smiled at a dog in the backseat of a car in the opposite lane doing the same thing. People didn't know what they were missing.

The taxi slowed in front of the office block. He yanked a couple of notes from his wallet and thrust them to the driver. "Keep the change."

He made his way slowly up the steps, but not as slow as he would have been moving three days ago. Somehow, the healing process continued. He sucked in a deep breath of city-rich air, then walked into the lobby where he took the elevator to the twelfth floor. The doors swished open. The logo of Gorsewell Productions emblazoned in eighteen inch gold lettering welcomed him back. Nothing had changed, except for one empty office across the hall from his own. He wrenched his gaze from the small section of the door that showed through the greeting glass panel. Sian wasn't coming back.

The doors to the reception area opened at his approach. He glowered at the empty reception desk. Where the hell was Evie?

The clatter of a book hitting the floor made him turn. Evie stood in the doorway of one of the offices, open-mouthed. She flicked at the droopy mass of spiked fair hair on her forehead. "Mr. Gorsewell. Oh, my, we didn't expect to see you for months."

"You know I don't like the reception desk left empty. You've got an assistant to do the menial tasks."

She bent to retrieve the dropped sign-in book, looked up from where she crouched, and flashed her baby blues. She stood, paced across to the desk on teetering glossy pink heels, and took her place. "Yes, sir. I know. Jess is out of the office at a medical appointment, sir. Mr. Astle wanted to see the desk book for a few moments."

"Then he should have dragged his sorry ass out here and not called you into his office."

"Yes, Mr. Gorsewell. I do apologize. I'll make sure it doesn't happen again."

He studied her raspberry-red cashmere sweater where it clung skin-tight to her rounded breasts. Were those silicone or not? Whilst mulling on that, he counted four links in the chunky necklace she wore. When her neck grew flushed, he raised his gaze. Her face, filled with such abject sincerity above the offering of her tightly swathed breasts, held a certain charm. He gave her a small smile. "I understand, Evie. I've been away and things have gotten sloppy. I'll have you back to your best performance by the end of the day. You can count on it."

Her peachy-glossed lips curved in a half-smile as she nodded. She took a very deep breath.

He fixed his gaze on the rise of her peaked nipples beneath the fine weave mesh of her sweater. "Good. Is Richard in my office or his own?"

"His office, sir. He's taking a call from the client in Chicago."

"I'll go in now. I want you to have all the information on the *Timeless* stats, plus initial identified post production concerns, and all you have on the next project ready in one file and emailed to me in half an hour. Right?"

"Yes, sir."

That lower lip of hers appealed, was cute in the way it trembled after she spoke. "Good. I've missed you, cherub."

She batted the mass of her mascara-coated lashes. "We've all missed you, too, sir."

"I bet you have. Coffee in fifteen minutes in my office. I'll have finished my discussion with Mr. Astle by then." He limped across to Richard's office. Not too much damage seemed to have occurred in his absence. Evie could be licked back into shape quickly.

Very tasty.

"Franklyn!" Richard came around from behind his desk with a smile and offered his hand. "I didn't know you'd be back today. How are you?"

"Improved." He shook Richard's hand. "How are things here?" Rather than use the stick for support he leaned against the set of drawers by the door.

"Ticking along. You know the *Timeless* project is complete. I've not long gotten back here from the hotel outside Darnwell."

"Yes. What's happening with the next?"

"I've, this minute, finished speaking with Karl. Everything is going to plan other than the exact venue for the shoot. I've been waiting in the hope of talking to you to finalize the arrangements."

"I know." He frowned.

"There wasn't much we could do about it, sir. The Darnwell house is unavailable for any more photo shoots. I'm afraid Mr. Johansson is implacable. I've managed to find another country house, and I hope you'll agree it's suitable. It's an unusual property, but it has the water features you wanted plus some mature woodland for the animal shots."

He arched an eyebrow. "Somewhere new?"

Richard grinned. "Oh, yes. It's in commuting distance, too, so we won't have the expense of hotels for the crew. The owner is very amenable. I think you'll like the place."

"If I do, then I'll say well done and you'll get your bonus a few weeks early."

"Thanks, Franklyn. I've got some still shots of the house and grounds in my files. Shall I mail them through to you?"

"Yes. I'll take a look at them today."

"Are you staying the rest of the day with us?"

"I'll be here till four. I've decided I'm returning but I'll take things steady the first ten days. Ten till four the rest of this week. I'll get in a little earlier next."

Richard shook his head with a smile. "There's no stopping you."

"I think you might be right there."

"I'll e-mail the images through to you now."

Franklyn stood upright from leaning on the top of the set of drawers and moved to the door. "I want the details of the advertising you've set up since I've been gone and the responses we've had. The company needs more work."

"Sure. I can get it all together for you before the end of the day. We've a very hopeful enquiry for a big project next summer, one I know you'll enjoy. The date would be within two weeks of Karl's shoot, a sharp turn about, but we could manage it, I'm sure. It's good to see you back."

"Fine. Thanks, Richard." He ambled back out to where Evie sat peering into her computer screen. "Oh, cherub."

"Yes, sir."

"You're to make sure Ms. Armstrong is taken off the payroll as of the end of last week. When Jess turns up, get her to clear Ms. Armstrong's desk if there's anything in it. Ms. Armstrong won't be back."

Evie's lips parted on a soft intake of breath. "Sian isn't coming back?"

"No."

"I have to say, I'm relieved at the news, sir. Ms. Armstrong seemed to think she was my boss for a while. There is only one boss here I've ever wanted to work for." The tip of her pink tongue skimmed her lower lip. The little tremble appeared again.

Damn it all, Evie looks hot.

He inhaled her fragrance and relished the scent of her arousal rising to him. "It's good to know I inspire some loyalty around this place." He would have leaned down to caress one of those pink cheeks, but with the stick and his sense of balance still off, he couldn't. "You've made my return sweet, cherub."

Her smile grew, and she sucked in a breath so her breasts swelled beneath the smooth sweater. "Yes, Mr. Gorsewell. Is there anything else I can do for you?"

"Just coffee"—he glanced at his wristwatch then back to her—"in precisely eight minutes."

He didn't wait for her reply, but made his way into his office where he opened one of the closed blinds, sat, and turned on the computer. Being behind his desk settled his earlier tension. The discovery of Evie's ample attractions proved an added bonus. Odd, he'd never noticed her until today. All he needed to do was tell her to wear red lipstick instead of the peachy gloss, and she'd look ten times more attractive. She'd never match the beauty of Sian, but her generous assets offered some compensation.

This time there'd be no mistakes, no waiting on the whim of a teenage girl, no need to coax or wine and dine. Evie was all grown up, and from the adoring look in her blue eyes, she'd not be too coy to start or end her working day with a screw in the boss's office.

Things were improving by the minute.

Chapter 19

Magnus turned off the taps on the step-down bath. He refilled the two champagne flutes, lit three large scented candles, then stripped off his clothes as he waited for Sian to join him. He called through to the turret bedroom. "The bath is ready."

She came in from the bedroom, her eyes widening at the sunken tub. The candlelight flickered in the gilt-framed mirrors and cast soft shadows over the stuccowork decorations on the ceiling and cornice. "This is wonderful."

"As are you."

Sian swept her hair up and shoved in a couple of twig-like things to hold it in place.

Exquisite.

He could never have enough of her. Eager to touch all the porcelain beauty she offered, he reached out for her. Smooth, supple, and warm, her hip graced his palm. She looked up, angling her head to receive his kiss. An electric jolt flashed through him at the touch of her tongue on his, the pressure of her breasts against his chest, and the little whimper she made as he caressed her thigh. He lifted his mouth from hers. "My woman, you are perfect."

Her moist lips promised more delight as she smiled. "Are we going to bathe?"

"Oh, yes. I want to talk to you."

"Talk?"

The expression she wore would rob a saint of chastity. "Yes." He took her hand, undid the belt at her waist, and slipped the silky robe from her shoulders. "Allow me to help you in."

She stepped down into the foamy water and sat amidst the bubbles in the huge bath. "Well?"

He draped her robe on a chair before he handed over her glass "I will keep my vow. We shall talk of nothing but us."

Her eyes shone glossy bright. "You've decided, haven't you? I will be your mate."

The innocence and enthusiasm shook him again. Tonight, he couldn't deny his need. This woman, his woman, she was the only one he'd ever wanted in this way. He pushed aside the fear of her recriminations a hundred years hence, the concern should they create another poor wretch such as he, and greedy to see her smile, he nodded. "Yes."

"When?"

"While we are here."

"How?" Her voice wavered.

His gaze lingered on her tight nipples peeking through the foamy water. "There is only one way I can make you like me."

"Yes."

"I will bite you." He lifted his gaze to hers. "I will become the…" He couldn't say anymore and reached for her hand.

"You will become the wolf here? No cage? No chains?"

"Yes."

She'd grown pale.

"I have much more control than I've ever achieved before. I truly believe I won't do more than make you mine." The promise rang hollow in the tall-ceilinged room.

"You've always been so insistent I chain you, cage you when you change."

His stomach rolled with the edge of fear in her voice. "That is at the full moon when the creature is at its strongest, and my control until now was minimal. With my new alpha strength, I'm close to peak condition and I feel certain I could manage the beast. I shall force it to obey my wishes."

Sian took a sip from the glass and then set it down. Her gaze returned to him and held his, flickers of light from the candles reflected in her eyes. "I'm not afraid."

How he wished she didn't look it, but her courage had captured him in the beginning and it conquered him again. "We will stay here a few days. There is so much to tell you, a great deal to show you while we are in the mountains. We have lots of time."

"If we do this here, will I change straight away?"

"Not immediately, perhaps this forthcoming full moon or maybe the next. The changes may make you feel a little ill at first."

"I don't care, Magnus. I want to be with you, like you. I want us to be together as we should be, in the same way your parents were."

"And so you will. But if we are a bonded pair, we will make a better job of leading a pack than my parents ever did."

"I don't want to hear anything like that, you promised."

He nodded. "Indeed I did, forgive me."

Her delicious low laugh echoed around the room. "You are offering me life near eternal, youth, love...and you ask me to forgive *you*?"

A sudden desire to do it now, to give her all of what she wanted, blasted through him, but he shoved the temptation away. "Yes, I ask you with all my heart to forgive me."

She got up onto her knees in the sudsy water, moved onto all fours at the other end of the bath, her eyes shimmering. "Hold me?" She crept toward him, smoothing her palms over his legs and up his thighs as she moved closer. Her water-warmed skin glistened pink. He had to touch her.

"Come to me." He sought her moist skin, clasped his palms around her hips to pull her forward so her slick flesh slid against his. "I need you."

The rigid nipple he sucked enticed him to taste more of her. Sian settled one thigh over his offering him easy access to her pussy. Her little groan at his light touch led him on. He traced his thumb against her clit and rubbed with a steady circular motion before slipping a finger into her heat where he probed slowly before returning his attention to her clit.

The moans and whimpers she gifted to him made him work twice as hard to pleasure her. Alternating feather light caresses with deep pressure inside her, he pushed for her responses. He so wanted her to enjoy this, and the next, every time they made love here, for this was where the first aspects of their true bonded link would be formed.

"Magnus, please."

Her pleading moan moved him, and while he suckled deeply at one nipple, he worked her hard with his fingers, relishing the silkiness of her arousal. The spasms inside her came half a second after her pleasured cry. He waited until the muscular ripples subsided and her breathing eased. "Rest now, while I soap you."

She still trembled as he lathered soap over her for the sheer, sensual pleasure of it. Little whimpers greeted his softest caresses during his tender massage of her neat row of nether curls. He glanced up to her closed eyes and smiled as he used the back of his hand to send a wave of water over her mons.

She opened her mouth with a gasp.

Delightful, and he would taste her later when he'd gotten her out of the
water. Giving her nipple one last little nip, he moved up to her shoulder
and tilted her head so he could kiss her. When he released her lips, he
moved to her ear. "You are mine, Sian, all mine."

"Yes, oh, God, yes."

The heat in his erection throbbed again, but not yet. He'd not take her
now. She'd be so much more responsive if he stoked the need.

* * * *

Nestled beside Magnus in the big brass bed, Sian studied his face in the
dim light from the window. Starlight etched his strong features as he rested
with his eyes closed. Their love making had left her satiated, filled with
a blissful sense of weightlessness, as though both her body and mind had
joined the constraint-free realms of the long lost gods. She watched his
steady breathing for several minutes, mulling on her questions prompted
by their earlier conversation. "Are you awake, Magnus?"

His eyelids rose, and he rolled onto his side to face her with a lazy
half-smile. "Yes."

"Tell me more please. Tell me about this place?"

"The roots of part of my ancestry lie in these mountains. Though this
was never home to my parents, some of those in my mother's family were
born here. The heritage from my mother means this place has a power
and importance to me, but there is far more for the one who I choose as
my mate."

She walked her fingers over the wide expanse of his chest. "We both
agree that's me."

A low chuckle from him pleased her beyond measure.

"Yes, you." He tightened his embrace about her. "My wild and
wonderful woman, you are my perfect mate."

She nodded. "And?"

"We we will climb Caer Howld. At the top there is a cairn from which
you must take a stone."

"Take a stone? Not add one?"

"Yes, take a stone. The alpha female of my pack has the right to take
and wear a stone from the founding place of my mother's family. It will
give you the right to dominance over the pack. Without such a sign, you
would have to fight to maintain your place. I'll not have that happen if
we can avoid it. "

A sigh she couldn't stop escaped her. "I'm not sure about the pack
thing, Magnus. Not if it means Franklyn being around."

"I know." He angled his head and swept a kiss against her cheek. "But we will be strong together. You will discover your place with ease. You will be the source of power in our pack."

"No," she whispered, resting her head against his chest to listen to his heartbeat. "You will lead."

"I will, but not without you."

"Tell me more, Magnus, please?"

"We will be one. We will hunt together, and we will have wonderful—"

"Wonderful what?" She pushed up from his chest to sit. "I don't want mysteries between us. I want to know."

"Experiences."

"Don't stop, there is more, I know there is."

"I can't say for sure. I've never had a mate. I don't know everything." He drew her down beside him and smoothed his palm over her hair. "Rest now. Tomorrow we will go into the local town. We'll pick up some climbing gear so we are both properly equipped to walk the hills and climb Caer Howld together. You can find out more about the mountains."

She didn't want to know more about mountains. Right now, it seemed enough he had made the decision she'd longed for him to make. He'd brought her here to show her these things, and most important of all, to make her like him. She squashed the word *bite* as it came into her mind. Enough for now. Her body still thrummed with the pleasure of loving with him, and for the first night since Franklyn's brutal invasion of her dreams, she understood there was a way to keep him from her. "Thank you." She pressed a kiss to Magnus's jaw.

"For what?"

"Making me safe."

"Ah, I will give everything I have, all that I am, to see you safe and happy."

A lump formed in her throat. "I know."

"Then sleep, together we will dream and love."

She closed her eyes. The weightless state led her fast into the dream world where Magnus stood, his arms open, waiting for her to join him.

The sky held no clouds. She inhaled the fresh salt scent of the ocean. This beach, where she'd first dreamed with him, had powder fine, damp sand. She squeezed it through her toes as, arms linked around each other's waist, she and Magnus walked toward the rills of turquoise water washing up on the shore.

"Why here?"

"Because here we are both happy and free."

"*Yes, and we've already made some wonderful memories of this place.*"
Magnus caressed her outer thigh with his palm as she strolled beside
him. "*Indeed. Tonight we can make more.*"

"*No interruptions?*"

He smiled. "*None. This place is entirely our own.*"

Chapter 20

Sian puffed out short breaths as they neared the summit of the mountain. Her waterproof gear rasped like crisp leaves as she walked. Though she'd thought the turf-covered slope gentle at first, as they headed up, more boulders of jagged-edged granite broke the green surface. The temperature plummeted as they neared the misty barrier to the summit. There wasn't anything gentle about this mountain after the foothills. Soon, they would truly be climbing.

Once they made it through the barrier of low cloud, she discovered a new world, one to make her mouth dry at its brutal majesty. Ice-filled small depressions amidst the rocks, and the little lichens looked as though they clung in terror to the rock face. The terrain below seemed balmy, easy walking in comparison to this rock-strewn incline they now faced. The way to the peak was near perpendicular in places. Magnus opened his pack. He took out the balaclavas they'd purchased and handed hers over.

"Don't worry. You have been stupendous so far. Put this on, you'll need it now, it's cold up here. We might even hit some snow. When you're ready, we can take the pace as slow as you wish. It's less than it looks, under two hundred feet." He took a length of rope from his pack. It would join them together for the remainder of the climb.

She donned the head covering and tugged the front down to offer him as broad a smile as she could before she put her helmet back on. Once Magnus attached the rope to her harness with the metal karabiner, she gave it an experimental tug. He'd shown her how strong the link was after they bought the kit at the shop. The rope, slender as it seemed, would hold her bodyweight with ease.

Her face warmed under the fabric but her eyes stung with the chill. She shivered despite all the climbing gear. She turned her back to the wind while she waited for Magnus to finish with the rope. The last thing she wanted was for him to think she was afraid.

Daisy Banks

"Ready?"

She nodded.

Half a dozen steps on, Magnus glanced back over his shoulder, pausing to wait for her.

A skitter of pebbles rolled beneath one foot when she placed it on a ledge. She stilled.

"Take it steady, no rush," he called.

Their progress slowed as she deliberated the best spot for each of her steps. Soon she needed hand holds, too. Her focus centered on following his lead, on finding safe purchase for her hands and feet. Time seemed to stand still as their way forward grew more difficult. She called, "Magnus, I can't. Truly, I don't think I can do it."

"One long pace and you're there. Take a good hold of my hand. I'll pull you up."

She peered down into the froth of clouds below the rock face, blinking hard in the frigid air. Stones lay everywhere on this section above the pale mist. Steel gray and streaked with white, they offered no crumb of comfort. Lifting her chin, she looked up. His outstretched hand reached toward her from a swathe of icy blue sky. Taking a deep breath, she raised her gloved hand to his. "Okay, but I think you'd best pull me up. Please, don't let me go when I reach you."

Seconds later, she stood wrapped in his embrace, her toes skimming the floor, her heart thundering as she pressed her chest against his. She opened her eyes enough to peek. "Oh, my God!"

"You're safe, quite safe. Nothing can happen. You can't fall."

The warmth of his voice and gentle words helped calm her. She took another quick peek. "Oh, Magnus!"

"This is the summit we've climbed toward. Today, you are its queen."

She clutched him tight. "I can't do the next bit."

"You must. You have to do this part."

She lifted her gaze as his fingers dug deep into her thick waterproof jacket. The far off peaks reflected in his gray eyes to taunt her. Somehow, she found movement enough to grasp the rope joining them.

"One stone from the cairn is all you need. Small or large, it matters not, but without it you will have to fight for a place that is rightfully yours."

The words ground like minced gravel into the wind.

As she removed one glove, she fought off all thoughts but finishing this job. Despite the bitter chill, her fingertips would find a stone quicker without. "Let me go," she whispered, shoving the glove into a pocket. "I can do this."

The words belied the truth in so many ways. Her knees locked and her stomach rolled. Every limb stiffened as if she'd been carved from stone. A sour taste came to the back of her throat. If she opened her mouth now, she'd puke. Tears, dried fast by the wind, sprang again as Magnus removed the protection of his arms from around her torso.

"Quickly, Sian. Do it now!"

Her heart hammering, she lurched up from the ledge to grasp onto the last two foot of the mountain. She gripped hard, wrapping one arm around the wedge of stone, for she had to hang with her feet swinging above the small ledge where Magnus remained.

Nothing stood between her and eternity. She held tight with her one arm while she reached up with the other and scrabbled about with her ungloved hand. Despite the cold, she used her fingers to feel for a loose stone amid a tiny depression. The wind tugged at her, howling as though her presence desecrated this venerated place.

She sniffed in the tears she couldn't shed. The very second she thought she must be defeated by the mountain and her fears, a fat pebble lodged under her hand. Grasping it fast, she swallowed down her triumph. Even though she had the stone, the danger remained. If she fell, she might drag Magnus with her in a tumble down the cliff face. She still had to get to him safely. She drew in an unsteady breath. There could be no elation until she stood in his embrace again, with both feet planted on the rocks, safe from the wind whipping at her, sheltered from the bitter cold that numbed her fingers and robbed her of her senses. Most of all, she needed his warmth to soothe her. "I've got it."

A second of adrenaline-filled terror as she let go and she slipped into his waiting arms. She clung fast to him until she could breathe easy again. She slid the stone into the smallest pocket of her jacket. Her movements jerky, almost uncontrolled, she tugged her thermal glove back on.

Somehow, she held it together until they descended the worst of the rocky climb and reached the grassy shelf beneath the clouds several hundred feet below the summit. Only there, did she sink to her knees. Tears rolled fast. Ignoring his reassurances, she sobbed, shoving the balaclava away from her mouth to ease her breathing. Finally, she calmed and swiped at her eyes with the back of her hand. "I'm sorry, but I've never been that afraid in my life."

Magnus knelt to put his arms around her. "I know, and you have nothing to apologize for. You are victorious. I am so very proud of you." He caressed her cheek.

Sian buried her head against his chest, dabbing off tears spilled on his quilted anorak. "Can we go down the mountain now?"

"Yes. You have what you need to claim your place."

She glanced up as he helped her stand. "I want nothing but to be your mate, you know it."

Magnus gave a slow nod. "Indeed, but now you have been tested by the mountain. You will be the alpha female of our pack for all time."

"I wanted it so I can be with you," she whispered.

"I know. When we get back to the cottage, give me the crystal." He slipped his arm around her. "I'll take your stone to have it mounted in gold for you."

"Gold?"

"Yes. Welsh gold. The last amulet made was my mothers, many generations ago. Now a new one is needed. The goldsmith will be as proud to make it as I am to have the ordering of it."

She stuffed her hand into her pocket and drew out the round quartz pebble. Sparks of light bounced back to her from the veining in the smooth stone. "I'll never forget the day I found it."

"I know, neither will I." Magnus bent and covered her lips with his.

All other sensations diminished but for his arm around her, the taste of his mouth, the heat of his tongue twined with hers, and the growing understanding of what she'd achieved. Magnus drew her closer still, deep into his embrace, so the wind no longer buffeted against her. "I want to have all of you."

She gazed up into the depths of his eyes.

"Soon."

"I know. I'm ready. I'm not afraid, I swear it."

Huddled next to him, she let go the pinnacle of Caer Howld and relaxed into his warmth. She clutched the pebble tight and allowed his body heat to seep into her chest before she relaxed enough to take his palm with hers and set the pebble in the hollow of his hand. His gray gaze locked on hers. Despite the climbing gear, the mist, and the plethora of her fears, the promise of his love filled her.

They took the first steps of their descent on the grassy slope beneath the rocky challenge, arms entwined as they headed farther down the hillside.

Each step on turf and stone brought the process of her change so much nearer in her thoughts.

The slope of the hillside decreased until, at the last, they danced their way down. They raced until, with a few feet or so of the descent left, he caught her to him. Her toes skimming the shale, slithering over the grass, she zigzagged with him as if they tangoed down the hill.

She screamed a victory yell as they reached the spongy turf of the valley floor. "Wonderful!"

"Yes, you are."

The laugh on his face stilled her. For along with the pleasure, amusement, and relief, she found something else. The gleam of the hunter sparked in his glance. "Tonight, Magnus?"

"If I have half your courage, yes."

"And if you don't?"

He smiled, pressed a kiss to her lips. "Then, you will sleep soundly until I do."

* * * *

Back at the cottage, Magnus stowed their climbing gear away. Once she'd unlaced her boots and taken them off, she stripped off the jacket so she could hurry up the stairs to the bathroom. She turned on the taps to run a hot bath. Though they'd had the heater on in the car, she still shivered. The cold from the mountaintop seemed to have sunk into her bones. The November sun had tracked fast through the late afternoon as they drove back.

"I'll make some soup for you while you bathe," he called up the stairs.

"I won't be too long, but I need to warm up." She closed the door and stared at her reflection until she had to wipe away a mist of condensation. Though she'd told him she wasn't afraid, right now fear looked back from the mirror. Not merely the aftermath of the grueling climb they'd made, but fear of tonight.

More than anything she had ever wished for, she wanted him to do this. Her courage mustn't fail. She had to trust him, totally. If she didn't, then everything between them would be lessened to the mere span it took her to get old. She screwed her hands into tight fists. Her shoulders grew rigid. *I love him. I know he loves me.*

"Then why am I so afraid?" she whispered. "He mustn't see how scared I feel." She turned away from the mirror and peeled off the body warmer, followed by the Meco shirt she'd worn for their climb, tugged off the grubby trousers and thick socks.

In the hope to find calmness, she poured half a bottle of lavender-scented oil into the bath and swirled it around in the water. The fragrance wafted up in the steam. Once the bath filled, she stepped out of her underwear and down into the warm water. Wrapping her hair up in a towel to keep it from the oil, she sank beneath the water, rested her head on the back of the tub, and breathed deeply.

Ten minutes later, she decided lavender was overrated. Even though her muscles had eased physically, the tight coil inside her remained. The slightest slip of her concentration led her straight back to gut-churning fear.

The bath water had cooled. The last thing she wanted was to grow chilled. She eased up from the tub and stepped out onto the soft mat where she dried off with one of the warm towels from the heated rail. Certain her silky robe wouldn't be enough tonight, she donned Magnus's bathrobe instead. Each movement slow and deliberate, as though she forced her hands to work, she cleaned her face, then dabbed with a toner before she rubbed in moisturizer.

She took several deep breaths, gathered up her discarded clothes, and put them in the laundry hamper. She teased the wide toothed comb through the hank of curls she held and glanced again in the mirror.

The heat from the bath had given her some color. She shook her hair around her shoulders. Yes, she could just about pass for normal.

I'm ready for whatever comes.

She opened the bathroom door, fetched her slippers from the bedroom, and made her way down the stairs.

A steaming bowl of soup sat waiting for her on the dining table, a large glass of wine beside it along with a folded piece of paper. She picked up the note placed by her spoon.

Eat, drink the wine, and go to bed. I'll be back shortly. Don't lock the door.

Her stomach rolled. Any vestige of hunger vanished. Had he gone to take the crystal this evening? When he came back, would he be Magnus or the wolf?

My Magnus-wolf.

She sat, picked up the heavy-bottomed wineglass, and took a gulp. The wine hit her empty stomach with a kick. The smell of the soup, a hearty meat and vegetable broth, sparked her need for food. She ate a couple of spoonfuls, but after they stuck in her throat, she could manage no more. A pity to waste the meal, but she took the bowl back into the kitchen and tipped the contents away. The wine would do for now. She swallowed another gulp as she walked to the stairs. She'd take the glass of wine up to the bedroom and finish the last of it there.

The curving staircase drained her strength as she made her way to the top. Perhaps it was one climb too many today.

Her eyelids weighed heavy as she sat on the bed. After another sip from the wineglass, she set it on the nightstand. A deep lassitude overpowered her body. She curled up, hugging the pillow against her, gave in the struggle, and closed her eyes.

Drugged.

She forced her eyes to open. The room wavered.

He'd put something in the wine.

Chapter 21

The bedroom light remained on. Sian must be asleep by now. He'd waited in the garden for half an hour since the light first showed. She would most likely think him a coward for sedating her, but it was the only way he could think to ease her fears and the pain he'd inflict on her tonight.

Memories of pain played over his flesh as if each of his limbs felt the shock of injury for the first time. Tonight he would hurt her. It would be impossible not to. The fierce ache in his gut returned. How could he bite her and not cause pain?

I can't!

He paced half the length of the garden and back. Each step, he repeated the instructions for how he must proceed. The wound had to be deep enough to draw her blood. He swallowed hard against the desire to lick his lips as though he might taste her. What if he couldn't control the bite?

Fear multiplied a thousand fold. Since his first kills, he had always bitten deep.

"Don't play with it, boy. Kill it!" The words of his father returned. Tonight he needed to have complete domination of the wolf's eagerness to offer a swift and easy death. He must taste blood but also exercise restraint in the same bite.

Sian is my mate, my woman, and I love her beyond measure.

The first stars shone.

As soon as he changed, he'd find a rabbit and try to bite without killing it.

The moon, the bitter mistress of his change to wolf form, slid less than half full from behind a thin cloud. He turned his back on it. Slowly, his breath puffing white in the cold air, he dragged off his clothes. He'd leave them in the waterproof bag he'd brought with him and collect them tomorrow. The idea of tomorrow wisped like a haze. He couldn't imagine what the new dawn might bring if he did as Sian wished. One thing was certain. If he didn't find the courage to go through with it now, he never would, and time, his old enemy, had a certain victory.

Uncertain if it were a good thing he could find no rage to prompt this transformation. All his concentration dwelt on the hopes in his heart, willing them to be stronger than fury.

His recollection of his battle to stop the transformation in the shower the morning he'd discovered Franklyn's foul presence in the grounds of the house returned, tonight a useful tool. Breathing slow as if meditating, he tried to focus on the sensations he'd known then. The fading vision shifting between his own and the sharpness of wolf perception, he blinked as the tower's thick stone wall shimmered. A stirring in his blood quickened his pulse. The familiar start to his change gave him hope. Prickles burned his skin. Blistering hot, his body burned within.

Slow as an old man, he curled toward the ground. The quicksilver race began with his low groan.

* * * *

Magnus sucked in the rich sweetness of the air as the thin, brittle shell shattered. Joyful, he stood on all four feet and shook himself.

Free.

Free to run.

Run and hunt.

The elemental elation throbbed through him. He opened his jaws for a blissful howl. The woods of his earliest youth beckoned. They would offer him all their wealth and beauty tonight. He spun away from the house with its prying lights, and raced as fast as he could toward the line of trees casting shadows.

Skidding to a stop, he sniffed to study the vale, the beautiful curve of hills as they merged above one long valley.

Sian's breasts.

Her breasts were smoother than this. The valley between them was always sweet-scented, offered peace, the place where he would rest his muzzle should his goddess allow.

He gave a snarl, shook his head, and sucked in a breath. The scent-laden air promised him game tonight, a chase worth the making.

Hunt.

Yes, hunt but not to kill.

His muscles twitched. A low growl rumbled in his throat.

Not kill.

Not kill!

He paced on, treading over the silky chilled turf until he reached the coarser growth beneath the trees.

The ripe scent of hind met him. Somewhere close. He peered at the earth.

Prints. Deer.

Tasty deer.

Cautious now, he moved to the rim of a clearing. Another waft of odor met him.

There.

Pale throated as the goddess.

Soft, sweet flesh.

Crouching, his belly close to the loamy earth, he crawled forward.

Hunt.

Bite.

Not Kill!

The creature bent her head, then turned as she nibbled at a stand of taller grasses beneath the tree.

Close enough to see the long lashes of the hind's eyes, the pale strip of her neck, he inched onward. One more move. He'd be in position to leap and bite.

Not kill!

I will not kill her.

Open mouthed, he leaped at the deer. He gripped the hind's supple, pale throat.

Her hooves flailed as she tossed about with a wild squeal. Feet scrabbling in the leaf litter, kicking up tiny stones, she bucked. She pushed. He held. She shoved. The whites of her eyes shone brilliant in the night.

Blood. The iron rich delight made him salivate. Tongue rubbing at the source, he sucked in the first thin spurt from the wounds in her neck.

Stop!

Let go. Let her run.

He relaxed his jaw. Gasping, he set the hind free.

She thrust away from him. Another of her screeches tore into the night. The heart-shaped white flash of her rear sped away as she ran for her life.

Dribbling for her loss, he sank down to the ground, aching but somehow pleased. The hind lived.

Time passed. The stars shone like his pride. He'd bitten but not killed. Idling in the cool wood, he ran his tongue over his upper lip. A sticky smear offered a luscious taste, but he needed something more. He hauled himself up from the chill, damp ground at the edge of the turf and eyed the house. Understanding came; all he needed lay inside. Now certain where he must hunt tonight, he turned and headed out of the woods toward his quarry.

A light from a half-curtained window in the round tower beckoned him. This night, perfection awaited him. He'd no need to trail the woods. The light would lead him to quarry with skin more yielding than the hind's. She'd offer more than the lick of blood he'd yet tasted.

Sleeping.

She awaits me.

I will make her mine tonight.

The goddess would be his. Her blood would be the exquisite culmination of all his desires his long life.

He picked up his pace to a trot and basked in the shivery sensation racing through him. Closer now, he discovered her scent. She led him onward. A long expanse of grass lay at the front of the house. A play of shadow leaves from the tall bush by the partly open door showed him the trail across the green. Although the house made him prick up his ears and bunch his shoulders, he approached the building. This night he would go inside. He must.

The thick door stood ajar. A beam of light from within beckoned. He nudged the heavy wood with his head. A board creaked, the sound echoing like a gunshot. Instinct set his muscles ready to fight. One thing gave him pause. Reassurance, too. The scent of the goddess. Licking his lips, he sucked in her unique fragrance.

One more step took him inside the house. Lost to anything but her lure, he followed the trail up a wooden staircase. His claws clicked on the glossy boards. Another door to nudge open.

The well of lamplight spilled out from the half open door at the top of the stairs, casting shadows on the wall and floor. His heart pounded with the delight of her. Tonight she would be his.

All mine.

A fresh growl rumbled at the base of his throat.

Every muscle quivered as he entered the room. He peered at her curled form on the bed and inhaled the perfection wafting from her flawless warmed skin.

Bite.

The force of the thought sent him floundering backward on the slippery floor.

Dare he?

He ran his tongue over his upper lip. A hint of hind.

Though she lay motionless against the pillow, he approached slowly. He sniffed the goddess-laden air.

Taste.

He must savor her.

The bed juddered as he mounted it. She lay so close he could admire the detail of her creamy skin, the shadowy vale between her breasts, and as he breathed in again, he luxuriated in the perfect richness of her call for a mate.

Saliva flooded his mouth.

A tremble like a shockwave raced over him, raising the guard hair on his fur. He leaned forward. He lifted his lips, using the tip of his tongue to sample her aroma. The pale wealth of her throat beckoned him. Nuzzling his head against her, he dared to lick a tiny part of her arm, then a little more, which robbed him of anything but the wish to taste her glorious flesh.

The exquisite flavor beneath her curved arm proved too much. Lapping rapidly, he moved along the exposed skin. His excitement grew as he found the folds of fabric fell away at his tongue's urging. He licked up to the whiteness of her throat, tasted the edge of her sweet-scented lip, before he moved back down again.

She gave a little moan. He waited.

The goddess moved, exposing one white thigh, offering him a hope of all he desired. Watching her pale face closely, he edged down the bed. He mustn't bite her throat or her shoulder. If he did, he would break her, but he must bite.

Bite.

Her thigh sagged limp. He clasped the muscle with his jaw. A shudder of delight shook through to the end of his tail. He positioned his teeth, set ready, and bit down until the sweetness of her blood oozed into his mouth.

Not!

Kill.

"Magnus." Her scream rang loud, but with one paw on her chest, he prevented her twisting away. She whimpered, but he clung to her thigh, salivating at the luscious glory.

Recognition appeared in her wild gaze as she pushed back toward the top of the bed, then her eyes closed and she lay limp in his grip. His goddess knew him. She favored him with her trust. Easing his jaw from the thick muscle of her thigh, he lapped once at the flow of blood racing down to the pale bedding. He gave a low-contented growl as he curled beside her beautiful body.

Chapter 22

Magnus arose from the bed. The sheet revolted him, mired with the dusty remnants of the powdery shell of his transformation and the stain of Sian's blood. Careful not to wake her, he shoved the bedding aside, reached out, grimy as he was, to check Sian's pulse. Firm and steady, a regular beat throbbed under his fingers. *Thank God, she still sleeps.*

The seeping puncture wounds in her thigh sickened him, but the worst—his bite—was over, and she would heal. Desperate she shouldn't wake to blood on the bedding, he worked around her to remove the top sheet and comforter as carefully as he could. He fetched a clean hand towel to cover her bruised and bloodied thigh. Anxious she shouldn't become chilled, he tucked her silky robe around her. He took the soiled bedding, along with his robe that she'd worn last night, into the bathroom where he dumped it on the floor, unwilling to put the bloodstained mess in the laundry hamper. He'd shower, dress, and after he'd checked on Sian again, put the lot in a bin bag. Sian didn't need to see any of it.

He showered quickly, washed his hair, doing everything he could to remove any trace of last night's occurrence. Certain he was clean, he dressed in jeans and a warm sweatshirt. One glance at the bed when he entered the room, and her hollow-cheeked pallor worried him. But she'd not lost a lot of blood, nor could she be in shock, for she'd barely woke but for the one gut-wrenching scream at his bite. He smoothed his palm on her cheek. The movement of her eyelids told him she dreamed. He prayed the dreams were sweet.

The dose of tranquilizer he'd put in her wine should wear off soon. She would open her eyes to a tidy room. He hurried to take the filthy bedding away, and after he'd turned the heating up another notch, returned with coffee, a large glass of water, some painkillers, and the first aid kit.

Her expression, even in sleep, had changed. She was rousing to pain. He hung his head. When she opened her eyes, he found their light dimmed.

She gave a small cry as she moved in the bed. "Magnus."

He got up from the chair where he'd watched over her and moved to sit on the bed beside her. "Drink some water for me. I have some painkillers for you, too. Can you manage to take them?"

She gave a little nod. "It was real?"

"Yes, dearest. Forgive me."

"My leg, it hurts like hell."

"I know. Here, take these—they will help the pain." He waited for her to sit up, wincing at each small movement she made.

"Bloody hell, Magnus, why my leg? I don't think I'll be able to walk."

The reasons he'd not dwelt on last night, he now comprehended. Some of what he understood he'd not tell her for she might be sickened by the thought. "I didn't want to break you," he whispered. "If I'd bitten elsewhere, I could have hurt you too much, may have snapped your bones."

"Give me the tablets, please." She held out her hand, and he passed her two of the powerful painkillers.

"I want you to drink as much of this as you can." He handed her the glass.

"I need the bathroom," she whispered, before she swallowed the tablets with a gulp of water. She passed the glass back to him. "I'll try to get up. Don't look so worried."

He moved to allow her to rise. "Do you need me to carry you?"

"No." She moved the towel he'd placed over the wounds. "Shit!"

He caught her as she swayed. "Don't faint."

She clung tight, her face ashen and her eyes wide.

Carefully he lifted her in his embrace, carried her to the bathroom, and set her down on the lavatory. "Do you want me to stay?"

She shook her head.

"You won't fall?"

"No."

Uncertain if he believed her, he backed off and left the room. While he waited, he sorted out clean linen from the chest at the end of the bed. He had the fresh mattress cover, a bottom sheet, and both pillowcases on the bed before he heard the door open.

She stood in the doorway to the bathroom, pasty pale, a sheen of sweat on her brow. "I can't walk—it's agony."

He raced to her, caught her in his embrace, lifted her, and carried her back to the bed. "I've found something warmer for you to wear," he said as he set her down. "A fresh bathrobe. Here, I'll help you put it on, then you can have some coffee if you wish, and I'll take a look at your leg."

"It won't need stitches will it?"

His gut churned. "No, but I want to clean the wound with a swab and cover it." He held her gaze. "You will heal within two or three days. Believe me, this wound won't be like any other you've ever had."

She reached for his hand after he'd slid her arm into the robe. "I hope so. Tell me it worked, Magnus. Please."

He finished helping her into the robe. Only a smear of blood marked the silky affair she'd taken off. "I promise you, the bite will have the effect we want. Would you like some coffee?"

"Hold me first, just hold me."

She shook in his embrace, and this close to her, he discovered a new aroma to her skin. "Yes, the bite worked. I can smell the changes within you already."

He accepted the warmth of her lips against his, and as tenderly as he could, returned the fragile kiss. They would rediscover their passion together later, in a day or two, but right now, he'd offer her all the reassurance he could. "I'm so sorry I hurt you," he whispered as they parted from the kiss. "I swear I will never hurt you again."

"It was necessary—you know it."

He cupped her chin in his palms, looked deep into her eyes, and found no resentment, only the clouds of pain. "You have gifted me so much," he whispered, bending to kiss her again. "You have my heart eternally."

"We will be together in every way."

"Yes." He kissed her again. "Now we must heal you. Coffee, and I'll attend to the damage."

Her chin trembled as he released her, but she nodded before he turned to the coffee pot he'd brought up to the bedroom. He poured her a cupful and took it to the bed. "Drink this. I'll look at your leg while you do."

She took a sip and looked away as he brushed the robe back from her right thigh. One of the wounds had closed already, the other wept a smear of clear liquid. The bruising around the puncture marks was deepest purple from the pressure of his bite. The discoloration spread from the top of her inner thigh down to her knee and from the front of her leg around to the back. "Keep still," he said, reaching for the first aid kit.

Sian faced the window, her gaze fixed. He opened some medicated swabs, and keeping his touch as light as possible, cleaned over the damaged flesh.

Her coffee cup trembled in her hand as he taped a non-stick dressing in place. "There. I'll finish making the bed and you can rest." He closed the lid on the first aid kit. He put a clean top sheet on the bed, then a blanket and a smoke-gray, satin counterpane. "Have you finished your coffee?"

She handed over the cup, easing back against the fresh pillow. "Do I have to stay in bed?"

He smiled. "For an hour or two. It will give me chance to make lunch. I'll carry you downstairs when lunch is ready."

"Okay." She took his hand. "I love you."

"I know it. I can feel it within me. Your blood and mine are mingling. You will feel my love within you."

"All the time?"

"Yes. We will be one in a way you've not yet experienced, nor I either. You will know the depth of my love, all my desire, and with your love I will be the happiest I have been in my entire life."

A little color had come to her face. The healing, along with their growing bond, raised his hopes that soon she would be well. "You are hungry this morning. I'll make us lunch and come to fetch you shortly. Until I do, I want you to relax and rest."

She nodded with a whimper as she turned onto her side.

He took one last look at her, picked up the coffee tray and the first aid kit, and took them downstairs.

* * * *

A lightness raised his spirit in the kitchen. A wonderful sense of triumph, hers, and the overwhelming sweetness of it brought a lump to his throat, not from his fear nor guilt, but a rich wealth of emotion. He'd not realized the sheer power of being with a bonded mate. If she swept through him like this now, how more powerful would their bond be once they celebrated it in wolf form?

His movements automatic, he loaded the dishwasher before he checked in the freezer. Sian would need meat in a way she'd not done before the bite. The desire for it might hit her today or tomorrow, but either way, he'd make sure there was plenty to satiate her hunger. Venison would do nicely for lunch. He could manage a red wine sauce and a few roasted vegetables, not that they mattered since meat would be what she wanted.

While the escallops defrosted, he prepared the vegetables in a roasting tray and set it in the oven. The venison he would cook in the red wine in a pan on the top of the stove, ten minutes or less for the meat.

She needs water.

He shook his head at the instant knowledge. Would their bond allow him to feel her this deeply always? He filled a jug and carried it upstairs to her. "I've brought you something to drink."

"How did you know? Thank you." She accepted the glass he poured and drank deeply. "I think it must be a reaction to the—"

"Tranquilizer."

"You know."

"Yes, I can feel it. I can feel your pain, too. Do you want more painkillers?"

She sipped the water. "Not yet. It's too soon. I'll be okay."

"Try to get some rest." He smiled. "Call me if you need me to carry you to the bathroom again." He headed back downstairs where he checked the oven. Everything looked fine so he went out to fetch the bag of clothes he'd left in the garden last night.

How different his mood was today than it had been in the moonlight. His fear gone, he could rejoice in the decision he—they—had made. He should have trusted her courage to accept him, and to take the step to join with him. They had so much they could share this week and for all time after.

He'd see her amulet made and present it to her before they left Wales. She could wear it instead of the key to the chains in the small room, where he had to be caged. He would teach her to hunt with him. Together they would be formidable. They had much to discuss about hunting. He picked up the damp bag of clothes and took them back in the house.

The smell of rosemary met him as he entered the kitchen. He'd time for a cup of coffee before he needed to do anything else to prepare their meal. His sense of peace grew deeper as Sian slept, and he could hardly wait until she woke again.

After his coffee, he set the dining table and put one of the fat cushions from the sofa on Sian's chair. As badly bruised as she was, she'd need the extra comfort.

A place at the back of his neck prickled.

"Magnus." The call came from above. She shouldn't be walking already. He hurried over to the stairs.

She stood at the top with a smile.

"What are you doing there? Shall I come get you?"

The smile spread, capturing his heart in a net woven of love.

"I'm ready to come down now."

"Your lightest whim is my duty." He trod the stairs fast, and at the top, took her in his arms, lifting her into his embrace. To carry her like this could become addictive. "You are all I live for."

Sian settled her arms around his neck, leaning her head onto his shoulder. "Good, but is lunch ready? I am ravenous."

He clasped her tight. "Ten minutes is all I need and everything will be perfect for you."

She gave a little yawn, stretched, too. "Fine. I can last another ten minutes. "But, Magnus, not much longer. I'm famished."

The hairs rose on his arms and at the back of his neck. He must feed her as quickly as possible or she might tumble so deep into the realms of the wolf, he might never get her back.

Chapter 23

Franklyn left his office door open, tossed his briefcase to the side of his desk, and yanked off his jacket. He gave his swollen cock a push as it strained against his trousers. All the way here, he'd envisaged screwing Evie until she drained him. She'd be here in five minutes. He moved a couple of folders off the desk before he strolled across to press the button on the coffee machine.

The door to the reception area swished open.

"Evie, cherub, in here," he called, stripping off his tie. "I like the way you're always ten minutes early. Dependable. Shut the door."

She came in, closed his office door, and turned. "Do you need me for something, sir?" Her smile spread as she looked up from under her lashes.

He fixed his gaze on her rounded breasts. Her nipples stood proud beneath her baby pink cashmere sweater. He smiled as he crossed the room to her and bent his head to whisper in her ear. Her heavy perfume wouldn't put him off. "I need to fuck you, Evie. I need it badly, and I am going to do it now."

Her glossy lower lip shone as she licked at it with her tongue. She blinked her thick jet-black lashes, and sucked in a breath when he slid his arm around her waist. Her heels grazed the carpet as he edged her toward the desk. She gave a little moan when they got there.

"Are you ready for me, sweet cheeks?"

"Yes, please, sir. Now."

He planted a palm in the middle of her back and pushed. Obediently, she bent forward, settling herself over the edge of the desk, offering the mounds of her ass that were outlined by the clinging fabric of her skirt.

His excitement shot up another notch as she gave an encouraging little jiggle. He shoved the material up so it rolled in a tube around her hips. The little underskirt with its pink ribbons went the same way, too, and he palmed his hands over her thighs, moving his fingers up to touch the appetizing pale skin above her stockings. A vicious throb pulsed in his cock. He rubbed her damp crotch and gave her clit a massage.

She liked it, making encouraging whimpers as she wriggled against his hand and squirmed like a snake.

Her silky underwear tore as he yanked at the sides to get it off fast. She gave an affected little squeal. She could forget that; he'd never liked screamers. He balled the scrap of satin in his palm and pulled at a thick hank of her hair until she lifted her head with a squeak. He shoved the cloth in her mouth. Her muffled oomph had his cock weeping for joy when she didn't spit the fabric out. He undid his trousers and snapped on a condom before he settled his cock at the entrance to her syrupy pussy.

"I promise you're going to love this, cherub."

He shoved forward hard inside her, using his hands to push the clingy sweater and her bra out of the way so he could grab handfuls of tit.

Her muted cries and heavy breaths, the way she answered each shove, added to the fun of thrusting in and out of her. He leaned down closer over the desk and buried himself in her. He clasped his fingers around the jiggling mounds of Evie's breasts. She bleated through the panties in her mouth. The noise grew at his increased pace as he humped her harder. Evie was easy to please. She came like a train.

The peak hit him fast. She thrust back at him. The muscles of her pussy contracted, clutching at his cock, tightening his balls. The pressure intensified until, with a yell, he spurted inside her.

He grunted, sawing in and out, prolonging the last seconds of pleasure. For three minutes, he found bliss, and then it was gone.

He pulled out.

Evie lay splayed over his desk breathing hard. He found detachment as he assessed all he could see of her body. The pale hummocks of her ass cheeks bore red patches, two round ruddy spots he'd made with the forceful slamming into her. Didn't matter.

He frowned at her pale ass. She'd a little unpleasant hair, too much for his liking. She could get rid of it today and book herself some time on a sun bed so she didn't look quite this slug-like. She wasn't a true blonde and definitely not a natural auburn.

The best cure for her was a Brazilian. "Don't move," he said, hauling his trousers up. He fastened the waist button and yanked up the zip before he planted his palm in the middle of her back. "I like to admire my work." She stayed splayed on the desk. He leaned heavy on the middle of her back as he bent to study her gaping pussy while she twitched like she loved it. "You can take a couple of hours out of the office this morning."

He dragged his wallet from his back pocket and set it on the desk beside her.

She tried to rise. He landed an open palm slap on her ass so she mewled like a cat against the ball of satin in her mouth. "Stay put and listen. You go to Darcy's on Blackthorn Street and get a Brazilian. You've time before lunch." He ran his fingers between her ass cheeks. "I want all this soft and slick the next time I stroke it. I want it sweet. If you get it right, I just might be happy."

Evie gave a shriek through the cloth in her mouth when he dipped his forefinger into her asshole. Her surprised squeal promised him all kinds of fun. He lifted his hand from her back and gave her another swat on the ass. "Up you get and off you trot, sweetie. You've no need for panties." He held out his hand.

Grabbing his palm, she pulled herself up from the desk.

"Spit," he said, offering her the bin as she took the balled up silk out of her mouth. "I'll have something much better to keep you quiet next time." He ignored her wide eyes, took a fifty-pound note from his wallet, and shoved it in her hand "When you come back from Darcy's you can come in here to show me exactly what it is I've paid for. If I like what I see, I'll give you a real good workout."

"Again, today?" she murmured. A light shone in her eyes when she smiled. She tugged to adjust her skirt. "You're wonderful, Franklyn."

"Yes, cherub. Off you go."

She sucked in a deep breath as she pulled her bra into place. Her chin quivered.

Right at that moment, he could have fucked her again. But his head clearing fast, he dismissed the notion. She didn't deserve more of him yet. "Go tell Jess she can cover for you while you pop out for something important."

"Yes, Fr—sir."

He held her gaze as she covered the satin bra with her sweater. "Don't you ever forget who's the boss here. Send Jess in here before you leave. I want a word with her."

"Yes, sir." She walked away across the office. He smiled to see her go because she stepped with a slight wobble to her paces, the walk of a woman with a well-fucked pussy, creamy in fact.

"Cherub?"

She turned to meet his gaze, her lower lip, not as glossy now, trembled still. "Yes."

He smiled and a sense of all being well with the world swept through him. "You send Jess in here, and do tell her I've discovered she's been a very naughty girl."

The baby blues flashed wide. "No!"

"Do as I've said."

"You can't want her, too."

He smiled. "Why not, cherub?"

"You— We—"

He gave a low laugh. "You mean I just fucked you? Yes, I did, and cherub, if you are a very lucky receptionist I will fuck you when you get back from Darcy's. Jess has nothing to do with you. Now, send her in here!"

Evie scuttled out the door.

The mood he'd woken in today had mellowed a little at Evie's compliance. She'd been salivating, certainly dribbling as he called her in here and whispered in her ear exactly what he wanted to give her. She should have said months ago what she needed. He'd have been happy to oblige. Jess, on the other hand, would be clearing her locker by midday.

The traitorous little bitch.

He settled behind his desk, flipped up the consul, and opened the damming e-mails he'd discovered last night. She'd ruined his whole evening, until he dwelt on how she would look when he told her she was fired.

"Evie said you wanted to see me, Franklyn."

"Pour me a coffee and then I want an explanation."

Jess moved to the coffee machine and poured. She'd paled a little, and his pleasure grew. She knew what she'd done.

He deliberately waited for another minute to tick by as she set the cup in front of him. She didn't meet his glance.

"I've discovered some e-mails you need to tell me about," he said after taking a mouthful of coffee.

"I don't know what you mean. What e-mails?"

He swiveled the screen around, and when she bent, he grasped her shoulder and yanked her forward.

"Hey!"

"Look!" He tugged her until her face almost touched the screen. "Four e-mails to your 'best friend in all the world.' Each one of them is full of information on our upcoming schedule!"

"So what?" Jess pulled back and pushed at his hand that gripped her shoulder. "Don't touch me!"

"Espionage is grounds for dismissal."

"What the hell do you mean espionage? All I did was send a couple of mails wishing Sian well as she wasn't coming back."

He dug his fingers deeper into her plump shoulder muscle. "You gave her everything the company is booked to do until the end of next year. I read the lot because you forgot to take off the copy to me, you silly bitch." He gave her a shove. She screamed as she tumbled backward. A sickening scrunch sounded when she whacked her head on the arm of the chair on the other side of the desk.

She didn't get up.

Red stained the carpet, pooled in strands of her burgundy and pink streaked hair.

He picked up the phone and called the emergency services to report the accident. "No, not the police, we need an ambulance only. The incident is an office accident. My colleague tripped and hit her head on the chair. She is now unconscious and bleeding on the carpet."

While he gave the address, he couldn't tear his gaze from the blood. Glossy at first, then dulling as it thickened on the charcoal colored carpet, the viscous liquid fascinated and lured him. He set the phone down, walked around the other side of the desk, bent, and wiped his finger into the pool. Cool, it coated his finger, and the metallic tang set his mouth watering. His brain screamed the importance of her blood.

He lifted his dripping finger to his lips and touched the tip of his tongue to the luscious deep red.

A powerful surge of need burned up from low in his belly.

Shaking with desire, he licked his finger.

An explosion of sensations tore through him.

Bliss.

Better than fucking. Better than Sian. Better than anything he'd ever tried in his life.

He dipped again and licked.

Ecstasy.

He wanted more and bent closer until he could lap at the edge of the rich puddle.

"Franklyn?"

At the sound of Richard's voice, he darted a glance to the closed door. Shaking with the lust for more of the delight, he took another sweep with his tongue. Despite the incredible lure of the taste, he dragged himself up off his knees and swiped at his lips with a handkerchief he pulled from his top pocket. "Richard, get in here. Something terrible has happened!"

The door swung open. "Oh, God. Have you called an ambulance?"

"Yes, get the first aid kit. We need to stop the bleeding."

"Sure." Richard turned to the filing cabinet and pulled out the first aid box from the top drawer. He bent beside Jess, tugged the green box open, and ripped open the biggest of the padded packs. "Here, try this. I'm not sure about pressure though, not on a head wound like that."

Trembles ran through Franklyn as he held the pad to the wound. "She fell backward. I couldn't stop her falling."

"It's okay. The ambulance will be here in a few minutes. It's not your fault. She's going to be all right. God, boss, you look white as a ghost."

"Sorry. It's the blood."

"Don't you faint. Here, I'll do it." Richard reached for the cotton pad. "You go out to reception. Evie's not there. We'll need someone to meet the ambulance crew."

He allowed Richard to take over and got up from his knees, breathing deeply at the exotic, tempting smell. "I'll go wait in reception." He ripped his gaze from Jess's bloodied hair. Of all the weirdness of the last few weeks, nothing had been this crazy. A fragment of disgust flashed through him at the matted length of bloodstained hair, but the sheer, sensual pleasure from the taste squashed any regret.

A need had sparked, and he'd find a way, any way he could, to satisfy it again.

Chapter 24

Sian sat at the table, facing the empty white porcelain plate. She toyed with her fork. Impatience coursed through her in an unfamiliar way. She couldn't ever recall being this hungry. Her stomach growled but a deeper need gnawed inside her. Magnus had said lunch would be no more than ten minutes. She couldn't bring herself to shout "hurry up," but she wished he would.

The discomfort from her thigh had lessened as the morning had progressed, and her recollections of last night grew ever stranger. The one thing she remembered clearly was his eyes, the wolf's compelling eyes. She inhaled deeply, and found the rich aroma of cooking meat. Saliva flooded her mouth. A trickle of dribble ran from the corner of her lips. She swiped at her chin with the back of her hand in case Magnus should see. The scent of the food overwhelmed her senses. Did he live with extreme responses like this all the time? She'd have to ask.

"Lunch." Magnus carried in a tray with covered dishes that he set down on the table. He lifted off the covers so steam and an exquisite fragrance wafted up. "Venison, a little red wine sauce, and some vegetables. Shall I serve?"

"Please." Trembles raced through her body, all of her snapping with tension. She watched each movement he made transferring the meat to her plate. Red, wine-red, blood-red, the venison filled her consciousness. Before Magnus had placed any vegetables on the plate, she lifted her knife and fork, cut a slice from the meat, and put it in her mouth.

"A little more?"

She nodded as she chewed. The savage delight of meat, of the hot juices running on her tongue, took her to a new level of bliss. Food had never tasted this good. Magnus added another escalope of venison to her plate and a few, very few, vegetables, then a little of the sauce.

"There is as much meat as you need. I want to make sure you don't stint yourself. The impact could be difficult if you do."

Mouth full with another chunk of venison, she nodded. Stint herself? He must be joking. If he knew this feeling, he'd not worry. She'd gorge on the meat until she couldn't eat another sliver.

Magnus took his place opposite and poured her a tall glass of water, before he served himself.

She gnawed at another hunk of the mouth-watering meat, swallowed, and raised her glance to him. The intensity of her need was scary.

"I know. The desire will pass. Soon you will find it becomes manageable. This compulsion is part of the process your body is undergoing. You will experience changes in all manner of ways. Do you want to ask me anything?"

Chewing and swallowing, she shook her head. "Not now, once I've eaten."

He smiled, and reaching out with his napkin, wiped her chin with the linen square. "Very well."

She simply must eat the rest of the venison before she could think of anything else. Her concentration fixed, she cut through the rare, bloodied flesh. Her stomach growled as she put another piece in her mouth. Often when they dined, she and Magnus chatted, but not today. She could do nothing but focus on the meat.

The moment of sufficiency came when she'd eaten the last piece of venison on her plate. Her breathing rate dropped back to some kind of normal, and she looked to Magnus. "Thank you. That was delicious. The most wonderful meal I've ever eaten."

"There will be more. Tell me, how do you feel?"

"Full."

He laughed. "Other than that, how is your leg?"

"Doesn't hurt as much." She struggled to find the words she wanted. "I feel alive, like I'm tingling with sensations. Smells especially are incredibly potent."

He nodded. "You are developing rapidly. Tell me of any need you have and I will fulfill it."

She lifted her glass and sipped. "I'd like to go outside, a walk or something. I feel like I need to be in the fresh air. I'd like to go to the woods."

"I understand." He set down his cutlery. "Shall I carry you upstairs and help you dress?"

"No, I think I can manage."

"Very well. You go and dress. I'll clear things away. I'll be ready to go when you come down."

She inched up from her seat, took a step, and when the wound didn't protest, took another. "Magnus," she said as he began to clear the plates, "you mustn't spoil me."

"Wrong. I can and shall spoil you to my heart's content. Go dress. I'd suggest not jeans or trousers. You don't want to chafe your thigh."

She climbed the stairs, washed, and sorted through a drawer to find underwear and a pair of long over-the-knee socks. She donned them along with a natural-toned suede skirt with a T-shirt and sweater. After she'd bundled her hair up with a large clip, she put on a little makeup, wrinkling her nose at the smell.

Would she ever get used to this level of physical awareness?

Since her overactive senses responded to the touch of the clothes, the smell of her lipstick, she decided against her normal perfume spray. It could prove too much to handle. Ready, but for her boots that were downstairs, she made her way back down. Magnus came through from the kitchen as she stepped on the final tread of the stairs.

"I'll get your jacket and boots." He fetched them for her, and after she sat, helped her on with both.

"Magnus, you can't keep this up. I can do things myself."

"Yes, but for today, I insist you allow me look after you."

She gave a little sigh. All his attention set her heart aflame. "This is crazy," she whispered.

"Yes, I know. I can feel it, too. I want you to think about something for the rest of the day."

"What?"

"The design for your amulet. The setting will be gold. Your stone will be the center piece, but in what kind of design?"

"Traditional, Magnus. I want something like your mother or her mother might have worn."

"Are you sure?"

She nodded and stood. "Yes, positive. Shall we go? I want to be outside."

"Very well. I'll take the stone to the goldsmith tomorrow. Come, just a short walk. I don't want to over tire you today. You have a lot going on inside."

"Yes, but I need some fresh air."

He took her hand and they left the tower. They strolled out, down the path to the end of the garden and across to the squashy turf to the woods.

The cutting chill of the breeze held the warning of frost, maybe snow. "Magnus, I can smell the countryside. All of it." She squeezed his hand tight.

"Try to pick one scent and concentrate on it. You'll find it easier if you do it that way."

She struggled to isolate one aroma in the complex amalgam, but finally chose one of the strongest in the interweaving blend. "I smell fox."

He took a deep breath and nodded. "Yes, perhaps you might find it if you follow the scent."

"Like hunting?"

"Mmm."

She angled her head, inhaling again. "This way."

The pungent lure ran like a thin skein of silk through the air. His hand in hers, she led him down the slope to the edge of the woods. "Definitely inside the trees," she said after a moment's pause. "Shall we go in?"

"Yes, as long as your leg feels up to it. Remember we have to return to the house and we've walked a distance already."

"Just a little more."

The trees offered protection from the wind's chilly bite, and the lure she followed grew stronger. Her steps, despite the heavy boots, were light. Magnus's smile offered approval and so much love. She paused in a little clearing with a low depression filled with leaf litter. "It's here somewhere."

"Look and feel, see if you can search it out."

The mix of aromas here threatened to swamp her, but she discovered the source and pointed to the hollow at the base of a large tree. "Inside. It's female."

"Well done."

"You knew?"

"Yes, but I wanted you to find it. You have. It's a vixen. I think you will prove to be a wonderful hunting partner."

"Hunting?"

"Yes, we will hunt together."

"Hmm. That means killing something, doesn't it?"

He squeezed her hand and moved to embrace her. "Yes. The concerns you have will not prevent you from following the nature of the wolf, but like me, you will hunt with purpose. I promise you, we will never kill indiscriminately."

A sudden tiredness robbed her of strength. Everything seemed so complex, and all in ways she'd not imagined. "I think it's time to go back," she whispered. "I'm exhausted."

Magnus kissed her, his lips offering not much more than a soft caress. "I'm not surprised. You have done very well today. You need to rest. I'll make dinner this evening, but I think you should sleep for a while." He linked her arm through his. "Can you manage the walk back to the house?"

"Yes."

Arm in arm, they strolled the route they'd come until they reached the rise up to the house. Her leg ached, the discomfort growing with each step. She gave a little wincing cry at the next step up the slope, followed by another cry of surprise as Magnus swept her up into his arms.

"I know you are in pain. Let me help you. "

The lassitude those words always induced silenced her. She rested in his arms. Her appreciation of his strength grew as he carried her up the slope to the rise and along to the round tower house. Inside, he set her on the square-backed sofa, slowly took off her coat and boots, and as she settled down, curling up with one arm around a fat squishy cushion, he covered her with a warm woolen wrap.

"I'll light a fire and you sleep."

She yawned as she closed her eyes. The pain in her thigh throbbed.

* * * *

The following day after she'd eaten a huge breakfast of bacon and eggs, Magnus left her to rest again, while he took the quartz crystal to the goldsmith. They should have the amulet back within two days, or so he'd said, and as long as she remained well, they would return to Darnwell then.

Well. She had never felt this healthy in her life. Energy soared through her in great gusts, followed by sudden spells of fatigue. Magnus said they would lessen and she would become more balanced. She hoped so. One thing concerned her, and she wasn't certain what to do about it. Since the night he'd been the wolf, they'd not made love. True, her wound hadn't completely healed. The bruising remained, though not as dark as yesterday morning. Perhaps they should take things steady for a few days yet.

She lay on the sofa and watched the flames in the hearth. The smell of wood smoke held a comforting quality. She'd sleep until Magnus returned, and then they'd have meat for lunch. Closing her eyes, she smiled.

Chapter 25

"Thank you, Cradoc." He accepted the box from the goldsmith who gave him a small bow.

"The honor is mine to make a piece to grace the throat of your lady."

Magnus nodded and opened the box. He inhaled, struck by the beauty of the setting. The design of the amulet, reminiscent of the one his mother wore, also had new elements, tendrils of gold wrapped like a shimmering caress around the stone. "Sian will be happy with this, I'm certain."

"Will you be needing more next year, sir?"

He shook his head. "There is no thought of young, not yet, not for some time."

"Very well, inform me or my son when there is, sir. We will make sure another nugget is available for use to make suitable items."

"Ever thoughtful as have been all you kin, Cradoc. I will contact you should Sian and I need to welcome infants." He closed the lid on the box and put it in his top pocket. He left the tiny workshop at the base of mountain where a waterfall spluttered down in graduated drops.

On the drive back to the cottage, he dwelt on the jewel Cradoc had made for the most beautiful mate any male had ever had. Sian had grown and developed so fast it took his breath. He'd helped her all he could. His desire she should make her first transformation with this coming full moon had seemed too much to ask, at first. But three days on, his certainty she would be ready and their bond celebrated, had become more than a hope.

Though she'd not questioned him about it, he could sense her disquiet. Although they lay wrapped in each other's arms each night, they hadn't made love. Nor could they until they bonded and mated in wolf form twelve nights from tonight. Each day without the joy of her body would seem twice as long as normal, but he would not interrupt the process of her changing, nor take the risk if she were satiated with him in her woman form, she'd not find him the mate she wanted as a wolf.

Tradition said they should wait. Even though it might be uncomfortable, he would do nothing to alter any aspect to their bonding ritual. All her other appetites could and would be catered for. When she transformed for the first time, she'd be ready to mate, if not yet breed, and he'd be waiting to fulfill her every desire.

A thrill shot through him at the prospect of a full bonding with her, of seeing her as a wolf for the first time, of discovering her scent and making her all his own.

His for eternity.

A prickle of sensation between his shoulders interrupted his joy. He glanced into the rearview mirror. A large four by four, black with tinted windows, trailed him. There was nothing odd about an off-road style vehicle following him along the country road, yet his senses screamed to beware.

He continued driving until he reached the turnoff to the single-track lane leading into the hills where the cottage stood. Indicating as late as he could, he turned into the lane and kept his view on the mirror. The black car crossed the top of the lane on the main road. He sighed. All this with Sian, perfect as he'd hoped, had made him defensive. Of course, it had. Any new bonded male was protective of his mate.

He parked the car, and eager to see if she remained well, as well as show her the jewel, he took the box containing her amulet into the house. She should have it now. He'd thought to perhaps make some kind of ceremony of it, but decided against the idea. Sian had claimed the stone from the cairn. Nothing else was needed; the jewel was hers by right. The stone's setting had nothing to do with the power of the crystal, merely enhancing by the offer of a beautiful backdrop to a powerful physical representation of her courage and ability.

"Hello," he said as he opened the door. She didn't lie on the couch in front of the wide hearth. Upstairs perhaps?

"Magnus!"

He strode through to the kitchen.

Sian stood at the table. Flour splattered over the tabletop. White flecks clung to her elbows and apron.

"What are you doing? Why aren't you lying down?" He wiped a pale smudge off her cheek.

"I'm making Beef Wellington. The beef was in the freezer, the pastry, too. I'll be five minutes. I've just got to seal the pastry. After that, the dish is ready to rest. I'll put it in the fridge, and it can go in the oven later." She brushed a dab of flour off her cheek with the back of her hand. "Don't look so surprised. I can't leave you to cook everything while we're here." "Very well, I'll wait until you have finished your task. I'll make tea. Once you've washed your hands, I can show you the amulet."

Her eyes widened a fraction. "Of course, I thought I'd have this finished before you returned. Five minutes or less. Yes, tea would be great." A softness appeared in her expression. "I want so much to see the stone again."

"And you shall. I'll leave you to get on with the Beef Wellington. I'll make us a pot of tea." He moved across to the counter where he filled the kettle with water. Sian clattered the pastry board on the table.

When the delicate fragrance of tea rose from the steaming pot, she came to stand beside him. "I've only to wash my hands and I'm ready."

"Cups today, not mugs," he said.

"Mmm."

"Go sit at the dining table. I'll bring the tray in. Would you like biscuits?"

She shook her head.

He finished putting cups, saucers, sugar bowl, and milk jug on the tray, then added a small plate of delicate shortbread, too. The water added to the pot, he took the loaded tray in his hands, following Sian out of the kitchen into the main room of the cottage.

Her gaze lifted as he set the tea tray down. A lump settled in the base of his stomach for she looked tired with dark shadows beneath her eyes. The green depths dazzled brilliantly, but not with a healthful glow. No, she looked stressed, on edge, as though she'd forced herself beyond her current limit. He reached for her hand. "Tea?"

"You're upset?"

"Yes." He poured a cup for her, added a little milk and one sugar lump. "I'm concerned you are pushing yourself too hard."

"I can't leave everything for you to do," she whispered.

"Sometimes, stubbornness can be the cause of a great many trials."

A rosy flush colored her cheek. "You think I am stubborn?"

"Yes, and presently it can do you no good. You have so much strength, but at times, misapply the quality, as in today's situation."

Sian sipped her tea. "I don't think I misapplied anything."

"I'm aware of that. You do know you are undergoing a rare and important process, yes?"

She squeezed his fingers tight and nodded.

"Yet despite this, you feel you must work in the kitchen like any cook I could hire for a few pounds. Now, do you see what I mean?" He held her gaze. "I want you to rest, to relax so this process makes the least demands possible on you."

"I'm not very good at being idle," she said, taking another sip of her tea.

He gave a low laugh. "Idle? Don't underestimate all going on in your body. I'm trying to ensure you are physically safe throughout the process and don't suffer."

"I know. I promise I'll go upstairs after I've drunk this. I'll sleep until it's time for dinner. Please," she whispered over the rim of her cup, "show me the stone?"

He went to the sideboard where he'd placed the parcel. Taking one of the red roses from the display there, he carried the flower and the box back to her. "Sian,"—he shook his head at her teary eyes—"you are overwrought."

She sniffed. "No, it's that I want you so much. I want to be your mate."

He set the parcel down in front of her, the flower beside it. "The amulet is yours as it should be. Look at it, please."

Seconds ticked by as he waited for her to lift the lid of the box. His certainty she would approve the design quelled his fears. He watched her every move, each muscle on her face, and his love rolled though him like a ceaseless tide.

"Oh."

He knelt beside her at the gentle murmur. "It is yours and will be yours forever."

She reached to touch the stone in its setting. So determined, so strong, yet she was as fragile as the flower next to the box. "Please, will you go to rest now?"

She closed her eyes.

He counted to ten before her dark lashes lifted.

"I think I need to sleep."

Determined to make sure she did as she'd said, he lifted her from the chair. She trailed her hand toward the amulet. He clutched her tight and took the box, too. "I want you whole and perfect as I know you can be. I'll not leave you alone again until you are—"

"Shh." She pressed her lips to his. "I will be well," she whispered. "I have my stone now."

"More than that." He squeezed her tight. "You have me. You will always have me."

"For eternity?"

"Longer if you wish." He pressed a kiss to her lips and carried her up the stairs as she rested her head against his shoulder.

He should have guessed. Every day of the process had seemed so easy, too easy. Possibly because her desire to become like him masked the depth of her body's effort, he'd not seen all he should. Until today. From now on, he'd be far more careful of her. "Beef Wellington, indeed." He shook his head.

"It will be glorious."

"Mediocre at best if I cook it. I have a poor hand for pastry."

Her gaze met his. "But you do so many other things so well." She pressed a kiss to his lips and another to his cheek. "My necklace is beautiful, truly the most beautiful thing I have ever seen. I'll wear it when I get up."

"Yes. Wear it when you wake and every day thereafter."

Chapter 26

The automatic black gates swept open. Magnus drove up to the house and parked the Range Rover by the portico. "Happy we are back here?"

"Yes, aren't you?" She studied his face and discovered from her inner sense he didn't feel any warmth in this homecoming. "This isn't a prison, Magnus, not any more. The house won't cage either of us. There will be no need."

He gave a sigh.

"It's not like it once was." She put her hand on his arm. "You won't be alone and we have agreed on how we will hunt."

"Yes, but I don't know if such an agreement will hold water with the wolf."

She laughed because a surge of energy swept through her, strong enough to challenge his doubts. "We will have to wait and see, but I am certain I am right."

"Ah, how I admire your certitude." He leaned across to kiss her.

An instant flame of longing burned at his least touch, and the kiss left her shaking. The surge of desire through her loins screamed for him to satisfy her hunger. "If you continue, you'll have me begging for more, which is hardly fair. There are still days to go."

"Another four days. Tomorrow we will be focused on the garden."

"And Martha Raynalds," she snapped.

"I will cancel the appointment if you wish."

She had no doubt he would do if she asked, but if she pushed him to it, she knew she'd regret forcing the issue. The exchange of emotion between them, the ever present sense of him within her, even down to basic day-to-day needs, still took some managing. The issue between them regarding Martha Raynalds brewed like a storm cloud covering the sun. "I don't want you to cancel seeing her. I'll try not to be—"

"You have no need to feel anything other than happy the walled garden will become what it once was." He reached out and caressed her cheek. "This time next week, you will know that for certain."

"Forgive me. It's hard to deal with how I feel right this minute."

"I know. I promise you no matter what I discover about the director of Green Girls, it will have no impact on us or our future together."

A wave of concern backed up his spoken promise. The pettiness of her angst regarding this young woman from the gardening company shamed her. "I'll try to do some growing up, Magnus."

He smiled. "Don't do it too fast." He got out of the car and walked around to open her door for her. Funny how she always allowed him do so. She'd never permitted anyone else to open her door, but with Magnus it seemed as right today as it ever had. She slid out of the seat into his embrace, and couldn't stop her need to press as close as she could to his body when she accepted the kiss he offered. The desire for time to fly, to allow them to make love again, squished all her thoughts of Martha Raynalds.

"I know. I ache for you." His warm breath brushed by her ear so she gave another shudder.

"This is pure torment."

The expression in his eyes told his agreement but she knew he'd stick to the tradition he had explained. She couldn't imagine a time when she wouldn't want him, as a human or in wolf-form. His wolf had her heart already, but Magnus insisted they wait. A huge sigh broke as he stepped away from her embrace.

"I'll get the luggage. You go in."

She turned and went into the portico. The front door opened. Mrs. Tyson stood waiting. The woman's gaze settled on the amulet where it hung against Sian's sweater, and she gave a smile. "Madam, welcome home."

No longer Miss Sian. Tyson knew or understood at a basic level what the amulet symbolized. "Thank you, Mrs. Tyson. Magnus is bringing the luggage. Has everything been okay while we were away?"

"Yes, madam. Will you want dinner this evening?"

"Please, tell Cook something simple will do. Hmm, yes, steak and a little salad would be fine."

"Very well, madam, I'll inform Cook. Shall I bring tea to the drawing room?"

"Thank you, yes."

Tyson nodded and left.

Sian took off her jacket and hung it in the large walk-in cupboard. Magnus joined her to hang up his coat. "I ordered steak for dinner this evening," she said.

He smiled. "A good choice. Cook knows to present it rare."

"Mrs. Tyson is now calling me madam. Is that who I am?"

"Yes, it is. Next week we will see about making the title legal as well as permanent."

"Marriage?"

"A formality surely. You expected it, didn't you?"

She shook her head. "The other process seemed much more important."

"Yes, of course it does, because it is. You are my mate, my woman, my she. You will be my wife in the eyes of the world." His eyes widened. "Should I have proposed earlier?"

"You might have asked," she said with a grin.

He took her hand and bent on one knee smiling, his eyes alight with humor. "My perfect, Sian, I ask you to make me very happy by agreeing to become my wife, immediately."

"Yes, Magnus. I will be your wife. I will be everything you ask of me."

His expression grew serious as he kissed her hand and stood to embrace her. "I will cherish you and our love as the most precious things in my life. What kind of wedding do you want, and when?"

"Soon and quiet, just us."

"Surely you'll want friends present. We will need witnesses, too."

"I'll think about it after the full moon."

"I demand you wear a wedding gown. There will be flowers and champagne. I have something very special in the cellar."

"Truly, you want the traditional style of wedding?"

He smiled. "I want whatever will make you happy, but I am certain you will be stunning in a wedding gown. We can hold the wedding here in the ballroom. I do know the name of the local vicar, or we could use a registrar. We'll marry the week before Christmas."

"I could invite a few people, Richard, Jess, and Evie, some of the staff I know well from work."

"Not Mr. Gorsewell?"

She shook her head. "No, not unless things have changed by then."

Magnus caressed her cheek. "I think things will have changed enough for him to attend our wedding quite safely. He must recognize me as his maker and you as my mate. You are as far above him as the stars. He will know it. When he witnesses our marriage, he fulfills his obedience to me, and in turn, to you as my mate." He tucked her arm through his, then glanced at the coats hung around them. "Forgive me. This really isn't the most romantic spot for a proposal."

She laughed. "I agree, but, Magnus, it doesn't matter. You see, being with you is more important to me than anything else in the world."

He bent his head and kissed her.

When they parted, she stood with her arms about his neck. "I think we should go and have tea before we become too involved here."

He smiled as he caressed a warm palm over her rear.

"Please, Magnus. I am suffering for you."

"I know. You're not alone in your need. Tea before, as you say, we are tempted beyond all constraints."

They moved in unison, steps matched as they walked out the door and down the corridor to the drawing room. The synchronization between them that Sian had found when they'd made love or in the moments after seemed to have become part of her, its powerful force as natural as breathing.

The love of the wolf, for the wolf, bound by a ceaseless energy from the life force in each of them, moved like a slow stirring in her core. His love, her love, his pain, hers, too, and everything else in the wide world of their existence would be shared.

A tea tray sat ready on the table in the drawing room. She sat and poured, then offered him a cup with the lemon he enjoyed and stirred a lump of sugar in hers. "Magnus, I want to concentrate on the full moon for the next few days rather than our wedding. Do you think it's right I should?"

"Yes. The wedding will be a celebration of our union. I'm glad you feel that way. The forming of our dynasty is very important."

"Dynasty?"

"Eventually." He sipped his tea. "However, I have every intention of purchasing an engagement ring for you next week. What would you like?"

She clutched the wrought gold amulet with her crystal inside. "This is all I need."

"So I am at liberty to select anything I think appropriate?"

"I know you are teasing, but yes, you are. Please, don't buy anything big or ostentatious. I'd like something suitable to wear all the time."

"I'll give it some thought." He set his teacup down. "Would you care for a short walk?"

She smiled. She'd entertained the idea of looking again at the walled garden before tomorrow, and he'd picked up on it. "Yes. I think we'll need Wellingtons, but I'd like a walk."

"We'll go look at the walled garden. I am sure we can think of some ideas to discuss tomorrow morning."

"Perfect." She set her cup down and they headed out to put on boots and coats.

Outside, she inhaled the rich fragrant air, the scent of pine strong from the woods, the combination from animals on the estate, too. Magnus put his arm around her shoulder, and together they strolled down the cinder pathway to the rear of the house, past the damaged section of the music room, farther along and up to where they could look down on the walled garden.

She took his hand in hers as she gazed at the small potting shed standing by one wall. The first time he showed her the garden, they'd made love in there. She sighed.

"Dearest, please stop thinking of sex."

Her cheeks tingled with heat. "I'm sorry. I couldn't help but remember the shed."

He gave a low laugh. "I agree, but please, try to think of something else."

"Right, I'll think about the fruit trees."

"Hmm, peaches. Soft, smooth, and juicy, with curves a perfect fit for my palm."

"Magnus!"

His laughter echoed as he hugged her. "Soon. You're right about the fruit trees, too."

"Glass house," she murmured. "We need to talk to them about maintenance, irrigation, pest control. You'd have to have at least two gardeners. Maybe more."

He leaned his chin on her shoulder and tightened his embrace, pulling her back against him. "Rather like an age gone by."

"Not really. A lot of estates make money from their gardens. You could, too."

"We could, but it's not necessary you know."

She turned her head to brush her cheek against his. "But if the garden produces fruits and vegetables, then there would be far more than we could use. You couldn't allow all of it go to waste."

"Hmm. Perhaps, as you suggested, we could find a ready market for produce. That's something else to discuss tomorrow."

"Agreed. Oh, rain." She blinked at the spatter of raindrops. "Back to the house. We'll end up soaked if we stay here."

Magnus caught her hand and they turned together. She broke into a run, and though she was certain he slowed his paces to match hers, they raced back to the house and dived into the portico, dripping wet.

"I hope it's not like this the night of the full moon." She shook her hair.

"It won't matter if it is. I promise you." His smile met her gaze, and his eyes shone with the light of desire. "We will love together. Nothing could stop me wanting you."

"Soon."

Chapter 27

Magnus glanced to the clock. They'd half an hour before Ms. Raynalds should arrive.

Sian had tapped her coffee cup with her nails for the last few minutes as she stared out the window.

"Would you rather I met with this lady alone?"

"No, not at all," she said. "I am intrigued."

He ran his hand over the length of her curls. Loose today, her hair hung past her shoulders, a silky temptation to his touch.

Sian glanced up. "Am I so very obvious?"

"I know you're disturbed. I can see and feel you're concerned about today."

She smiled. "Along with a few other things."

"Yes. Is there anything I can say or do to help?"

She shook her head. "No, I know what's to come." Her gaze met his and claimed his heart anew. "Mostly."

"You know how important you are to me." He bent and brushed a kiss against her lips. "Later today we'll meditate together and find each other when we do."

Her cheeks rounded as she puffed out a breath. "Dreaming is easier. The meditation is so hard."

"You need to still your mind of other concerns."

A knock at the door silenced them both. Mrs. Tyson came in. "Ms. Raynalds is here, Mr. Johansson. I've shown her into the drawing room. I said you'd be with her in a moment or two."

"Thank you, Mrs. Tyson. We'll be there directly." He clasped Sian's hand and tugged her up from her seat. "Are you ready?"

"I'm all right. Don't worry about me."

"Good."

They strolled to the yellow drawing room. He turned to her, his hand on the door handle. "Last chance to do something different."

"No, Magnus. I want to meet Ms. Raynalds with you."

Her courage still took him by surprise at times. He hoped it always would. "Very well, we'll go in." He opened the door and walked through. Sian followed a footstep behind. One look and he understood. "Good morning, Ms. Raynalds. I'm Magnus Johansson. This is Sian."

"Hello, Ms. Raynalds," Sian said. "A pleasure to meet you."

"Hello, Mrs. Johansson, Mr. Johansson. This is a wonderful estate."

He took in her slate blue eyes, the fair hair a match of her grandmother's in color. He didn't correct her about Sian, time would make her statement true. "I'm pleased you have found it so. Would you like coffee or shall we go directly to the walled garden?"

"I'd prefer to look at the garden. I like to get my first hands on impression, that way I have ideas to give you to think about after I leave today. We can discuss other things later."

"Very well. We'll get coats on the way." He took Sian's hand, led her and Ms. Raynalds out and down the corridor. Sian gave him several curious glances as they put on their coats and headed out of the portico. They waited for Ms. Raynalds to get her Wellington boots from her van, and once she'd donned them, they all strode along the cinder path.

"The walled garden was at one time the powerhouse of food production for the house," he said as they strolled to the garden. "It has sadly been untended for over half a century."

"But if the foundations are still good, it can be resurrected, Mr. Johansson. I assure you. Our company has worked on two projects of a similar nature. After assessment, we may find some of the plants can be rescued or reseeded."

"Oh, good," Sian said. "There are several fruit trees I hope might be salvageable."

"Specialty ones?" Ms. Raynalds asked.

"Yes, peach trees."

"We might be lucky, Mrs. Johansson."

Sian glanced to him, and he gave a slight shake of his head while he concentrated on the sheer wealth of energy from this young woman striding beside them. The quality he'd found attractive in her grandmother oozed from her also. This close to the full moon, with his senses prodded by the forthcoming change, and Sian, too, he discerned something more from Martha Raynalds. The call of blood kin. This woman carried a part of him in her genes.

"Here we are," he said as they reached the top of the rise where they could overlook the whole of the walled garden spread below. "As you can see, there is a great deal that needs to be done."

"Good heavens, it's huge. I've not seen a plot this large in sixteen years in this business."

"Is it too big to work on?" Sian asked.

"Oh, no, it will be a wonderful project to complete. The sheds are still useable?"

He heard Sian's little cough and immediately said, "Yes, though they could all do with a little work."

"This is excellent. The brickwork all looks good, too. The Victorians knew how to build to last."

"Part of the garden dates from the late eighteenth century," he explained. "There was a hothouse at the far end of the south wall. I have photographs of the garden before it fell into disuse. You could look at them if you wish."

"Would you like us to do a complete reconstruction of the garden as it was, sir? Or would you like to put your own stamp on the garden?" Ms. Raynalds asked.

He looked to Sian. "I…we would like to have some input in the ideas for the planting, yes?"

"Yes," Sian said. "I've a lot of questions I'd like to ask when we go back inside."

"Of course, Mrs. Johansson."

"Would you like to go down into the garden, Ms. Raynalds?" he asked.

"Please, I'd like a brief look around, and please do call me Martha, if you would."

"Very well, Martha. This way." He led her and Sian down the path and through one of the gateways into the garden. Sian squeezed his fingers tight.

"Look at this." Martha tapped at one wall of the arched gateway. "Best bonded brickwork. This garden must have been a top example in its heyday. I'll take a quick stroll down along the rows if you don't mind."

"Of course, we'll wait here."

The young woman strode down the path at a fast pace.

"Tell me?" Sian said.

"I believe my first inclination was correct."

"But she doesn't know?"

He shook his head, watching as Martha bent and then crouched to look at something in one of the beds. "No. Perhaps Dorothy didn't tell her anything. I don't think she knows about her heritage."

"Do you think she's like...us?"

"No, not quite, or not yet."

"Yet?"

He linked Sian's arm through his. "It may be she could be awakened by something to that part of her heritage. I'd need to research it to discover if it were possible."

"Oh, she's coming back. You'll have to tell me more later."

"This is a fine garden, simply begging to be put to rights, Mr. Johansson. I'll be very happy to take on this project if you wish me to."

"Then we'll make our way back to the house where we can discuss some ideas, perhaps some rough figures, and a timescale for activities." He turned with Sian back toward the house. "Sian has a list of questions prepared, I believe."

"Of course." Martha strode beside them. "A quick estimate, I'd say there is approximately a year's work to get this back to planting readiness."

"And the fruit trees?" Sian asked.

"There are some viable, but they'll need a lot of pruning, feeding, and general babying to get them back to their best. You've one or two breeds I've only seen recorded in Victorian head gardeners notebooks. I'm going to enjoy this project."

"How big a team will you need for the work?" he asked.

"I'd say five permanent gardeners from my team, and extra staff for the heavy work as it comes up. I'll work section by section, you see, not try to do everything all at once."

"Hmm, I think that's a good idea," Sian said. "The work would all be quicker if your team were local."

His heart sank. He'd no way to warn Sian against what he simply knew she'd propose next.

"Of course there are staff quarters over the stables, aren't there, Magnus?"

He nodded. "They haven't been used for some time. I don't know if they'd be suitable."

"But we could look at them and see, couldn't we? Would your team prefer to live on-site for the project, Martha?"

The tall fair-haired woman stood still. "I can certainly ask. We have used a similar arrangement in the past on one project with the team members on-site for the week and off to see family at the weekend."

He blew out a deep breath and looked to Sian. "After Christmas though, Martha. Work begins then."

"Yes, Mr. Johansson. Due to the size of the garden, it will take at least that long for me to draw up plans for your approval. I made my estimate of working in December before I'd seen the size of the plot. I'll visit several times during the month I would think, with your approval."

"Excellent. We'll go back indoors and get coffee."

The three of them headed toward the house, discarded muddy Wellingtons and their coats, and made their way to the drawing room. Sian rang for coffee.

He sat opposite Martha. "It's obviously too early for a detailed costing, but I would like an estimate as soon as possible, and a list of staff numbers. Arrangements would have to bed only. I've a limited kitchen staff."

"I understand. Provided there are cooking facilities in the accommodation, my team will be happy."

"Good. As to the overall cost of the project, I'll await your figures."

"Do you want me to source period planting for the garden, sir? I'm afraid if I do, it can add to the price."

"Sian, what do you think?"

A trace of color highlighted her cheeks. "You must forgive me, but I've no idea what kind of money we're talking about to do this work. I think some original varieties of plants would be ideal. We also need to look at how we are going to utilize produce when the garden bears fruit."

"Don't worry about the money. If we are going to do this, then it must be paid for."

"I would suggest contacting local restaurants in the area as they are often the ones who will take smaller quantities of top grade fruit and vegetables in season," Martha said. "There's no shortage of good restaurants in this locality. If you discuss the idea with several chefs and find out what they may need before we plant, we could base some of the planting according to what they may require."

He glanced to Sian as Mrs. Tyson came in with a tray of coffee and biscuits.

"Thanks, Mrs. Tyson," she said. "Would you tell Cook I'd like to have her ideas on fruit and vegetables for the walled garden if she'd share them with me?"

"Of course, madam. I'll tell her you asked."

Sian picked up the coffee pot and poured. He stood to take a cup and pass it to Martha, then picked up one for himself. "I think the best thing regarding the planting will be to discuss it with Sian who will research the possibilities of retailing the produce."

"I will?"

"Yes. I already have the orangery as a project to oversee."

"Okay." Sian turned to face Martha. "If you can get the details to me before the end of December, that would be great. Send me an e-mail regarding dates you might want to return to visit the garden. I'll also make sure the accommodation block above the stables is made ready for you and your team. How many was it again?"

"Five permanent gardeners will make up the main team for the duration of the project, with a possible addition of up to ten for occasional periods, Mrs. Johansson. I'll have a detailed schedule for you before Christmas."

"I'll look forward to seeing it."

Martha nodded. The charming, broad smile reminded him so much of Dorothy, he looked away.

"One thing I should have said earlier... I don't know if you've ever heard of it, but my team and I tend to find our planting work produces its best results if we time it to moon rhythms. You won't have any objection to us working in such a way will you?"

Sian glanced across, and he shook his head to still any response she might make to the request. He sipped from his coffee cup, gaining time to make sure his voice held no hint of his surprise. "No, Martha, we won't mind. We quite understand the importance of moon rhythms."

Chapter 28

Magnus opened his eyes at the bleep of the alarm from Sian's phone. He roused from the deep meditative state he'd striven to find for the last two hours. Sian sat opposite, her eyes gleaming in the gloom. He'd not found a link to her as he'd meditated. She'd remained bundled in the here and now, a captive to her nervous fervor. He ached for her apprehensions, but tonight he understood each nuance of her fears. He could do nothing, it would seem, to give her peace.

He doused the scented candle on the small table between them. Her idea, and one he'd enjoyed. He offered her his hand. "I think we should go now."

Silent, her eyes fixed on his, the depths shimmery as a mirror, she reached up for his fingers and grasped them tight in hers. "I feel so strange."

A jolt of panic hit him. Surely, she couldn't have begun the change already. He searched her gaze. "We must hurry if we are to go to the pagoda."

Their decision to use the pagoda had solved the problem of where to go this full moon for her first change to wolf form. He led her quickly out of the secret door. They sped down the path, hurrying over the slippery grass slope down toward the causeway on the lake. He inhaled deep, sucking in great breaths of the chilled night air. Sian's breaths rasped loud as she did the same. The flicker of change in his vision to the sharp focus of the wolf altered his conscious thoughts. He slowed his pace, but a snap of sensation bit.

"We must run."

Sian's breathing grew faster, and a tremble ran through the fingers he clutched with his. She reached the bottom of the slope in front of him and yanked him along. They stumbled together over the causeway, slippery with the frost coating from the bitter night.

The moonlight hit him full-on as he paused to take a breath at the end of the causeway. Agonized by the white light, he writhed as the scraps of his skin opened to the moonbeams. With the last of his strength, he pushed Sian inside the pagoda and onto the day bed. He followed her and sagged to the floor, unable to stop the quicksilver race over his body.

* * * *

Inhaling deep, he uncurled to stand on his four feet and shook himself to free his fur of any detritus. The aroma he discovered in the air sent a shiver over him. The richness of female scent surrounded him. He nosed the cushions, sniffing at the shards of thin shell that crumbled at the touch of his breath. The heady mix of her scent set his blood pounding with need. He yowled with anticipation of finding her. She must be close by.

He sniffed the floor.

A howl echoed in the distance, but not hers. He lifted his head, searching the wealth of odors. No female would offer a challenge like that. He turned and paced out of the pagoda into the wealth of moonlight reflected from the lake. Trotting over the causeway, he inhaled again and found the sensual trail of her fragrance. His fur bristled when another call echoed in the woods. He must find his female, claim her, and his territory from some interloper.

He opened his mouth wide to allow the layers of aroma to fill not only his nose, but also his mouth, so he could sample every scent on the wind.

The night smells of the familiar surroundings held all manner of joys, but the fragrant track of his female led him onward and along the edge of the lake toward the woods. She had headed this way. She sought the protection of the mature trees in the woods across from the lake. Something had frightened her so she didn't wait for him to emerge from his cocoon.

A fresh howl, its raw savageness echoed into the night. The owner of that voice might be the reason she fled. This time he answered the challenge. He stretched his neck and opened his throat so his howl flooded out. The power of his wolf voice soared to the stars with the strength of his reply. Silence followed. He headed along the path and up to the tree line highlighted by the moon.

The she-scent he followed grew stronger, graced with high notes from her scent marking. He salivated at the sweetness of each mark he discovered. The first trees she'd sprayed proved so delightful he circled each, breathing the gorgeous fragrance in several times until he'd no choice but to leave his scent, too, combined with hers. He pressed on but at a slower pace to make sure he wouldn't miss any of the sensual joy as he journeyed to discover her. The small glade awash with moonlight made him pause. He could not only smell her, but also heard her shallow, quick breaths.

There.

Her body hunched. Her lustrous tail tucked under tight told of her fear. The exquisite and gleaming pale coat, accented with red tips on her flanks and tail, shone in the light.

Not fear of him.

The unknown howler in the starlight had caused her to feel threatened. He'd show her she had nothing to fear.

They belonged in these woods together.

He inhaled and drank in the sight as well as her fragrance. Her green eyes shone and her gaze remained on him. The narrow, pale, furred face, highlighted with darker red tones, tilted after a moment of recognition. She deliberately angled her head, eyes downcast, so he could approach unchallenged. He ached to touch the rich lushness of her pelt, to sidle up beside her, to persuade her she was his and his alone.

Drawing closer, he paused and inhaled several times. A low rumble of appreciation burbled in his throat.

She turned away from him, the sweep of her flanks and her beautiful lustrous tail glistened in the moonlight.

A throb surged in his flesh as the corner of her pink tongue swept from the edge of her mouth and swiftly licked her lips. She stood, emboldened by his presence, perhaps. Delicate, on slender limbs, she took one pace away from him. Her muzzle lowered, she glanced back over her shoulder, enticement in the play of her every muscle. She headed out of the glade moving fast weaving her way through the trees. Her swift steps took her into the deeper woods.

The chase was on, and he'd no doubt it would have only one culmination. He raced after her and caught a quick flash of her long tail as she sprinted ahead. Her short yip, as she dashed away, beckoned him to follow, pleaded for him to catch her. The invitation to join her and romp among the leaves this winter night couldn't be refused. He wanted to play with her until they both lay breathless. Then he'd curl next to her and listen to her heartbeat.

A joy he'd never known before lured him onward. Her rich scent offered the promise of more. Nothing could be more enticing than the way she flicked her long tail and wafted her fragrance toward him.

High pitched and closer, a series of howls soured the night. The calls carried an ominous threat, one of battle. He answered again, sending a deep-throated response to whoever dared invade his territory.

A shimmery, lighter sound answered him. This seductive series of barks didn't come from the owner of the original threat. This call came from his female, and her note of impatience drove him on. He would have her close enough to stand in his shadow if this other male dared to interrupt their courtship. The race to find her took on fresh urgency. He wound his way through the trees fast to reach her before the other male could find her. A fresh howl disturbed the night.

His quarry stood nearby, her sides moving quickly as she regained her breath. He gave a low growl, and she spun to face him, her eyes fixed on him. The mischief from earlier had gone, replaced by wariness he'd hoped not to find. He took a step closer. She lifted her upper lip, revealing one of her long canines.

He licked his lips, then yawned, offering her a display of his teeth. Stepping closer, he barked. She swept her gaze to the floor and angled her head away. The gesture, a subtle but submissive welcome to his attentions, lured him closer still. When he reached her, he stood a whisker's length from her mouth. She leaned in closer, then flicked her tongue once against his muzzle. He opened his mouth and caught her nose between his teeth as gentle as if he held a cloud.

Her little yips floated like music. Lost to the beauty of her fragrance and the wonder of being beside her, he licked her nose, her muzzle, the dark fur outlining her eyes and back to her lips.

She angled her body in line with his until they stood shoulder to shoulder, hip to hip, though she had nowhere near his bulk. He stroked his head along her neck and she returned the caress with a low rumbled sigh.

"*Sian.*" The name whispered in his mind, softer than the rustle of the breeze in the wheat fields, velvety as the furry hide he rubbed against. "*Sian-wolf.*"

"*My Magnus-wolf.*"

The words invaded his mind and they spun in his consciousness, prompting him to find a way to reply with his thoughts alone, something he'd never done before. "*My love.*"

Warm, smooth, and tickling, she used her tongue to lap at this face, over his eyes, along his jaw, right to the edge of his lips. A sweep of desire raced through him, and he ached to mate with her. He inhaled again, desperate to find if she might be ready for him to mount her. She gave a small pup-style yip and nipped at his ear. Obviously not, but they had days to enjoy each other. Before the end of the moon's influence, they'd mate.

She rubbed her shoulder and hip against his, licked his face until he could stand the teasing no more. He nudged her hard enough so she rolled over onto her side. He stood legs astride her where she lay and proceeded to lick down her throat. By the time he reached her belly, she whimpered, and enjoying her pleasure, he continued. She rolled back and forth, her front paws crossed as he nibbled at her.

Her little cries became a whine until finally he relented and allowed her up.

"My goddess."

Her brilliant eyes looked deep into his.

A sound he'd never heard before in this form reached him. Her laughter. She turned from him and raced between the trees. Her spine sinuous, her shoulders and hips, rippling in enticement, she ran. He followed, eager to enjoy this chase through the moonlit woods.

Her screeching yelp brought him up short in a scatter of dirt and plant debris.

She lay, cowering under the heavy foot of a gray wolf with white banding. One who snarled, his back humped in aggression as he bared full canines in an open-mouthed snarl.

Playtime was over.

Chapter 29

She stilled the desperate need to escape and made whining mewls of submission in a plea for her captor to ease the painful grip holding her to the woodland floor. When he did, she'd turn and rip his throat out.

The big gray male above seemed to hear her thoughts because he added more weight to her burden. He pressed down heavily on her with his front paws, and growling, he showed her a deadly set of vicious teeth.

A dribble of his saliva hit her eye and made her blink.

The gray male howled.

She shivered, unable to fight or escape his weight.

A second of despair passed before an answering snarl came from across the way, and pinned as she was, she tilted her head so she could see the wolf of her longings. She wanted to be his, to mate with him, to lie in the deep darkness next to his heat and rest her head on his shoulder. Her vision bleared. She scarcely had enough breath for a whimper.

"Be still. Don't look at him. You're mine!"

She shuddered at the words from the gray wolf who shoved her spine into the dirt. Recognition hit. *"Franklyn."* She'd never be his, not this side of paradise. All her hope of happiness lay a few steps away.

"Magnus!" The name ripped from her mind, tore its way out, bloody and desperate. She twitched in the aftermath.

"Let her go, Gorsewell, your grievance is with me."

His calm words stilled her terror. She closed her eyes from the revolting view of the gray wolf's erection as he stood over her chest. Both his front paws pressed down harder and she struggled to breathe.

"She'll run if I let her up."

"So? If you try to take her, I will kill you. If you try to make a move to harm her more, I will kill you. Are you ready to die this night?"

She sucked in a gasp as the pressure on her chest eased a little.

"You don't have the courage to fight me. You're all talk."

The bunched shoulder muscles and raised lips over fierce teeth said the gray wolf lied. Magnus would fight. The heaviness of the gray's weight forced a whimper from her lips. A snarl rang in her ears and made its way into her chest. She closed her eyes and lay limp as one dead.

The gray wolf holding her eased more of his weight from her with a tentative paw. *"Come take her corpse from me!"*

A howl to fill the cosmos shook her bones. Franklyn-wolf leaped. She rolled away. Magnus-wolf met the attack as the gray smashed into him. He spun, dislodging his foe, who sprawled heavily before jerking upright.

Crouched less than a tail length beyond the space where the two of them fought, she screeched a howl. At least her wolf knew she still lived and would help him if she could.

Dust, leaves, twigs, and dirt flew about them. Each slash of claws hissed with a weight-laden *woosh* through the air. Snarls and howls stung her ears.

She scrunched her body tight and didn't breathe as finally one of them made contact. A spray of blood spattered against a low-lying oak branch. The gray wolf lifted red-stained claws high in the moonlight. Each tip dripped a scatter of scarlet blood beads, and he screamed his triumph before diving deep into the shadows, slashing down another blow.

The night shook with the power of the snarls, the grunts drawn from each by the pain from biting injuries. Back and forth, they moved fast as they fought. Every time Magnus seemed to have a grip on his foe, Franklyn, his head blooded by a wound, somehow slithered free.

She struggled to control her need to enter the battle, to protect the male she wanted from further harm. Crouched on all fours, her belly pressed to the ground, she jiggled her body weight from one side to the other while she waited, seeking a space to join the fray.

The gray wolf suddenly stilled, all its muscles rigid. The ruff of fur stood, and a sudden spray of urine gushed. She turned her face from the stench, but desperate to see what had happened, she swiveled back.

"One move and I will take your brain and eat it."

The words echoed like a chorus about the woods. The gray wolf had frozen, its head caught between Magnus-wolf's powerful jaws. It didn't move.

Gladness filled her heart.

"If I press here, you will be dead. Are you ready to die?"

Shrill whining came as the answer. Magnus-wolf flipped its victim around in response, his toothy grip still obvious as loose soil swirled from the scrabbling claws of the other wolf. Another rash of yaps and whimpers, each higher pitched than the last.

She couldn't bear the pitiful squeals. *"Stop!"*

Teeth barred as he gripped his prey tight, Magnus-wolf met her gaze with one golden and rich. *"He would have raped you, killed you perhaps. Are you certain I should simply allow him to go?"*

She bowed her head. Whatever he thought to do, she'd agree. A quickening of fear returned at the memory of Franklyn-wolf holding her pinned to the ground. She swept her glance away from the blood-laced grasses, from the dark patches on Magnus's beautiful apricot-tipped fur, the slowly spreading stain and drip of blood from the gray's ears.

"Walk back to the lake. I'll find you there."

She nodded, and turning into the nearest path among the trees, she left the two males alone.

Not many steps on, a screech sent the birds up from their night nests. She hung her head. This night, the prelude to their bonding, should have been filled with love and the sweetness of brilliant moonlight, not this ugliness making her shiver. She sucked in another breath as the next wild cry echoed up to the stars. She couldn't bear it.

"Stop. Please, Magnus. Stop."

She doubted he'd hear her, and even if he did, he wouldn't stop. Dragging her steps, she found herself at the edge of the woods, moonlight still glossing a thin sliver of the lake. She walked until she could lie down on frosty turf in the last scrap of the silvery beams.

The wind raked over her, battered against her, and she closed her eyes, burying her nose between her furry paws. Her stomach churned as she waited, breathing out smoky white puffs into the night air.

"Beloved?"

She lifted her head from the warmth and looked at his bloodied mouth. *"You killed him?"*

"No. I allowed him to live." He sank down beside her.

The stench of blood and urine overwhelmed his powerful fragrance. She nosed him, pressing lightly against his thick fur. *"Franklyn-wolf is gone?"*

He gave a low grunt when he rested his head against her shoulder. His pain thudded through her, but the gashes and slashes would heal. She tilted her head to touch her muzzle to his despite the smears of blood. *"I love you."*

"I know. We must move."

"Why?"

Daisy Banks

"We can't rest here." He lifted his head and pointed his nose toward the pagoda on the lake. *"In there, until the day is done."*

She looked up to the sky. The moon had tracked across and sunk beyond the trees. Her first night in wolf form neared its end. *"Will we dream together?"*

He hauled himself up, a little unsteady. She stood beside him, ready to help if he needed her to, and shook her head at the savage slashes down his flank. Their slow paces matched, they walked in union as they headed toward the causeway.

Pausing at the lake edge, Magnus-wolf lapped water, then led her across the wooden boards and into the shadows inside the pagoda. He slumped down in the corner. She joined him, nestling close despite the smell of the fight still clinging to his fur. The short November day must pass before they could run through the woods together again.

She yawned, curled up, and wrapped her long tail over her face. Magnus-wolf shifted until she lay in the curve of one of his front paws. The rest of his body warmed her as he pressed himself against her.

Tomorrow night must be sweeter than this one had been for they would be alone together in the moonlight.

Chapter 30

She woke to the warmth of his tongue against her lips.

Soft gold with brighter flecks, his gaze searched hers.

She yawned.

"Run with me." He swiped his tongue up the side of her face again. Warm and fragrant, his caress sent a shock of sensation through her body.

The luxury of peace, of his touch, of the shimmer of moonlight through the open door—all of it stole any concerns from yesterday. *"Catch me."* Her thought danced away between the shine and shadows.

He batted her with a padded paw, his demon sharp claws sheathed to stroke her. *"Wanton. Run with me."*

Her body flashed with brilliant sparks of lust at his lightest caress. She sucked in a deep breath, filled with his enticement, and stood. Arching her back, she stretched her legs.

His hungry groan echoed around them in the shadows.

She turned to meet his brilliant golden gaze as it locked on hers. *"My beautiful she. I need you."*

A sudden flashback to the woman Sian made her wobble. Shaking her head, she blinked until her vision settled to that of the wolf. *"Magnus, my mind keeps swapping."*

"You need something other than fear to pin you to the here and now. Run with me."

She sidestepped his closeness, twisted and hopped, for his feet stepped in between hers no matter which way she moved. Finally, with his low, grumbling, pleasure growls in her ears, she managed to get to the door with him half wrapped around her. The lure of him urged her to slide against him. They needed more room.

The moonlight beckoned, but her ache for him kept her steady, waiting for him to stand beside her, shoulder and hip aligned. Her body tingled when he joined her, his hip nudging hers, his eyes fixed on her as he rolled his shoulder to massage hers. A flood of her scent mingled with the powerful wave of his.

The thick aroma of mating wolves increased her arousal.

"Run."

She did, streaking away from him as fast as she could with the one intent that he should follow her. The light from the full and fat moon beamed off the lake, illuminating the trees on the horizon as she headed toward them. The sound of his breathing, as he ran behind her, told her he was no more than a pace or two from catching her.

His paw snagged her back foot. She rolled, tumbling over and over until, her breath fast and her heartbeat quicker, she stilled. Magnus-wolf stood over her, tilting his head down so she could lick at his muzzle should she wish. *"Too slow, my she."*

Her gaze remained locked on his, fixed on the promise of love. All her nipples tingled. Her cry, half howl, half moan, tore into the night.

The one comfort she could seek was from him, yet at this moment, her fear robbed the peace of love from her. She fought to find herself within the wolf, or the wolf within herself, and screeched into the night. *"Help me."*

"Be mine. All mine."

"Always." His scent as he rubbed against her, stroking her fur the wrong way, smoothing it down after, stoked her desire. Heat flashed through her, centering in her loins and heating her belly. She stroked her neck against his and pressed her flank against him.

He breathed, opening his mighty jaws. *"You taste so good."*

The aroma in the air came from the lust for him coursing through her body. She needed him to satisfy the longing deep inside.

She flipped her tail under his nose. His low-throated growl showed his pleasure.

"Now, Magnus."

Their shadows, cast by the brilliance of moonlight, combined as he mounted. His breath rushed past her ear and she bore his weight on shuddery paws. Above, the stars swam in the blackness as she accepted him, tilted her head with an ecstatic howl and thrust back toward him. *Yes!*

Time ceased. Nothing in her life as woman or wolf had been as vital. Every part of her body tingled with the frenzied blasts of satisfaction that didn't stop even when Magnus-wolf stilled, panting above her.

He nudged her with a gentle nose, so she lowered herself to the ground with him still buried deep within her. *"My life is yours, my mate."*

Warmth cocooned her. His fur beside her silky soft, his tongue rasping against her face, his body twined with hers, his erection buried deep within, all swamped her in delight. *"I am yours forever."*

"Until the world stops turning."

She groaned and growled as she closed her eyes. They would pleasure each other every time the moon became full.

They remained locked together, blissful, sharing the mutual delight of their bonding as the moon tracked across the sky. Tonight the bright moonbeams danced on his fur and hers where the strands mingled.

Never could she have enough of him. Always she would long for him. She whimpered when finally he withdrew and left her body bereft without him as part of her.

"You are mine and me. I am yours and you. Feel it."

She reached up to lick his face. The sensation inside her so powerful she could barely lift herself from the turf that their combined body heat had warmed. *"Will it always be as intense as this?"*

"Yes."

Another attempt and she managed to stand. She stared into his golden eyes where she found the mirror of herself. All her love and need, desire and hope, a myriad of emotions centered on this one man, wolf. *"You are my mate. Let's hunt."*

The passionate bonding with Magnus-wolf altered everything. They shared every sense as they hunted. He moved with her as they padded over the grass and into the woods. No challenge from Franklyn-wolf rang tonight.

"No, he is not dead. He will return here, but only in answer to my command."

She hoped Franklyn-wolf's return wouldn't be for a very long time yet. Instinct made her turn her head at the exact moment Magnus-wolf did. He shot off at a race, and before she could blink, all three rabbits feeding in the moonlight succumbed to the swiftness of the wind raised by his paw. The little creatures froze briefly, as if surprised to be dispatched, before they fell, dead. He brought one over to her and deposited it at her feet.

While he returned to fetch the others, she ate, snapping small bones and pulling away chunks of fluff to get to warm meat. Tasty enough in its way, but she'd hoped for a bigger meal. After eating, they ran through the woods together, him in front and then her. They raced each other, skidding down the slope where they rolled amidst the crisp leaves together. Her heart, still full of him from their coupling, soared with the compulsive joy of being with her mate.

Daisy Banks

This union between them, forged by their link and their mating, would grow stronger. The love wrapped around each of them, a gift from the other, would swell and bloom like a mighty tree in the forest. They would be one.

Magnus-wolf nuzzled, offering her sweet caresses with his lips and tongue. She arched her neck so he could continue in his attentions.

The moon moved across the sky, and with the first hint of approaching dawn, they returned to the pagoda. She took a long drink from the icy lake water. Inside the shelter, they settled together in the corner. Magnus-wolf curled his body around her.

One night remained before they would leave their wolf-forms behind. *A pity.*

Chapter 31

The third night, the moon glossed shadows across the lake made a monstrous creation of the wolf pair mating, again. He couldn't tear his gaze from the pale she-wolf with the red highlights to her fur, the larger male thrusting fast into her. The pair seemed oblivious to everything but fucking, just as they had been last night.

He inched his wounded paw forward, and as another rat raced along the run, he jabbed it. For a second, the squirming creature squealed out the last of its life skewered on his longest claw.

Still, they mated on the slope by the lake. Envy swept through his every bone at the rising intensity of her pleasure cries.

She should be mine.

Absently he snapped off the head of the rat and dumped it with the others.

Mine.

A kind of choked tremble ran through him. He gnawed on the bloody opening of the rat's neck. The pile of heads had grown in two nights. Stupid creatures, they should have at least noticed how many of their brethren he'd eaten, except the heads, not the heads.

The female's high-pitched cries reached a desperate level.

He sniffed. The rich, ripe scent of Sian, the alluring fragrance of her sex wafted across to torture him from the other side of the lake. Her body should be warm and willing with his. She should be screaming out her pleasure for him.

Yet here he lay, barely able to walk. He'd crawled into this drainage ditch at the end of the fight with the yellow wolf. Exhausted, bleeding, terrified a lesser beast would discover him weakened as he was and take the opportunity to end his first full moon, along with his life, he'd huddled in the mire. The wounds had improved a little but never would he forget who made them and how, nor could anything ever make him lose the memory of Sian's betrayal. She had walked away.

His fur bristled.

The pair across the lake howled their pleasure still.

Won't they ever stop?

He'd show them. He'd change back to himself soon. How he knew, he couldn't say, but he would. When he did, he'd find a way to show them he wasn't beat. If Sian had become wolf, then so could other women, lots of them. He'd find out the way to do it, and he'd make sure he had mates enough to howl into the moonlight like she did.

The hunger he'd experienced this full moon would be satisfied once he'd healed. He'd learn the things the big yellow wolf knew and he'd learn them fast. This so-called leader would wait a long time for him to return here. He spat a bit of rat bone out and peered again at the shadowy pair mating across the lake.

They could fuck each other stupid.

Never would he think of Sian as special again—she wasn't, not anymore. When he did get her, and he would, the best joy he could think of was to mate with her, then after tell her she meant nothing.

A growl formed at the back of his throat as he swallowed the last of the rat. The next full moon, he wouldn't return here. He'd find his own hunting grounds and a worthy mate. Not a prancing little bitch-wolf like Sian, no. Once he found out how to do it, he'd get a female much better than her.

While they were busy across the water, he made the effort to stand. He needed to get out of here before the moon was gone. His limbs trembled with the strain. The savage wounds had ripped the strength from him so he couldn't hunt or think of anything but his pain. He'd heal, though. The last two days his condition had improved by the hour. Tonight, he was fit enough to limp back to the city and get ready for the changing moon. If he had a little luck, he'd find something better to sustain him than rats.

One last look showed the pair of them now lying together, still joined. The male's haunches juddered as, yowling in pleasure, he filled her and licked at her muzzle. Revolting, vile. They'd both be sorry. He'd see they got everything they had coming to them. He'd destroy them, make them pay for all the hurts they had inflicted on him.

He staggered along the drainage ditch, stepping though the rank waterlogged mud and muck. *Oh, they'll pay.*

The climb out of the ditch nearly finished him. He had to lie down and rest, his breathing raw and savage. He shook from the sheer effort, but he'd done it. If he could do this as badly mauled as he was, when he healed, he could do anything. He glanced to the moon. There would be time tonight to get back to the city.

The call to come here had been so powerful the first night he'd changed. His journey from the city sped by fast as he'd raced to follow the trail back to the grounds of this house. The return home would take a lot longer but he'd do it.

* * * *

The city scents offered a richness he'd missed the last two nights. This would be his hunting ground from now on, and damn Magnus Johansson. Silent but for the occasional pained whimper, he made his way in the darkness, slunk past sharp neon streetlights keeping to the deepest shadows he could find. He'd discover places in the city to hunt when he got stronger. Plans romped through him for hunting sites, for prey, and for satisfying the nagging lust deep in his belly, the need for meat, blood, and bone. The other desire would be satisfied, too.

A surge of energy like he'd felt when he had raced to Darnwell shot through him. *Yes, here I'm on home ground.*

This place, this world, it would be his. If he stayed here, there would never be a need to be a part of the vileness of Darnwell. One day, he'd wipe the place from the face of the earth. Lifting his chin, he howled to the last of the moon this night.

Dawn wasn't far off. He needed a place to hold up until the transformation happened. He could feel the strange prickling inside his skin as he had when the change to wolf overwhelmed him. Scenting the air, he moved a little faster to reach his apartment. The garage would be the perfect place. He attempted a run, but his muscles screamed in protest. *Soon, I'll run again.* The eastern sky had lightened with the first glimmer of day. He whined in pain when he jumped up to the open skylight window. He wormed his way through and fell heavily to the floor beside his Porsche.

The last scents he registered were polish and oil as he curled in a ball to wait for what must come next. The return to human form.

Chapter 32

Sian stared at the pills in the foil. Three days missed. The problem hadn't entered her head in all the anticipation of the full moon, in the joy of becoming Magnus's mate. She squeezed the amulet she wore. The incredible experience of bonding fully with Magnus proved so much more than she'd imagined. Even now, two days after they'd returned to human-form, she recalled with exquisite detail how they had loved together as wolves. She would have to resolve the issue before next month's full moon. One day this week she had best visit the doctor. Though Magnus had spoken of them founding a dynasty, which obviously meant children at some time, she'd rather think of the event a ways off in the future.

She swallowed the contraceptive pill with a swig of coffee before she headed to the study to see how many replies she'd had from people she'd invited to the house for the wedding. Once she'd dealt with them, she could concentrate on the walled garden project. Magnus, in a lighter mood than she'd ever seen before they bonded, had gone out, not to the local town but farther. He'd not be back until this evening. With her ring.

Magnus had not said he'd buy her ring today, but she knew. The thought exchange between them had deepened as he'd told her it would. They could almost speak without words at all. In less than three weeks, they'd be married. She'd organize the flowers and her gown before the coming weekend. Hopefully, Richard and Jess would be the witnesses. She'd not heard back from either yet. She'd called Jess several times, but the call diverted to voicemail each time she had tried.

While she printed out the two plans for the garden Martha had sent, she flicked through several pages of wedding gowns on the computer. She'd have to make her choice in the next day or so. Her excitement about the wedding had hardly built. It truly did seem as Magnus had said, a celebration of their bonding. The ceremony would join them legally, but with him linked so deeply into her mind, she didn't think they could be much closer.

The printer finished churning. She took the sheets from it, sat, and following the numbers on the pages, laid them out on the floor to create the full design. All of it looked good, and she could hardly wait for the project to begin. She'd another addition to the garden to make, too, one Magnus had come up with as they bathed together when they came back from the transformation.

The pagoda, though useful this last month, had its limitations, and Magnus wanted a secure place for them both. Though they'd not discussed his reasons for the need, she understood. Franklyn would be back at some point, he'd have no choice, and she'd never feel safe with him around. The idea of an underground retreat appealed to her. A manmade set of caves or caverns would be perfect. The garden company could work on the project, too.

Her phone gave a sheep "bahh," and she picked it up. "Hi."

"Sian, I got your e-mail. I'd be happy to be a witness at your wedding."

"Thanks, Richard. I'm thrilled you'll do it. I'd much rather have you than anyone else. Tell me, is Jess on vacation or working abroad? I can't seem to get hold of her."

"She's in hospital still. I'm sorry I should have sent you a message."

"Hospital!"

"It's been crazy here the last few days with Franklyn out of the office. Jess had a bad fall at the end of last week. Cracked her head open on the arm of a chair. There was blood everywhere."

"How is she?"

"Recovering but there is a possibility of permanent damage to her mobility."

"Shit!"

"If you want to go see her she's in St. Agnes's Hospital. Ward fourteen. Upper level."

"Yes, sure. Do you think she'll be able to be a witness?"

"No idea, but I'd suggest asking an alternative person because she might not recover in time."

She sighed. "Poor Jess. I'll go visit her this week."

"I'm looking forward to the wedding, Sian. I can't wait to see you roped and tied."

"No, it will be a traditional affair, nothing like that," she said and laughed with Richard.

"You want the band to play. They enjoyed the shoot so much because of all your hard work, I reckon I could get them to come back and play for you."

"Fabulous, you ask them, then get back to me. I'll be thrilled if they can play."

"Sure. I'd better go now, the office phone is blaring. Talk to you soon."

"Cheers, Richard." She ended the call and wondered how poor Jess had fallen so hard to do so much damage. Another hospital to visit. She'd go Wednesday afternoon, depending on the visiting times. They might need another person to be a witness. Maybe Magnus would have an idea of someone he could ask. Her one relative wouldn't be able to do it. Great Aunt Wendy was in her late eighties and suffered with such bad Alzheimer's, she didn't know who Sian might be.

If Dreams would play for the wedding, she'd ask for her favorite track from the *Timeless* album. The music would fit perfectly with the dress she'd decided on, the one with the intricate ribbon fastening all the way along the spine. The front of it looked utterly demure, simple and sweet, but the back showed another side. If she wore it with elbow length, lace, fingerless gloves, it would look fabulous. Yes, the outfit would work the way she wanted. She could have the lilies she'd decided on, white and tiger lilies—fabulous.

Such a darn pity about Jess. She crouched back down to go over the plans Martha had sent her again.

* * * *

"Hello. Where are you?"

She looked up from the computer at Magnus's call. Darkness had set. The light from her screen reflected in the windows. "In here."

"There you are, not working still surely?" He reached for her and hauled her from the chair into his embrace.

"Wedding things. I've got thirty replies from guests who will join us. Dreams, the band who played here for the *Timeless* film are going to come play for us. Richard sorted it this afternoon. He will be a witness. Jess can't be, though. She's in hospital."

"What a pity about your friend, and what a lot you've accomplished since I went out this morning."

"I've picked my gown, my flowers, and ordered both. I've also evaluated the garden plans and e-mailed Martha a lot of questions."

"I see, yet while you have been so busy all I have done is chosen your ring."

"I knew you would! Can I see it?"

He set her down and bent onto one knee. He took her hand, and with his other, presented a small green leather box. "For you, my perfect bride."

How strange her fingers trembled now. They hadn't when she first touched her amulet, but while the gold-encased crystal was a part of her, this ring meant something different. She opened the case. "Oh, my."

"Do you like it?"

The rectangular emerald set between two baguette-cut diamonds sparkled in the light from the lamp on her desk. She smiled. "It's perfect."

"Not too big or ostentatious?"

"No, neither, it's beautiful."

"Allow me to put it on your finger?"

She nodded. "Yes, Magnus."

He took the ring from the box and slid it on to her finger. "Not too tight?"

She shook her head. "It's perfect."

"I agree. The stone is flawless. I can see you like it."

"Oh, yes. Thank you so much." She reached up to kiss him, slid her arms around his neck, and pressed her lips to his. He tightened his embrace around her so her body molded to his. The fragrance of his cologne, appealing as it was, couldn't hide the more tasty scent of Magnus. Her body responded to the smell of him, the taste of him, and she gave a little whimper.

"Now?"

A kind of low growl rumbled at the back of her throat as she shoved his jacket from his shoulders and tugged at his belt. The craving for him hit her as strong as it ever had.

"Here." He nudged her back toward a chaise in one of the alcoves of the study. She fumbled, reaching to stop herself falling.

Magnus thrust her skirt up out of the way.

"Yes, now!" Desire shot through her. Instant arousal hit a fresh high. She wriggled to help him drag off her thong.

He caressed her clitoris, but she needed all of him. "Don't wait, not today."

His smile offered the promise of pleasure as he lowered the zip and kicked off his gray flannels.

She clawed at his back through his shirt as he entered. The sheer power of him silenced her pleas. The chaise creaked, offering an accompaniment to the rising rhythm.

Each thrust shoved her further along the route to fulfillment. She gasped for breath. Her nipples burned at his touch.

"I love you."

She fell.

Over the edge and burning like an ember from a bright sun, the energy consumed her cries.

"Yes, for me!" He thrust again and groaned as he joined her delight.

She clasped him tight against her as their breathing slowed. "Magnus."

"I adore you. We will love together forever."

She opened her eyes and looked into his. The light she found there made her smile. "I darn well hope so, otherwise we could both be very miserable."

He offered his hand as he withdrew from her. "We will always be one. No matter what."

"Hmm, I think I need to talk to you about that."

"At least give us time to be married first. Things may have changed by then."

She reached up to kiss him as he adjusted his clothes. "Yes, they may, but there again they might not."

Magnus clasped her hand and lifted it to his lips. "Whatever befalls us, we will face it together."

She brushed the wrinkles from her skirt and picked up the discarded panties. "Yes, agreed. I'm so happy to be with you."

He smiled. "I know. It's time we went down for dinner. I've news to share with you."

A sense of wariness lifted the fine hairs on the back of her neck. "What's this news?"

His dark gaze held hers. She wasn't the only one wary. She clasped his hand and squeezed. "Tell me, Magnus?"

"I've received a communication from my father. My parents will attend the wedding."

"Oh, my God."

Meet the Author

Daisy Banks writes sensual and spicy romance in the Historical, Paranormal and Fantasy genres. Daisy is passionate about her stories. Her focus is to offer the best tale she can to readers. Daisy is married, with two grown up sons. She lives with her husband in a converted chapel in Shropshire, England.

Turn the page for a special excerpt of Daisy Banks's

Timeless

Their love will be eternal, the legend says...if they survive.

Lonely and forced into a life of secrecy, four hundred-year-old Magnus finds Sian--the sexy music film producer who's working in his house--tough to ignore. As she resists his alter ego when he invades her dreams to seduce her, her innate powers astound him and his need only grows. In dreams or reality, he's determined to make her his. She is meant for him alone.

Independent, hard-working Sian has hopes and plans for the future that include the stately house at Darnwell. Not its aloof owner. She's there to acquire the home for a video shoot, nothing more. By day, each layer she explores in Magnus's grand old home with him leads her deeper into love. But by night, he seduces her in her dreams, gives her ecstasy like she's never known. Then she learns his secret: Come the full moon, she is the only one who can control his wolf curse. First though, she has to survive it.

On sale now!

Chapter 1

A teeth-rattling knock battered the door, startling Magnus awake. He hauled himself from the comfort of the wing backed porter's chair, glanced at his watch, and exasperation rising, stalked over to open the door. A chill blast hit him. Raindrops pelted the marble tiled portico, spotting his polished shoes.

He sucked in the cold air, speechless at the sodden young woman who stood before him.

Clutching the neck of her coat and dabbing her cheek with a tissue, she seemed unconscious of his gaze. Runnels of water dripped from her brandy colored curls to form tiny puddles on the shoulders of her coat.

"Miss Armstrong?" he asked.

Her bright green eyes flashed up at him as she wiped a raindrop from the end of her nose. Once she'd flipped back her lapels, she shook her shoulders, splattering more water, and smiled with slick, pink shimmering lips.

"Mr. Johansson? Hi, I'm from Gorsewell Productions, I believe you're expecting me. Sorry I'm a bit late. You know, you're not on the GPS. Hell of a place to find, this, but I made it through the sticks at last." She held out a black lace, fingerless gloved hand in greeting.

The sharp rainstorm hadn't dampened her sultry tones. They slid over his skin to leave a wave of gooseflesh. His irritation she'd arrived over two hours late ramped up a gear. Not only was she behind schedule, but hardly his idea of an executive producer. Her disheveled, bawdy looks belonged to one of the long vanished waterside stews he'd once reveled in.

"Miss Armstrong, how do you do?" As he shook her hand, flames of sensation eddied on his skin. Her smooth, pale, lace covered flesh nestled briefly in his palm. He took his hand away, flexed his fingers to ease the scorching flickers around his hand.

"I'm fine, and yourself, Mr. Johansson?" Hoisting a large bag on her shoulder, she took a step, edging him back, allowing her to enter. The portico door slammed shut, its eighteenth-century glass rattling.

"I am quite well, thank you," he said.

Without the buffeting wind to drain it away, her fragrance teased like an invisible mist in the air as she stepped into the hall. Sensual, like her voice, warm, feminine and appealing, the scent of her stoked the dormant need he'd squashed for decades, kindling life where none should be.

The thick, damp curls reached almost to her waist as she tilted her head back to gaze up to the gilded ceiling. "Awesome," she murmured, and he nodded, though it wasn't the view of the familiar ceiling prompting his agreement.

Here stood the worst surprise he'd received this millennium. But he'd spent years working to build up immunity to her kind, and this exquisite little dolly mop wasn't about to break through his shell.

Straightening, she slid the strap from her shoulder and dumped the sports bag on the polished mahogany floor. "Is it like this throughout?"

Teeth clenched, he winced at the thought of one of the bag's metal clips tearing into the wood, now silky smooth after restoration. Thoughtless wench.

"Yes." He lifted the bag and set it on the marble topped hall table. "My home is over four hundred years old, a rarity which follows the Baroque style. Much of it is now very close to the original standard of craftsmanship. May I take your coat?"

He approached, and a tiny flicker appeared in her eyes. Her pupils expanded a fraction, the first step in an ancient dance, and her response thrilled him in a way it had no right to.

Miss Armstrong slid the coat from her shoulders, and his neck muscles bunched in tension. The garment, a garish neon pink darkened by rain, was lined in heavy purple silk. A lovely foil to her pale skin, more of which was revealed by the way the scarlet bolero draped down so low, exposing one naked shoulder. He'd nearly forgotten the appeal of such skin. Porcelain, yet far more delicate than the object itself, and not icy cold, but warmed with the flush of lifeblood.

He hung the coat in the vast closet, stifling the vortex she'd raised in him.

She swiveled on crimson patent, six-inch heels that could also damage the floor. They were somewhat at odds with her olive-green leggings, which ended mid calf, leaving an expanse of rain-dampened flesh. Pale flesh, spattered with tiny dark specks she must have kicked up on the cinder path while running from her car to avoid the rain.

She flipped open her bag, took out an iPad and stared around her again. "Perfect." The word oozed from her like a low satisfied purr, and provoked his instant response.

Shock radiated through him. He wanted her, all of her. This moment, he could revel in taking her and enjoy a taste of paradise.

Swallowing his desire, he fought to master his thoughts, while she stared up at the painted panels in the interlaced plasterwork moldings above the stairs.

She must go. He'd show her the rooms he'd discussed with the owner of the company then send her packing.

An age or more had passed since one such as this had disturbed his equilibrium. A flash of need ripped through him. He'd been unprepared to receive her, hadn't expected such a creature. What had happened in the world, he should have to deal with the likes of her?

He stepped back, turned past the tall, long case clock, and entered the main hallway, where he placed his hand on the comforting familiarity of the rosewood handrail.

This visitor dazzled like an exotic butterfly. In her thigh skimming, mustard yellow tutu with its froth of spangled lace trim, she emanated life, exhaled vitality with each breath as she stepped toward him, tilting her shapely head to view the paintings. The hairs on the back of his neck rose. Too late, he fought her careless snare, for pure unadulterated passion coiled from her.

Here walked one worthy of the chase as he'd once known it.

He gestured to the ceiling and the corridor, which led to the main rooms of the house. "I thought you would find the house suitable from the information I received when I contacted Mr. Gorsewell. I take it, he's briefed you."

Her concentration fixed on the ceiling, she nodded, moistening her sugar pink lips with the tip of her equally pink tongue. He glanced away, but his gaze had reached into the deep shadow of ripe cleavage revealed by her corseted bodice. An unwelcome shudder ran through him. Someone ought to explain to this little hussy how to dress for a business meeting.

He dragged his mind from her attractions. This remained business, no matter how outlandish or desirable the company's representative might be. Commerce had always struck him as a sordid affair and until recent years, he'd rarely engaged in it. This afternoon's only objective must be the promise of a large amount of easy money to top up his funds so he could continue renovations on the house. The fact Miss Armstrong oozed the sex appeal of a lively whore had nothing to do with it.

Business. That's all. He'd spent too long in control of things to let them slip now.

"Well, Mr. Johansson?" She looked over her shoulder, arched a smooth dark eyebrow, shook her small digital camera at him and followed up with an encouraging little smile. "You are going to show me around, so I can make some notes and get a few shots?" The way her lip curled up at the corner tore at him. The tiny movement invited him to so much more.

"Yes, of course. As you are so late in your arrival," he said, unable to resist the challenge.

Yet she simply shrugged the one naked shoulder and gave him a sultry smile.

"I suggest we start in the ballroom. It's the largest room in the house, and you might find it the thing your company wants. If you'll follow me, Miss Armstrong."

A pity she had to walk behind him. There would have been a kind of pleasure in watching her walk before him. The short tutu skirt would flick and entice with her swaying steps.

His effort to banish such thoughts brought a film of sweat to his upper lip. Her heels tapped a call to arms as he led her down the corridor to the double doors of the ballroom. Perhaps too busy looking at the ancestral portraits, so far, she'd not uttered a word.

He opened the doors and heard the soft catch of her breath as he ushered her through. This room instilled such reactions. How many times had he seen it? And still he marveled at the symmetry and glory of the gilded decoration.

Mirrors lined three of the walls, giving him the added discomfort of being able to view all of her as she stepped forward. The red bolero clung to her small, narrow back and enclosed the contours of her well-rounded breasts, which the tight-laced bodice did nothing to disguise. A hint of the outline of her nipples against the silken fabric made him roll his tongue against his teeth.

If he'd found her in St. James's Square in his youthful wanderings, she'd have cost five guineas, maybe more.

"Good God, I'd not expected anything like this," she said.

He nodded. How could she have expected perfection like this?

The panel of French windows onto the terrace did not give enough light on such a gray day. While she stood wide-eyed, he flicked on the switch so the eight crystal chandeliers sprang to golden life.

"Will this room suit your purposes?" He posed the question as she busily scribbled notes. She held the thick stylus at an unusual angle in her lace-clad hand. Long, square tipped nails, shiny with crimson gloss, sent his pulse pounding. He licked his lips and forced the ache down to a manageable level. Her visit must be a short one, for he could bear her company no longer. A flash from her small camera startled him back to her presence.

"We can get at least a half a dozen good shots in here, a masked ball type thing," she murmured, speaking almost to herself. "Do those doors open?" She strode across the polished floor to the doors, pausing briefly to snap another photograph.

"Yes, they lead to the terrace and there are steps down to the formal gardens." He followed her quick pace. "Would you like to see?" At last, something which gave him some illusion of a business arrangement.

She gave a little sigh, as though he were too slow to understand what she wanted. "Please, Mr. Johansson. I do have a job to do. Not that I want to make you feel as though we'll invade your home, but I need to get the schematic for this over to Franklyn before the end of the month." She quickly thrust one of the French windows open. He ignored her jibe, but added it to her list of imperfections. Late, dressed like an expensive trollop, she must be the most unprofessional individual he'd ever met, and appeared far too swift in her assumptions.

"Of course, Miss Armstrong, forgive me. When one has lived in a home so long, one feels every guest should be given time to enjoy its delights."

Her eyes narrowed. The pink lips pursed, yet she nodded. "I'm sure. However, my job is to find if it's suitable for a music video shoot, Mr. Johansson. I'm not here to assess the individual merits of your home or its decor."

She stepped out onto the terrace, despite the rain, and made her way over to the large, ornamental terra-cotta pots standing at the top of the steps leading down to the bowling lawn. Rain drops gathered like tiny pearls on her glossy red shoes.

"These are good. I could probably use them," she said, nodding toward the sweep of the steps and taking more photographs. "Do you have a maze?"

"No, I have never felt the need for one."

"Pity, I could have done something with one. Never mind. Is there anything more you think would be suitable? Remember, we are looking for gothic horror, at this point. Though of course, things can change." She headed back into the ballroom.

He followed and did his best to maintain his composure. This young woman seemed to have no qualms at suggesting his home might not suit.

"May I suggest the library?" he said as he closed the French windows behind them.

"Sure, lead on." Her heels tapped across the floor, and he caught up to her. As they walked out of the ballroom and he led her down the corridor to the next room he believed would be suitable for the project, he noted one of his strides matched two of hers.

"Excellent. Now this is something special." She patted the Louis XIV desk in the library before taking a shot.

"I'm pleased you approve."

She ignored his words, took three more pictures and made notes. "I'd like to see the kitchens?"

The request startled him. "Why? You don't intend to use them, do you?"

"Please, don't plan my job for me. The kitchens, Mr. Johansson? Which way?"

"Very well, follow me." Irritation prickling, he led her out of the library. Her conversation proved nil and she bordered on rude. He ought to have guessed the true magnificence of the house would be wasted on these music industry types.

They descended the green, wrought iron spiral staircase to the kitchens. The rain-dampened ringlets of hair moved as she paced quickly through the door he held for her. The image of those lustrous coils wrapped tight around his hand as he tilted her head back to taste her mouth hovered. Swiveling around to face him, she seemed to pick up his thought, and a further widening of her pupils sent an electric hot flash to his groin. She blinked slowly.

Interesting. The barrier she drew against him when she closed her eyes proved surprising. Whether she knew it or not, she'd raised her hackles. Well, that wouldn't last long should he choose to take her.

A surge of all the needs he'd subdued through the ages rocked him. Half an hour in her company and his control could be challenged to this level of extremity? Base, lustful instincts bubbled, powerful and infuriating. He waited for her to speak, but she didn't.

While she glanced about the room, he squashed his thoughts, and though it proved a kind of torment to do so, drank in as much detail of her dainty--though strangely clad--form as he could.

"Maybe we can use this room. Put the main lights on for me?" He did as she asked, and her smile curved her cheek. "Yes, just right. Lovely."

The stylus moved quickly over the computer pad she carried as she made more notes. "Okay, last request. Master bedroom, or the one you think best for us to use. Obviously we don't want to tear you from your bed when the film crew gets here." A slight breathy laugh, telling him more than she'd intended, followed her words. She wasn't immune from him any more than he was from her. She'd absorbed his need as naturally as the air she breathed.

"I'll show you the main guest room. The master suite is not available. No amount of money could make it so." He held her green gaze.

"Oh."

The soft response surprised him. Since her arrival, she'd strode through his home like an advancing army. But let her think what she would. He'd not have her prowling through his most personal space, not with an iPad in her hand. A riot of images of her naked on his bed, her pale skin flushed and rosy with desire, her glossy mouth open in pleasure, her hair a flame on his pillows, rushed through him so he nearly gave up the pretense of humanity and hauled her into his arms. The control he exerted, the result of years of practice, made his palms damp.

She needed to leave.

"This way," he said, and led her out and along the corridors back to the central stairs.

"Do you actually live in this palace?" she asked.

"Yes, I've lived here for some time." He left it at that.

"Staff?" The camera clicked again.

"A couple of dailies, housekeeper and cook. Neither is here this late today," he said as they walked up the stairs. Her hand, long nails the same shade as droplets of sweet fresh blood, trailed along the glow of the polished banister. Incredibly provocative.

"They won't be wanted on the days we film. The band wouldn't like it. Everyone is vetted before they take part in a shoot."

"I see. Will the group object to my presence in the house? I, of course, won't disturb their work."

"No, that'll be fine, Mr. Johansson."

"Here, this is the main guest suite." He indicated the intricately carved door.

She reached out to cup the polished brass handle.

"Please, go in." He said no more and waited for her to enter. The enticement of her fragrance had worked on him all the way here, and he wanted to memorize her true scent. He'd know her again anywhere.

The animal stirred within. A smile curved his lips. He'd find her no matter how far away she might be, and when he did, he'd need no introductions.

Holy Angels, not now! Not again. Never!

He'd sworn it, and lived with the oath so long.

She paced about the room, nodding. "Fabulous, just the kind of thing I want. I'll sort the right soft furnishings." Her eyes sparkled as she took in the massive four-poster bed with its elaborate drapes, and she snapped more photographs. She tapped out a quick set of notes, and he enjoyed her concentration.

The delicate form of her features intrigued, at odds with her rather brash manner. He forced himself to observe because if he didn't, the tortuous images of her minus her bizarre outfit might take control and he'd make them a savage reality.

A small wrinkle formed at the corner of her eye with her smile. "Okay, thanks a lot. I think we can certainly say this will be the place to shoot the *Timeless* film. I'll email you with all the major details at the beginning of October, though the tech guys will need to visit before I can finalize everything." She flipped the computer closed. "Franklyn will discuss finance with you. He supervises all that." A little shrug of her shoulders followed, and he watched like a man starved of beauty. "I don't ever get involved with the money side of things," she said.

"So, when can I expect the film crew? Do you have any idea?" Soon, thankfully, she'd leave. He breathed a small sigh of relief, though he still warred with the creature within.

"End of October I would guess, maybe even Halloween. This place is perfect for it. We could have a fantastic Halloween party once we finish the shoot."

A shiver ran over him. Impossible. Not that night, no matter by what name she called it. There could be no worse night for them to come here. He would be at his weakest, the monster as strong as it could ever be. "I won't agree to the date."

"Now, hold on. Franklyn said you were open to reasonable requests," she said.

"No, Miss Armstrong, not that day, or night," he snapped, and silenced her.

The air crackled with the challenge she stared back. But he sensed when her opposition disappeared, though he could still scent her unwillingness to acquiesce. An involuntary spasm twitched in his hand. She was so primed for the next step. But he wasn't, never would be again. "You are ready to leave," he said.

Her eyes flashed, widening at his tone, and for the first time since she'd stepped into his house, her composure faltered. Perhaps she'd made an intelligent perception, discovered all was not as it appeared.

"You may bring the crew in the night before or after October thirty-first, but not on the thirty-first, Miss Armstrong. I'll show you downstairs." A small kernel of warmth grew in him, as she compliantly nodded. He remained in command of himself and his world.

"I'll need to arrange for the technicians to view, especially the lighting manager," she said, hurrying after him as he strode down to the hall.

"You may email me possible dates for their visit." Through the window, rain fell again from the lowering sky. As she zipped her bag closed, the sound dragged his gaze back to her.

Luscious, lovely, so youthful and ripe, she flaunted her vitality. The thought tore through him so he had to clear his throat.

She must leave, and now.

He helped her on with the still damp coat, and while she tugged the belt tight about her, had to resist the urge to touch it.

"Bye, Mr. Johansson, I'm sure we'll meet again," she said, offering her delicate hand.

The skin of her fingers, soft and supple, the warm, lace covered palm rested in his a second too long. "Goodbye," he said with a last look, drinking in the wide, coal black pupils centered in the dazzling green irises of her eyes. A picture of them stayed with him as he closed the door behind her, and her fragrance still pooled about him.

Hunger for her rose, hot and almost unstoppable. He shook his head. "We'll not meet again if I can help it. Not tonight, not later. Not ever would be better."

Miss Armstrong would be forgotten, in a few weeks. Perhaps by the end of the month he'd not even remember the delicate flush on her cheek or the fiery corkscrew curls twining over her marble-pale shoulder.

Fixated as a drowning man watching a life belt drift away, he stared through the window at her shimmering crimson heels as she skittered down the driveway to her car.

www.ingramcontent.com/pod-product-compliance
Lightning Source LLC
Chambersburg PA
CBHW020609270626
47155CB00022BA/1540